Carol Townend was born in England and went to a
convent school in the wilds of Yorkshire. Captivated
by the medieval period, Carol read History at London
University. She loves to travel, drawing inspiration
for her novels from places as diverse as Winchester
in England, Istanbul in Turkey and Troyes in France.
A writer of both fiction and non-fiction, Carol lives
in London with her husband and daughter. Visit her
website at caroltownend.co.uk.

THE KNIGHT'S FORBIDDEN PRINCESS

Carol Townend

MILLS & BOON

First Published in Great Britain 2018
by Mills & Boon, an imprint of HarperCollins*Publishers*
1 London Bridge Street, London, SE1 9GF

© 2018 Carol Townend

ISBN: 978-0-263-93285-0

MIX
Paper from
responsible sources
FSC C007454

This book is produced from independently certified FSC™ paper
to ensure responsible forest management.
For more information visit www.harpercollins.co.uk/green.

Printed and bound in Spain
by CPI, Barcelona

For my editor, Linda Fildew,
who listened very hard (and incredibly patiently)
when I was developing this story.

I'd also like to thank Joanna Maitland
and Sophie Weston of Libertà! Their sparkles
were invaluable. They know what I mean.

A thousand thanks.

Chapter One

❦

1396—Castle Salobreña in Al-Andalus—a watchtower overlooking the port

The eldest Nasrid Princess was feeling rebellious. Today, she was using her Spanish name rather than her Moorish one. Today, she was Princess Leonor. She was supposed to be taking her siesta on a pile of tasselled cushions by a latticed window, yet sleep was miles away.

The two other Princesses were dozing nearby. Thanks to the Sultan's orders, the shutters of the pavilion were firmly closed and, unhappily for the three Princesses, the breeze was too weak to work its way through the lattices. The heat was suffocating.

Leonor lifted the edge of her veil to fan herself and the chink of ruby and pearl bracelets echoed softly around the pavilion walls. With each breath, the gems decorating the fringe flickered like fireflies, and tiny rainbow-coloured lights danced over the tiled floor. Leonor frowned at the evanescent colours, at the brilliant arabesques patterning the pavilion walls, at the script flowing neatly over the door arch. 'There is no victor but God,' it read. Her frown deepened. As if she or her sisters could forget. 'No victor but God' was the motto of the Nasrid dynasty.

We are in prison. Our father has imprisoned us at the border of his territories. Will we ever be free?

Princess Leonor itched to toss her veil aside, but her father, the Sultan, may blessings rain upon him, had forbidden it. The three Nasrid Princesses were not to be stared at.

In truth, the Sultan himself was the only man alive to have seen their faces. Men in general, including even the hand-picked guards on duty outside their apartment, were forbidden to look at them. To all intents and purposes, the Sultan's daughters were invisible. Sometimes Princess Leonor felt as though she didn't actually exist. It was as though she had winked out of sight, like a real firefly.

She gripped her fan. It had been an age since she and her sisters had heard from their father. Did he intend to keep them locked out of sight for ever? The thought of spending her whole life in a jewelled cage was unbearable; something had to change.

Since Leonor was the eldest Nasrid Princess, perhaps it was up to her to see that it did.

She drew in a breath of warm air and gazed through her veil at a beam of light slanting through the latticed shutter. The shutter—yet another barrier to keep her and her sisters safely out of sight—was pierced with pretty stars. Leonor loathed the sight of them. Dust motes hung in the air. The light quivered and was darkened by a swiftly moving shadow.

A seagull outside? An eagle? It was too hot to move.

If I open the shutter, I could see the harbour below.

Not that Leonor was meant to do that. It wouldn't do for the Sultan's daughter to lean out of the watchtower window; it wouldn't do for a Nasrid princess to be seen.

But the heat! Holy heaven, she was melting. If she opened the shutter, just a chink, there would surely be some breeze. The latch was within reach, the latch that she and her sisters were forbidden to lift. Dropping her fan, Leonor stretched out her hand. Even the metal was warm.

She hesitated, picturing the castle walls straggling downhill towards the sea. The pavilion was situated in a remote tower overlooking the port—this window had to be well out of the guards' line of sight. Who would know if she opened the shutter?

If anyone on the quayside glanced her way, all they would see was a veiled woman in the distance.

Leonor lifted the latch and pushed at the shutter. Light poured in. And sounds! Sounds that the shutter had muffled—the braying of a donkey, the cry of a gull, the creak of a rope. Her pulse quickened. Silk rustled as she pushed to her knees. She leaned her elbows on the embrasure and looked out.

The wind toyed with her veil. She could smell salt and fish. And down there—seen through the film of her veil—the harbour teemed with life. There were so many people! Ordinary people who walked freely about her father's kingdom.

Out to sea, a ship moved steadily across the water. Hampered by her veil, Leonor couldn't see the detail, just the shape of it, its sails filled with wind. Even the ripples on the water were blurred by her veil.

Her throat ached. Gritting her teeth, half-expecting the heavens to fall, she reached for the hem of her veil and tossed it over her head.

The heavens didn't fall, but she blinked. Everything was so bright!

The sea stretched on for ever, it seemed, its surface gleaming like beaten metal. The sun sparkled on the swell and gilded the leaves of the palm trees. Best of all, Leonor could feel the breeze caressing her cheeks. It was cool, a touch of paradise and infinitely better than her stupid fan. Bliss. When a gust of wind caught a lock of hair and tugged it free of its pins, she held in a delighted laugh.

Below her on the wall walk, the thud of heavy boots sounded a warning, a guard was doing his rounds. Hand over her mouth lest she draw his attention her way, Leonor held herself still. Her heart thumped in time with the marching boots. If the guard heard anything and leaned over that merlon, he might catch sight of her. For her sake as well as his, it wouldn't do to be seen, but she couldn't tear her gaze from the harbour below. Paradise was surely looking at the world without a veil. Just this once. There was so much to see. A large galley had docked and was unloading its cargo. No, not cargo exactly. Merciful God, the men walking down the gangplank were chained together in a long line. *Chained.*

Goosebumps ran down Leonor's back. Was it a slave ship? There were slaves in the castle, but they were well cared for. Leonor had never seen anyone chained like this and what she saw appalled her.

Those men…poor things. Their bruises spoke of heavy-handed beatings by the brutes in charge of them. A powerful-looking prisoner in a crimson tunic was helping one who looked to be barely conscious. The beaten man stumbled, fighting the drag of his fetters, and it was clear that he was only standing thanks to his friend's supporting arms. It was odd though, something was very out of place. Most of the prisoners were remarkably well dressed.

Leonor's gaze was drawn back to the man in crimson. He stood taller than his companions, with strong, wide shoulders. As she studied him, the word 'warrior' jumped into her head. Not that Leonor had ever seen a warrior close to—her father, the King, may he live for ever, would never permit it. But that man, yes, he must be a warrior, his physique was truly remarkable. The wind was playing in his wavy dark hair, teasing the edge of his crimson tunic.

Leonor glimpsed a flash of gold and her eyes went wide. He was wearing a gold ring. Goodness, who was he? Why hadn't the ring been stolen by his captors? As she stared harder, she noticed that the man's crimson tunic was embroidered with gold thread. She looked at his neighbours and found more signs of wealth. Silver gleamed on the belt buckle of a man in a blue tunic. The man who was hurt also had a gold ring on. These three looked more like princes than slaves. Why were they chained? It didn't make sense.

Angry voices floated up from the quayside. An overseer cracked his whip and Leonor bit her lip as an agonised groan reached her ears. The injured man stumbled again, the chains jerked and the line of prisoners came to an abrupt halt.

Leonor quite forgot her place and leaned right out of the window. She was no longer the Princess Leonor who should know better than to show her face outside. She was simply a soft-hearted young woman frowning at a sailor for whipping a man who could barely stand.

She wasn't the only one to be so affronted. As the whip lifted a second time, the tallest captive, the one in crimson, rounded on the overseer.

Leonor's nails bit into her palms. Anger darkened the face of the warrior-like figure and he stepped directly into harm's way. The whip snaked towards him, and when it struck, he made no sound. He looked furious. Furious and proud. Something lodged in Leonor's throat. Even in his anger, that man was devastatingly handsome. No slave, he.

Who were these men?

Leonor suddenly recalled hearing her duenna, Inés, muttering to one of the servants. There had been talk of Spanish noblemen chipping away at the edges of her father's territory. There had been fighting and prisoners had been taken.

Thoughtfully, Leonor stared at the quayside. Prisoners, not slaves. Likely they were being held hostage for the ransom they would bring. Her father, the Sultan, peace be upon him, owed tribute to the neighbouring kingdom of Castile. Ironically, the tribute was intended to serve as a sign of goodwill between the Kingdom of Al-Andalus and the Spanish kingdom. That clearly didn't stop her father capturing Spanish lords and using them to gain ransom to pay that tribute.

Behind her came the rustle of Granadan silk, her sisters were awake.

'Leonor, your veil!' Princess Alba's voice held censure. 'Come away from the window!'

Leonor shot a glance over her shoulder. 'If you lean out far enough, you can see the harbour,' she said casually.

'But your veil! What if Father finds out?'

The youngest Princess, Constanza, came to stand at Alba's side. 'Father would be very angry. Inés has warned us about what might happen if—'

Leonor made an impatient gesture. 'Forget the veil, it's impossible for anyone in the castle to see this window, the line of sight is quite wrong.' She beckoned her sisters over. 'A galley has docked, and I think it's brought captives from the fighting.'

Princess Alba caught her breath. 'Spanish knights? Here in Salobreña?'

Princess Constanza simply stared.

Leonor smiled. The Princesses' mother had been a Spanish noblewoman and Leonor's sisters were as curious about Spain as she was. Sadly, the Queen had died before the Princesses had reached their third birthday and they could barely remember her. Leonor had faint recollections of a dark-eyed woman holding her hand; of a soft voice singing lullabies; of the tinkle of golden bracelets and the whisper of silk slippers on marble floors. Shadowy memories that prompted a strong interest in the part of her heritage that was lost to her. Her mother—a captive—had become the Sultan's favourite. He had made her his Queen. Leonor ached to know what her mother's life had been like before she had been captured.

All their companion Inés would tell them was that their mother's Spanish name had been Lady Juana. Inés had been their mother's duenna—her governess and companion—before they'd been taken by the Sultan. After the Queen's death, Inés had been given charge of the little Princesses. Unfortunately, she was closed as a clam, and she refused to reveal Lady Juana's birthplace, just as she refused to give the Princesses their mother's full name.

Inés must have been sworn to secrecy. Perhaps she was afraid.

None of which stopped Leonor wondering. What family had Lady Juana left behind? Had she fought to return home? Had she found it easy to adjust when their father had made her his Queen?

'Spanish knights?' Alba took a tentative step towards her. 'Leonor, are you sure?'

'Look for yourself. You can see quite clearly from the window.'

Alba twisted her fingers together. 'Leonor, if you can see the ship and the quayside, it follows that someone down there might see you. Put on your veil!'

With a shrug, Leonor turned back to the window. 'The people on the quay will be ignorant of Father's rules about veils. And even if they are not, how will they know who we are? We are too far away.'

Leaning out quite shamelessly, she watched the chained men, focusing once more on the man in crimson as he helped his friend limp along the quayside. She couldn't seem to help herself, he fascinated her. It was somewhat unsettling. Vaguely, she was conscious of first Alba and then Constanza coming to kneel beside her. A couple of swift, sidelong glances told her that her sisters were not in as rebellious a mood as she, their veils remained firmly in place.

She hid a smile. Veils notwithstanding, both sisters were leaning out over the windowsill, just as she was. They too stared down at the quayside.

'We must be quiet,' Leonor murmured. 'The guards...'

Alba nodded and the Princesses watched in silence.

Alba let out a soft sigh. 'One of them is injured.'

'The man in the green tunic, aye.'

'He is fortunate to have friends with him.' Alba paused, she sounded rather breathless. 'They are handsome, don't you think?'

Leonor's cheeks warmed as she gave a quiet laugh. 'Aye. Not that I am an expert in such things.'

'I wonder who they are.'

Leonor kept her voice low. 'Inés mentioned border skirmishes, that's why I think they're Spanish noblemen. Knights who've been captured.'

'Could they be related to Mamá?'

'Who knows?'

On Leonor's other side, Constanza kept her lips firmly shut. She too seemed to be watching the captives, but with Constanza one could never be sure.

Rodrigo wrestled with his fetters, caught Inigo's arm and kept him steady. Already Enrique, distracted by something on the ramparts of the tyrant's castle, had let go of him. Surely even Enrique could see that Inigo was on the point of losing consciousness?

'For pity's sake, Enrique, show some gratitude, lend Inigo a hand.' Rodrigo's voice was brusque, he couldn't help it. Grief and anger were taking their toll; it was hard to think of anything save the awful truth.

Diego was dead. His brother was dead.

Rodrigo's guts rolled. He was having a hard time accepting it, but his brother—no more than a boy—had been killed over a few yards of thistles on a patch of barren borderland. He narrowed his gaze on Enrique and tried not to think about the fact that it had been Enrique's foolhardiness that had got them into the mess in the first place. Recriminations wouldn't help. If they were to get out of this in one piece, they must stick together. Pointedly, Rodrigo rattled the chain that linked prisoner to prisoner. 'For pity's sake, Enrique, think. If Inigo stumbles again, that whip will fall on us all.'

Enrique threw a surly look in his direction and grasped Inigo's other arm. 'Inigo should have stayed at home. You all should have done. I would have been all right.'

Rodrigo's chest ached. That almost sounded like an apology. Certainly, it was the closest Enrique had come to admitting that if he hadn't filled young Diego's head with dreams of glory, Diego would be here today. It was too late. Whatever Enrique said, it was too late for Diego.

Enrique was responsible for Diego's death and their party's capture. Fool that he was, he'd hurled himself into battle early and Diego—too green to know better—had followed. Rodrigo had flung himself into the fray in a vain attempt to save his brother; Inigo had joined him, and shortly afterwards they'd all been captured.

However, there was nothing to be gained by raking over old coals. They were the tyrant's prisoners, they needed each other. Who knew what

Sultan Tariq might do? Until they were free, they had little choice but to stick together.

Rodrigo and Enrique half-dragged, half-carried Inigo along the quay.

Shadows were short, the port of Salobreña was hotter than an oven. As the captives were herded along, then made to stand next to a pile of fishing nets, Rodrigo suppressed a sigh. The sun was almost directly overhead. His scalp itched and his red tunic was dark with sweat. He swallowed painfully, his throat dry as parchment. 'I'd sell my soul for a drink,' he muttered.

Inigo mumbled something that might or might not have been agreement and sagged a little. Rodrigo propped him up.

'What will they do to us, do you suppose?' Enrique murmured, a slight crease in his brow.

'The Sultan's treasury is empty,' Rodrigo reminded him. 'He is desperate for money so he can pay his tribute. I'm confident we will be taken into honourable captivity until our ransom is paid.'

Enrique's brow cleared. 'Negotiations shouldn't take long. Mother won't allow Father to sit on his hands. I reckon I should be free in a couple of weeks.'

Speechless at Enrique's self-interest, Rodrigo shook his head and drew in a steadying breath. Enrique was his cousin, but if it weren't for the family connection, Rodrigo would have nothing to do with him. Particularly now Diego was gone.

Enrique glowered. 'What?'

'I was thinking about Diego.'

Enrique flinched and Rodrigo was taken by a powerful urge to hit something. Preferably his cousin. Grief. Fury. Telling himself that starting a family brawl on the quayside would get them nowhere, Rodrigo turned his attention to their surroundings.

Diego would want him to keep his wits about him. His brother would want them—yes, even Enrique—to get away from Al-Andalus in one piece. If a chance to escape presented itself, he'd take it.

Methodically, Rodrigo studied the port. He was looking for weakness, for anything he might turn to their advantage. There hadn't been many guards on the ship, but chained men weren't hard to control. It might be different here.

He swore under his breath. Hell burn it, even if they were presented with the chance to escape, they couldn't take it. Not until Inigo's leg healed. Not with Enrique proving so unreliable.

After their capture by the Sultan's forces— Rodrigo sent Enrique another dark look—the three of them had taken pains to stress their noble lineage. The grim reality was that they'd been caught fighting to win back land on the tyrant's borders, and to avoid summary execution they'd told the Moorish commander that they'd pay handsomely for their release.

Salobreña Castle loured over the port, solid

and imposing. It looked impregnable, not that
Rodrigo wanted to break in. If they were to be
lodged in honourable captivity in the castle whilst
they waited for their ransoms to be paid, he would
be looking for a way out. Inigo might heal quickly.

A flag hung limply from a flagpole, the
colours—red and gold—those of the Nasrid dynasty. Rodrigo ran his gaze along the length of the
curtain wall as it wound down the cliffs. There
were several watchtowers, the nearest of which
was close to the port. Interesting. If they were to
be lodged in the castle and if they did make their
escape, the location of that tower might be useful.

'Dios mío.' Enrique gave a low whistle, he had
followed Rodrigo's gaze and was staring at the
nearest watchtower. 'There are women up there.
Look, a shutter is open.'

Something fluttered up at the top of the tower.
For once, Enrique was right. A latticed shutter
was indeed open and three women were leaning
out of the embrasure, watching the harbour. Two
of them were wearing veils, the other—Lord, if
Rodrigo's imagination wasn't playing tricks with
him and at this distance he couldn't be sure—the
one without a veil was a beauty.

Rodrigo caught the flash of dark eyes, of a jewelled bracelet and a shining black twist of hair. A
low murmur reached him. He'd probably imagined the murmur—the tower was surely too far
away for him to hear anything over the lap of the

water and the clanking of prisoners' irons. The dark-eyed woman seemed to be watching him. Her friends too were looking their way.

'Who the devil are they?' Enrique asked.

Rodrigo made an impatient sound. 'Saints, Enrique, how would I know?' He made his voice dry. 'They could be the tyrant's daughters.'

Enrique's mouth fell open. 'The Princesses? Truly?'

'Enrique, I wasn't serious.' The Sultan was rumoured to have three identical daughters whom he kept in pampered seclusion in Salobreña Castle. Personally, Rodrigo was sceptical. He stared at his cousin. 'Don't tell me you believe that folk tale about the three Princesses.'

Their conversation roused Inigo from his stupor and he squinted up at the tower window, blinking sweat from his eyes. 'Princesses? Where?'

Rodrigo sighed. 'There are no princesses, Inigo, it's just a story.' Surely no man, not even a tyrant like Sultan Tariq, would incarcerate his daughters in a castle and never allow them to be seen?

Inigo stared up at the tower. 'Three princesses, Lord.'

Inigo's voice was little more than a drunken murmur, which was understandable. He *was* drunk— on pain, on fatigue, on thirst. They all were.

'There are no princesses, Inigo,' Rodrigo said firmly. 'Likely those girls are the castle cooks.'

'They don't look like cooks to me.' Worryingly, Inigo was slurring his words. 'I know a silken veil when I see one, I know the glitter of gold. Those are the Princesses. The one without the veil looks as though she's come straight from a harem. I bet the others are just as comely.' Inigo paused. 'What luck, there's one for each of us.'

Enrique let out a bark of laughter.

Rodrigo sighed. 'Inigo, you have a fever.'

Enrique's chain rattled. The line was moving again, they were being prodded and gestured towards a paved square that opened out just off the quayside. Rodrigo took Inigo's arm to help him keep pace.

'How's the leg?' he asked, more to keep Inigo conscious than in expectation of any reply.

'Throbs like fury.'

Inigo looked like death, sweat was pouring from him and, despite the heat, his face was pale. At least he was making sense, Rodrigo was amazed he'd remained conscious this long. 'When we get to our lodgings, I'll see they fetch you a healer.'

'You think I'll get one? Don't want infection to set in. I'd like to keep my leg.'

'You'll keep it, never fear.'

Inigo's gaze held his. 'You're certain?'

Despite his doubts, Rodrigo put lightness in his voice. 'Certain. Only one leg, only half the ransom. They need to keep you whole!'

Inigo's lips twisted and he glanced back at that window. 'What do you think his daughters look like close to?'

It was on the tip of Rodrigo's tongue to say that the Princesses would probably be ugly, buck-toothed hags when it occurred to him that Inigo probably needed a little fantasy. They all did.

He kept his voice light and smiled. 'Eyes dark as sloes and lips like rosebuds. Their hair will reach beyond their waists—it will be smooth as black satin and scented with orange blossom. Their bodies will be soft and curved, and their skin—'

Madre mía, what was he doing? Clearly the shock of Diego's death was taking its toll. Sultan Tariq's troops had killed his brother; Inigo was wounded; a ransom was being demanded for their safe release and here he was fantasising about three princesses who might not even exist.

Enrique tugged on the chain, causing Inigo to stumble. 'Don't stop, Rodrigo, I was enjoying that. You'd got to the Princesses' skin.'

Rodrigo ground his teeth together and man-aged—just—not to hit him.

Chapter Two

❧❧❧

Entirely focused on the knight in the red tunic as he helped his companion towards the square, Leonor didn't hear the pavilion door open.

'Princess Leonor!' Inés stood in the door arch, her hands on her hips. 'My lady, what *are* you doing?'

Veiled in the same way as the two younger Princesses, Inés was known to most in Salobreña by the Moorish name of Kadiga. It was a name given to her by the Sultan when she had first arrived in the palace with the Princesses' mother. However, shortly after their mother's death, Inés had told the sisters that she much preferred her old Spanish name. Consequently, whenever they were in the privacy of their apartments, they called their duenna Inés.

Leonor rose from the cushions and faced her. 'How do you do that?'

'Do what, my lady?'

'You always know which of us is which. It doesn't seem to make any difference whether we are veiled or not. How do you tell us apart?'

Leonor and her sisters were triplets and were as like as peas in a pod. The three of them had hair that was long and black, with the sheen and texture of silk. They had dark lustrous eyes, prettily shaped mouths and teeth as white as pearls. The only difference between them was a slight variation in height. Leonor was the tallest, then came Alba, and finally the youngest, Constanza. Aside from their height, see one Princess and you've seen them all.

Inés had always been the only person in the castle who could tell them apart. That she could do so even when she was looking at them from behind was astonishing.

'You are all equally beautiful, that is sure,' Inés said. 'However, you are my girls and I love you, that is how I can tell you apart.' She gestured at Leonor's exposed face. 'Princess Zaida, you will not distract me. Why is your veil pushed back?'

Leonor grimaced. By using Leonor's Moorish name instead of her Spanish one, her duenna was reminding her, not very subtly, that it wasn't wise to go against Sultan Tariq's orders. Guiltily aware that Inés might suffer for Leonor's disobedience, and that the poor woman must live in fear of what would happen to her should the Princesses rebel in earnest, Leonor bit her lip. 'My apologies, Inés, but I am no longer a child.'

'That is open to question.' Inés tipped her head to one side and hardened her voice. 'What isn't open to question is that you have removed your veil. You cannot have forgotten the Sultan's command that you remain veiled when you leave your apartments, and that includes when you are in this pavilion.'

'Have pity, Inés, no one comes here and the port is like a furnace. Even the palm trees are melting. I'm suffocating.'

'That is irrelevant. You are a Nasrid princess and you must obey your father.'

'Father might try wearing a veil in this heat and see how he likes it,' Leonor muttered.

'I beg your pardon?'

Leonor heard the fear in her duenna's voice and the old guilt stirred—the idea that their faithful duenna might have to suffer their father's wrath was simply unbearable. With a resigned sigh, she caught the edge of her veil and drew it back over her face.

The veil settled. Perspiration immediately prickled on her brow, even though her veil was light as gossamer.

'Thank you, Leonor.' Inés drew closer, her skirts dragging on the floor tiles. She touched Leonor's arm and her voice warmed, becoming almost conspiratorial. 'What were you looking at, my dear?'

'A galley has docked. We were watching the captives come ashore.'

'Captives?'

'We think they are Spanish knights,' Alba said. 'They must have been captured in the fighting.'

Inés went to kneel on the cushions and peered out the window. Leonor knew she'd see nothing, as the prisoners would have reached the square by now. Where were they being taken? The castle dungeons? Where else might they go—was there a prison in the town?

The Princesses were rarely allowed out. Though they'd lived in Salobreña Castle for years, they knew nothing about the actual town. Leonor couldn't help but wish that, whatever happened to those Spanish knights, the one in crimson would be able to care for his friend.

'The quay is empty.' Inés jerked the shutter closed and the pavilion dimmed. 'I have to say I doubt the men you saw were truly Spanish knights.'

Constanza let out a soft sigh. 'They were most handsome, Inés,' she murmured.

Constanza sounded bright, almost happy. With a jolt, Leonor realised that her sister hadn't sounded half so animated in, well, in months. Clearly, Leonor wasn't the only one to feel shut in. And through her filmy veil she would swear she could see Constanza blushing. Constanza, of all people, blushing!

Inés made a clucking sound and shooed them towards the door. 'Handsome—*pah!*'

Leonor caught her duenna's hand. 'Inés, where are those men being taken? Will they be put in the dungeon?'

'My lady, the whereabouts of a few Spanish captives is not your concern.'

The glass beads on Constanza's veil sparkled in the light, she was shaking her head. 'How can you say that? Inés, you are Spanish by birth. Our mother was Spanish. Those men might be relatives.'

Inés froze. 'My lady, they are not relatives.'

'They *could* be, couldn't they?' Constanza continued.

Leonor blinked. Of the three Princesses, Constanza was the most biddable, the quietest one. Indeed, apart from her lute-playing, she was so quiet that most of the time you would hardly know she was there. It was good to hear some life in her voice. Good to think that the Spanish captives had brought a blush to her cheeks. It was almost as though her youngest sister had suddenly woken up.

Leonor turned to their duenna. 'Inés, you must understand, seeing those men has made us curious. You came to Al-Andalus with Mamá, you must remember what life was like before you entered our father's kingdom.'

'I remember nothing.' Inés frowned. 'And even if I did, the Queen was a Spanish noblewoman, that is all I am permitted to tell you.'

'Her name was Juana. You did tell us that,' Leonor said thoughtfully. Seeing those knights had made her realise that her mother's background needn't be shrouded in mystery. In the world beyond her father's kingdom, there must be many people who knew her mother's history. 'Lady Juana. And I think you are forgetting something else. We were small at the time, but I remember it well.'

'Oh?'

'You said that Lady Juana was betrothed before she fell captive to Father.'

Inés took a hasty step backward. 'I did not. I wouldn't dream of being so indiscreet.'

'You told us Mamá was betrothed, I remember it distinctly.' Leonor nodded towards the shuttered window. 'Don't be afraid, I won't carry tales to Father. But you must see I am hungry to learn all I can about Mamá. What happened to the nobleman to whom she was betrothed? Who was he? What was he like? What did he do when Mamá was captured? We long to know more about our Spanish side.'

Slowly, Inés shook her head. 'No, you do not. It is no longer your heritage. My lady, I regret having told you anything, and I shall say no more.'

Leonor clasped her hands in front of her. 'Just

our mother's full name, Inés, that is all that I ask.
Our memories of Mamá are so meagre. We are
her daughters, surely you can tell us where she
came from? She was Lady Juana of...?'

Putting up her hand in a gesture of rejection,
Inés turned sharply away. 'You are the Sultan's
daughters and I have already told you far more
than is wise. Come, we must return to your apartments in the keep. Before you know it, it will be
time for the evening meal. Alba, it's your favourite, spiced fish with rice.'

'Inés, *please.*'

Inés stiffened her spine and Leonor understood
her pleading was in vain. Leonor was no longer
talking to Inés, her beloved duenna, she was talking to Kadiga, Sultan Tariq's faithful servant. And
Kadiga was displeased.

'Princess Zaida,' Kadiga said, in her formal
voice. 'This conversation is unseemly, and if you
continue in this vein, I shall be forced to conclude
that you need disciplining. Your father, the Sultan, will need to be told. He will be gravely dis-
appointed. For your sisters' sake, if not your own,
you must put your mother's ancestry out of your
mind. Such curiosity is not healthy—for anyone.'

Healthy or not, Princess Leonor's curiosity
could not be curbed. How could she stop wondering about her own mother's history? Impossible. However, since it was clear that further

argument with Inés would achieve nothing, she curbed her tongue and followed her sisters back to the apartments. As soon as the Princesses were safely inside, they removed their veils. Here at least, where they were waited on by trusted maid-servants, there was no need for concealment.

The afternoon dragged. Leonor paced around the fountain in the central courtyard as the spray turned to gold in the sunlight. Constanza toyed with her silver lute and Alba stared moodily out of the window. The shadows lengthened. Constanza's music filled the air and even though she knew it was forbidden, Leonor's thoughts kept returning to her long-dead mother.

Sight of those Spanish knights on the quayside seemed to have unleashed the rebel in her. Might those knights really be her kin?

At the least, one of them might have heard of their mother. The disappearance of a Spanish no-blewoman, even if it had been almost twenty years ago, must have caused a stir. Leonor would give anything to meet one of those men and speak to him.

Alba and Constanza didn't have to say a word for Leonor to know that they too were thinking the same. That was the way it had always been. They knew each other's thoughts so well that speech was scarcely necessary.

Evening came, and the Princesses lay on their silken cushions as their meal was spread before them. Leonor ate sparingly, barely noticing that the fish was spiced with cinnamon, or that the rice was flavoured with saffron, her mind was too busy for food. Where had those men been taken? Were they being well treated? If they were waiting to be ransomed, they would surely receive proper care. She hoped so. It was disturbing, not knowing. Had the knight in crimson secured help for his wounded friend? Were they being fed?

When figs were placed before her, Leonor peeled one with a silver knife and ate it absently as she pondered the likelihood of that knight knowing about a Lady Juana who had been stolen away by Sultan Tariq. It must have caused a scandal at the time.

Leonor set aside her knife with a sigh. It wasn't likely that those men would be relatives.

She felt oddly nervous, as though she was on the verge of making a momentous decision. Her stomach was in knots and, most curious of all, her hands were shaking.

There must be a way to use the arrival of the Spanish knights to learn more about Mamá. This was a rare chance to talk to someone who might have heard about Lady Juana. If she let it slip by, she would never forgive herself. She had to speak to one of those prisoners.

The image of the knight in the crimson tunic came into focus at the back of her mind. Despite his chains, he had an air of command about him.

Mind working furiously, Leonor pushed the fruit bowl towards Alba. 'Figs?'

Alba shook her head. 'I'm not hungry.'

Leonor frowned and glanced at Constanza. 'Constanza? Figs?'

'No, thank you.'

Leonor stared at her sisters, both of whom ached to know more about their mother, just as she did. She clenched her fists. She was going to speak to that Spanish knight.

And if her father found out? Her heart thumped. She opened her mouth and swiftly shut it again. The knots in her belly were warning her that she was on her own with this. It was too dangerous to involve anyone else. If she was caught, she alone must bear the blame. Her plans must remain secret.

She glanced towards the door arch. Inés sat in the outer chamber, keeping close to her charges, as usual. Her father's habit of punishing servants for the Princesses' sins meant Leonor couldn't discuss this with Inés either.

She toyed with her eating knife. Watched and guarded as they were, it wouldn't be easy.

Yet somehow, she must manage it without inflicting her father's anger on someone else.

Her gaze lit on a curl of manuscript next to Constanza's lute.

A letter! She would write the Sultan a letter.

With luck, she'd never need to dispatch it, and

the letter could be kept purely as a safeguard, in case she was caught. The Sultan's wrath was legendary, and if Leonor was discovered to have visited the prison, she doubted he would listen to reason. He might, however, read a letter, especially one she had written before speaking to the knight. The letter would set out most clearly that she had acted alone, and it would stress her fervent wish to learn about her mother's family. The Sultan must be made to understand she couldn't rest until she knew more.

'Inés?'

Inés appeared in the door arch. 'Princess Leonor?'

Leonor smiled. 'Please fetch another lamp. I shall need parchment, a quill and some ink.'

Her duenna's eyebrows rose. 'You wish to write?'

'Aye.'

'Very well, my lady.'

Shortly after cockcrow, Leonor was waiting behind a group of soldiers as the door of the prison scraped open. It had been surprisingly easy to persuade a castle guard to escort her there. The man she had approached—Yusuf—clearly had no clue he was speaking to one of the Princesses. He'd been eager to earn a little gold and no questions had been asked. So here she was, heavily veiled and disguised in the clothing of a maidservant.

Despite the ease of getting to the prison, Leonor was shaking from head to toe. If the Sultan found out… None the less, she had convinced herself that the letter she'd tucked into her jewel box would exonerate Yusuf from all blame.

The soldiers in front of her were laden with sacks of bread and flasks of ale for the prisoners. Also waiting to go inside were a handful of people who undoubtedly had paid handsomely to visit the noble Spanish captives. Leonor did her best to blend in and prayed no one noticed how much she was shaking.

Unhappily, she was the only woman and she soon realised that was enough to attract attention. Her throat was dry. This was the hardest thing she had done in her life. Not knowing what to expect, she forced herself to step into a stuffy corridor. Yusuf kept close.

They passed through another door and entered a room filled with many prisoners. Sight of so many men crammed together turned her insides to water. The smell was appalling; it caught in the back of her throat, so sickly sweet it was hard not to gag. Death crouched in every corner. Sounds were ugly. Someone was screaming in pain. Gaunt and hungry men swore at each other as they elbowed each aside to get to the food. It was grim beyond her worst imaginings.

These were her father's enemies.

Leonor's stomach lurched as it hit home. God

have mercy, these men were here on her father's orders. This was what her father did, he imprisoned wealthy enemies and held them until a ransom was paid for their release.

When a harsh remark was directed her way, Yusuf pressed close and muttered for her to hurry. Leonor didn't need reminding. This was no place for a woman, that much was plain.

'I'll be quick,' she whispered.

Hairs prickled on the back of her neck, the pinched faces of the captives scrabbling for bread told her that some had scarcely eaten in weeks. And these were the fortunate ones. She wasn't going to think about what happened to those without the means to pay any ransom.

She had long been aware of the Sultan's cruel streak. She had always resented the way he insisted that his daughters passed most of their days locked in their apartment like birds in a cage. But this! It was hard to take it in.

Her father governed Leonor and her sisters with an iron fist, but still the Princesses had been granted their moments of freedom. They'd been given gifts and privileges.

A couple of years ago, they'd learned to ride. Three beautiful grey ponies had arrived at the castle and that summer, on moonlit nights, the veiled Nasrid Princesses had ridden out accompanied by a troop of household knights. Naturally, they'd had to ignore their escort of knights, and the only person who could speak to them had been the eunuch acting as their riding instructor. It had been such a joy to escape the castle for a while. And the Princesses had learned to ride well, albeit in the darkest hours when no one was about to see them.

Leonor stared about her at the men her father had incarcerated and her throat worked. It was hard to accept that the charming and amusing father who occasionally appeared to shower his daughters with silks and jewels was the same man who lodged his noble captives in so rank a place.

As she struggled to reconcile the two images of her father—the generous parent and the cruel tyrant—her head began to throb. It was so confusing.

Willing herself to focus on finding the knight in the crimson tunic, Leonor searched the room. Luckily, in the sea of chaos—of wounded, haggard men—that bright tunic was easy to see. She found him kneeling at the side of his injured friend. She stepped closer. His tunic was somewhat the worse for wear and his dark, handsome face was tight with worry. Was his friend dying?

The heat was a curse. Rodrigo had spent the hours of darkness persuading Inigo to drink enough to make up for what he was losing in sweat, yet despite his best efforts, Inigo had tossed and turned for most of the night.

It wasn't surprising. Rodrigo and his comrades had been housed with about thirty other captured noblemen. It could be worse. Crucially, there was a roof, which meant there was shade in the day. Naturally, the windows high up in the walls were barred, but they were above ground and they let in both air and light and that was a blessing. Despite this, the stench was overpowering. Rodrigo didn't like to think what an underground cell would be like.

Vaguely, he heard the prison door open. Rodrigo was aware of the rush to get to the food and pushed himself to his feet. He wasn't interested in food though. Inigo was no better and Rodrigo was damned if he was going to lose Inigo as well as Diego. Rodrigo had to find the doctor who had ministered to Inigo the previous evening. The man had promised to return.

Ah, there he was, among the visitors. As soon as the doctor crossed the threshold, a babble broke out—shouting, coughing, groaning.

'Doctor! Over here!'

'Doctor, please!'

'Help me, Doctor!'

In the general melee, Rodrigo got to the man first, practically dragging him to where Inigo lay stretched out on some sacking by the wall. Other captives crowded close, some were curious, others clamoured for the doctor's attention.

The doctor scowled and waved the crowd back.

'Be silent,' he said. 'Give us space to breathe. I will see to the rest of you shortly.'

The hubbub faded.

The doctor crouched down at Inigo's side and touched his forehead. 'How's his fever? Did it abate after he drank that infusion?'

Rodrigo shook his head. 'He's been hot as a furnace all night.'

The doctor gave him a sharp look. 'He's not spoken? Has he roused at all?'

'No, I had to force the drink down his throat. I'd be grateful if you would take another look at his leg.'

The doctor sat back on his haunches. 'I stitched it most carefully. And that poultice is best left alone.'

'I would prefer if you checked it, and I'd like him to have fresh bandages.' Rodrigo spoke firmly, he'd seen a man lose a leg through neglecting to care for a wound and he wasn't going to allow that to happen to Inigo. There would be no more deaths, not if he could help it.

A wave of grief swept through him. *Diego.* News of his brother's death would kill his mother; had it reached her already? Rodrigo had bribed one of the Sultan's officers to send his brother's body home. Was the officer honourable? Would he do as he was asked? Rodrigo had no way of knowing.

'Very well.' The doctor held his hand out, palm

up. 'For another examination and fresh bandages, I need further payment.'

'You want more? Good God, I've already given you my gold signet ring.'

The doctor gave a regretful smile and glanced pointedly at the other prisoners struggling to catch his eye. A trooper was doing his best to ensure they waited their turn, but it was clear he was fighting a losing battle.

The doctor spread his hands. 'It's hard to perform miracles, my lord. This is not the healthiest of places. In my view, your friend needs more infusions to bring down his fever. That will cost you.' He stood up and prepared to move away. 'So, unless you can pay, there are others who require my services.'

Rodrigo and his friends had no coin, their purses had been taken the moment they'd been captured. They'd only been allowed to keep their rings as proof of their identity and status. Rodrigo's gaze landed on Inigo's signet ring. Like the ring Rodrigo had given the doctor the previous day, Inigo's was pure gold. Rodrigo had balked at taking it whilst Inigo was unconscious, which was why he'd given the doctor his own ring. Now, it would seem he had no choice.

Reluctantly, he reached for Inigo's ring.

'That will not be necessary,' a gentle voice said.

A small hand reached out and a jewel-encrusted bangle was pressed into his palm. The scent of orange blossom, as refreshing as a breath of spring air, surrounded him.

Rodrigo's jaw dropped. A woman? Here? He scrambled to his feet and found himself staring at a mysterious, feminine figure. She was swathed in black from head to toe. Everything was hidden, even her eyes were lost behind a full veil. Clearly, she'd been there long enough to overhear his conversation with the doctor.

'The doctor will accept this as payment for treating your friend,' she insisted, in a soft, faintly accented voice.

This mystery lady spoke Spanish? Rodrigo was gazing bemusedly at her when the doctor whisked the bangle from his palm and hunched over Inigo.

'Sir, I am charged to question you.' That small hand emerged briefly from within the folds of the woman's all-encompassing gown. She beckoned at a guard who was standing so close he had to be her personal escort, then she and her escort headed for the door.

Two soldiers appeared and Rodrigo was marched out into the corridor.

Chapter Three

Leonor's pulse was racing. She could hardly believe what she'd done. She, a Nasrid princess, was alone in a cramped prison cell with four men. Alone and unchaperoned.

Her hopes had risen when she'd realised the Spanish knight had parted with his own ring to pay for help for his injured companion. He might be her father's enemy, but he was obviously loyal to his comrades. With luck, he'd be grateful about the bangle and would be forthcoming when she asked him about her mother.

Folding her hands tightly beneath the maidservant's veil, she turned to Yusuf and switched to Arabic. 'Be so good as to take the other guards outside. Wait for me there, I shall call you when I need you.'

Yusuf hesitated and for a dreadful moment Leonor's skin chilled. If Yusuf refused to leave her, she would achieve nothing. She wouldn't be able to question the knight about her mother within Yusuf's hearing, for if Yusuf understood that she was asking about the Sultan's dead Queen and her family, he'd be bound to tell his commanding officer. Then word would soon get back to her father. And that letter in her jewel box wouldn't help her; she'd been deluding herself to think it would.

But it was too late for second thoughts. The die was cast and it was imperative that Yusuf leave her alone with this knight.

Yusuf eyed the knight's chained wrists before giving a curt nod. 'As you wish.'

'My thanks.' Leonor let out a sigh of relief and Yusuf marched out with the other guards.

The knight shifted. 'If you want any sense out of me, you will need to speak Spanish.'

'That is not a problem, sir.'

Dark eyes looked her over so thoroughly Leonor felt herself flush from head to toe. She was thankful for the heavy veil.

'I assume you gave me that bauble because you need my help in some way,' he said.

'You are astute, sir.'

'No serving wench would have such things to give away. May I know to whom I am addressing?'

'I... No.'

He gave her a curt nod. 'Very well. Lest you are curious, I am commander of the King's garrison in Córdoba. Rodrigo Álvarez, Count of Córdoba, at your service.'

It was a good sign that he had told her his name and Leonor felt herself relax a little. She even took a step closer. *Rodrigo Álvarez.*

His hair was disordered and in need of a wash. Light from a narrow window fell directly on his face, allowing her to see the hollows under his eyes and a haze of dark beard. His eyes were almost black and fringed with thick eyelashes; his gaze was intent and focused entirely on her. His tunic was torn and dirty, and his wrists rubbed raw—they'd been chafed by his chains. His mouth edged up at a corner—it was a smile, yet at the same time, it was very definitely not a smile. Beneath it, she sensed dark, swirling pain and implacable fury. This man loathed her father, if he knew her identity, he would probably tear her limb from limb.

She lifted her gaze back to his eyes and her stomach clenched. She was astonished to discover that she didn't feel fear when she looked at this man, though what she did feel was something of a mystery.

Revulsion? Possibly, because he was very dirty. Oddly, she didn't think it was revulsion. Whatever it was, it unsettled her.

His mouth tightened. 'Don't tell me the Sultan has taken to allowing his prisoners a little pleasure.'

Behind the veil, Leonor stared. 'My lord?'

'Never mind.' He leaned a shoulder against the wall, studying her with those penetrating dark eyes. 'You said you were charged to question me. As you see, I am entirely at your disposal.'

'Thank you.' Leonor hesitated. This man made her nervous in a way she had never felt before. For once in her life, she was grateful for her veil. Of course, she'd never conversed alone with a strange man before, it could simply be that. None the less, here in this cell, her veil was a welcome refuge. The Count wouldn't know how nervous she was. 'My lord, I am charged to ask you about events which took place nineteen or twenty years ago.'

'Twenty years ago? You intrigue me. Although I must tell you I was but a stripling then, so I doubt I can tell you anything.'

'Hear me out, please,' Leonor said, and the words tumbled over each other in her anxiety to get at the truth of her mother's history. 'It concerns a Spanish noblewoman called Lady Juana. She was captured and brought to Granada.'

Lord Rodrigo didn't move, save to narrow those dark eyes. 'Captured? Twenty years ago?'

'Yes, my lord.'

Leonor held her breath as something—a shadow?—flickered across his face. Shock? Astonishment? It was hard to say. Notwithstanding, a ripple of excitement ran through her. Lord Rodrigo knew something about her mother, of that she was certain.

A heartbeat later, his expression was once again inscrutable and the doubts rushed back. Had she imagined that look?

'It might help if you had the name of this lady's family.' His voice was dry and brusque.

'My lord, that is what I am sent to discover.'

His frown deepened. He pushed away from the wall and loomed over her, solid and imposing. 'Who wants to know about this Lady Juana? Your mistress?' He paused thoughtfully, his eyes as hard and unyielding as stone. 'You?'

There it was again, that flash of pain, that deep anger. Leonor resisted the urge to back away. Swallowing hard, she shook her head.

Even through the veil, his eyes held hers. 'Who are you, mistress? Have I seen you before?' There was another pause. 'In a tower overlooking the harbour, perhaps?'

Leonor's heart jumped and for a wild moment she thought that sharp gaze had pierced her veil. Count Rodrigo couldn't possibly know that she had been looking out of the pavilion window that day. He had been too far away to see clearly, he had to be bluffing.

She lifted her chin. 'I am of no consequence, my lord. I am merely an intermediary sent to question you. Lady Juana was taken from her homeland.'

'You are certain she was born outside Al-Andalus?'

'Yes. I am hoping to…to contact her family.'

'I grant you that Juana is a popular name, but you will have to give me more than that.' A dark eyebrow lifted. 'Where was her home? Did she come from Castile? Aragon, perhaps?'

Unable to dismiss the idea that Lord Rodrigo had heard about her mother's abduction, Leonor twisted her fingers together. If only she knew more about the world outside her father's castle. Until this moment, she'd never realised how ignorant she was. She'd been educated, yes, but in a limited fashion. Her world was the world of the harem. It was, so Inés had told her, more cloistered than that of a nun in a convent.

She was so eager to learn but, over the years, her questions about her father's kingdom and the lands beyond his borders had gone unanswered. She'd heard about the frontier skirmishes, but she had very few facts.

'I am not certain where Lady Juana came from,' she whispered. Although Inés had refused to talk about her mother's birthplace, she had once let slip that she herself had been born in Castile. 'Possibly Castile.'

The Count gave a quiet laugh. 'Castile is vast, that's not much to go on.'

His chains chinked. Frozen by a combination

of shock and fascination, Leonor watched as he took her hand.

She stopped breathing. No man, save her father, may he live for ever, had ever touched her. Of course, Count Rodrigo wasn't touching her skin, the cloth of the veil lay between them. Even so, it gave her a jolt to feel that strong hand on hers.

She jerked free. 'How dare you!'

Somehow the Count caught her hand again, even going as far as to raise it to his lips. When he kissed it through the veil, a disturbing bolt of energy shot through Leonor's veins.

The effrontery!

'It is forbidden to touch me, my lord.' Again, she wrenched free.

Straightening, the Count retreated to his position against the wall, eyes fixed on hers. 'Forbidden? By whom?' To her alarm, a triumphant smile flickered into being. 'I believe I know who you are.'

Leonor closed her eyes. 'You can have no idea.'

'But I think that I do.' He leaned in again and lowered his voice. 'Your questions betray you, Princess. All of Christendom knows that Sultan Tariq stole a Spanish noblewoman named Lady Juana and made her his Queen. It was the scandal of a lifetime. And who else but one of his daughters would want to know about that long-dead Queen?'

Heart in her mouth, it was a moment before

Leonor trusted herself to speak. Count Rodrigo mustn't realise he had stumbled on the truth! The last thing she needed was for her father to find out from someone else that she had been visiting the prisoners. 'You are wrong.'

'Show me your face.'

'Never.'

'You are one of the Princesses.'

'I am not.'

'You, my lady, are a liar.' Count Rodrigo's voice was little more than a whisper and yet she had never heard anything more threatening. 'Won't you tell me your name, Princess?' He laid his hand on his heart and gave a slight bow. Filthy and dishevelled though he was, she had never seen anyone look less subservient. 'I swear not to tell anyone you have been here, your secret will be safe with me.'

Thoughts in chaos—what had she done?—Leonor swept to the door and reverted hastily to Arabic. 'Yusuf, we're leaving.'

Rodrigo Álvarez, Count of Córdoba. The name reverberated in Leonor's mind as she hurried back to the apartments. Absently, she rubbed the back of her hand. It still tingled. Count Rodrigo hadn't touched her actual skin, yet her hand was all hot. How could so slight a touch affect her so strongly? What might it feel like if he kissed her skin, rather than the veil?

Her sandal caught on a flagstone and she missed her step. The feelings that the Count had unleashed inside her were astonishing, although she'd be the first to admit she hadn't been sure what to expect. She'd imagined him to be— what?—overbearing, like her father?

Count Rodrigo had been angry and resentful and not a little intimidating. Yet, filthy and half-starved though he was he, he'd kept his anger in check. He'd been more thoughtful and courteous than she'd dared hope. And that wry smile—why, at times, he'd even seemed amused.

How would Father have behaved in like circumstances?

Leonor wasn't sure, but she was fairly certain that her father wouldn't have been half as forbearing.

The Count did have a certain rough charm. Thoughtfully, she glanced at her hand, it felt as though it had been branded. Lord Rodrigo's kiss had branded her. Did all men have this power? Was this why her father denied his daughters the company of men?

Abruptly, she shook her head. That couldn't be the reason she and her sisters were kept in seclusion. It was more likely their father was saving them for some dynastic alliance.

Leonor had reached the sun-warmed courtyard near the rosemary bushes when Inés stepped out from behind a pillar. Her duenna wasn't wearing her veil and her face was chalk white. In her hand was the letter Leonor had written to her father.

Heart plummeting, Leonor glanced at Yusuf. 'Thank you, Yusuf, that will be all.'

Inés stalked up and took Leonor's elbow in an iron grip. 'Come with me, young lady.'

'You've been through my jewel box!'

'You left an anklet in the bathhouse, I was tidying up after you. And a good thing too.'

'You've read it?'

Inés watched Yusuf's retreat, pursing her lips until he had left the courtyard. 'Indeed, I have.'

'Inés, it's addressed to the Sultan, not you.'

'You've been into the prison! What were you thinking?'

'Inés, I never intended to send that letter, unless…' Her voice trailed off.

'Unless you were caught?'

'Yes.'

Inés brandished the letter. 'Are you aware that this puts Yusuf in grave danger?'

'I—'

'Did you know he has a wife and children?'

'No, I didn't. However, I don't believe the letter puts him in danger. I take responsibility for my actions. I made a full confession.'

'Sultan Tariq is not a confessor. Forgiveness does not come easily to him.' Inés snatched Leonor's borrowed veil from her head and her lip curled. 'What is this rag? It's not fit for a Nasrid princess. Where did you get it?'

'I shall not say.'

Inés glared at her. 'It matters not. If your father had received this letter, he would have had the truth out of you soon enough. And then the owner of this veil would be lucky if she received only a thousand lashes.'

Inés's tone of voice was colder than the snow lying on the peaks of the Sierra Nevada. Leonor felt terrible. 'I realised my mistake once I got to the prison, but by then it was too late to back out.' She gazed earnestly at Inés. 'Please be calm. No one discovered me, we can destroy the letter and no harm done.'

Inés gave a brusque headshake. 'I cannot believe what I am hearing. Princess Zaida, your behaviour is beyond unseemly. You tricked your way into the prison and spoke to an enemy captive. Further, this letter betrays an appalling want of responsibility. It condemns Yusuf; it condemns the maid who lent you her veil; and it condemns me. I have done my best with you. As the Sultan's daughter, you should know better. Do you hate me so much?'

'Of course I don't hate you! How could I? You have been a mother to us, you have taught us so much.'

'Not enough, apparently. Were you really prepared to bring your father's wrath down on the entire household simply so you may flirt with a stranger you glimpsed on the quayside?'

Leonor bit her lip and surreptitiously rubbed the back of her hand against her gown. 'I wasn't flirting.'

'Then what were you doing, pray?'

'Asking about Mamá.'

Inés put her hand to her throat. 'You talked to a foreign captive about the Queen?'

'Inés, please understand—'

'Enough! My lady, you need to know that the Sultan forbade me to tell you and your sisters anything about your mother.'

Leonor's eyes widened. 'What? You weren't to tell us anything?'

'I am afraid not.' Inés lowered her gaze. 'Over the years I have told you far more than I should.'

'Why did you do it, then, if you fear Father so much?'

A sparrow flitted across the rosemary-scented courtyard and vanished into a bush. Inés sighed heavily. 'I missed home and the three of you were naturally so curious—I couldn't help myself. It was a grave mistake.'

'Does Father know you taught us Spanish?'

'Faith, no! He'd kill me if he found out.'

Guilt lodged, heavy as a stone, in Leonor's belly. 'I am sorry, I didn't understand.'

'What's done is done.' Inés looked warily at her. 'You spoke Spanish to that nobleman, I expect?'

'Aye.'

Inés gave a heavy sigh, her eyes haunted. 'Did he know to whom he was speaking?'

'I… I am not sure.' Leonor stared at the ground. She couldn't bring herself to admit that the Spanish Count had indeed guessed her to be a princess. 'I said nothing of who I was.'

'Yet you asked him about Lady Juana and you addressed him in Spanish.' Inés let out a great sigh. 'Dear Lord, our idyll is ended.'

'Idyll? What idyll?'

Inés released her and straightened her back. 'I shall see you later. My lady, I shall destroy this letter and then I must write to the Sultan myself.' She gave another sigh. 'I have delayed writing to him, I should probably have written some months since. However, I can delay no longer, the three of you have outgrown my tutelage.'

Leonor felt as though a shadow had passed over the sun. She caught her duenna's sleeve. 'What do you mean we have outgrown your tutelage? Inés, what will you tell him?'

'Sultan Tariq made me swear to tell him once the three of you reached a marriageable age. Clearly, that time is upon us. I shall inform him that he is best advised to visit his daughters as soon as his duties allow.'

Marriage. Leonor toyed with her remaining bangle. Part of her was relieved that her letter would never reach her father—the last thing she wanted was for anyone to suffer for her desire to learn about her mother. On the other hand, she wasn't ready for marriage. Neither she nor her sisters had any experience in dealing with men. Other than bearing a man heirs—and even on that score Leonor was woefully ignorant as to how that might be achieved—the Princesses knew little of what a man might require in his bride.

'Father will arrange for us to be married?'

Inés grimaced. 'Possibly,' she murmured. 'Although it is equally possible that the Sultan will want to keep you pure.'

Leonor felt herself tense. 'What does that mean?'

'The King might not wish you to ever marry,' Inés said. She wasn't meeting Leonor's eyes and somehow that was more worrying than anything.

'Please continue.'

'I am not certain I can. It was something I was told years ago, and I am not sure I believe it.'

Leonor had never liked not knowing what her future might be. If her father was arranging her marriage, she hoped to have a say in the choice of her future husband—she wanted to get to know him before they married. She had fretted about this for years and in all that time it had never occurred to her that her father might not want his daughters to marry at all.

Father might not want us to marry? Inés must be wrong. What were they to do, if they weren't to marry?

'Inés, for the love of God, you can't leave it at that. What were you told? Does Father plan to have us married or not?'

Inés stared bleakly at her feet. 'After the three of you were born, Sultan Tariq consulted his astrologer and your horoscopes were cast. The Sultan was advised that once you and your sisters reached marriageable age he should be watchful. The astrologer warned him to gather his daughters under his wings.'

Leonor frowned, it all sounded extremely ominous. 'To gather us under his wings? What on earth might that mean?'

'I'm sorry, my lady, I have no idea. However, since you have clearly reached marriageable age, I have no choice but to write to the Sultan and inform him of that.'

Worry scored lines on Inés's face. Leonor forced a smile. 'I understand; you must write to Father.'

Her heart felt like lead. What would the Sultan do? Were she and her sisters to be kept closeted all their lives? Was that why they'd been kept so ignorant of the world? She touched the back of her hand where Count Rodrigo had kissed it and, for the first time in her life, looked into the future with fear in her heart.

Leonor had always assumed she would one day be married. Never in her worst nightmares had it occurred to her that all that lay in front of her might be a life of pampered imprisonment.

Such a life would shrivel her soul…it would kill her. She must have some say in her future. She must.

No one told captives anything. A month had dragged by and Rodrigo was tramping wearily along a dusty highway, one in a long line of prisoners headed for God alone knew where. He was covered in grit and his skin itched. The sky was a solid block of blue. The heat had been building all day and Rodrigo's clothes were drenched with sweat, he felt as though he was locked in an oven.

Instinct told him this was the road to Granada, but the terrain was unfamiliar and the guards resolutely uncommunicative. Not to mention that there was the language difficulty, neither Rodrigo nor his friends knew more than a couple of dozen words of Arabic.

Inigo walked along in front of him. And Enrique? Rodrigo trained his gaze on the front of the line, but his cousin was lost behind a curtain of dust. The three of them had spent most of the time since their capture trying to keep together and it wasn't easy. Just then, Inigo glanced over his shoulder and sent him a terse smile.

Praise God, Inigo's leg was improving every day; the wound hadn't festered and his limp was barely noticeable now.

Salobreña lingered in Rodrigo's mind as a stinking hellhole, he wasn't sorry to leave it. His lips twisted as he thought back to when they'd been herded into the prison yard. Inigo hadn't come back to his senses until long after that mysterious young woman had given her jewelled bangle to pay for further treatment. Rodrigo hadn't told Inigo about her largesse, although since then not a day had passed without her slipping into his thoughts.

That husky voice was unforgettable. And, despite his mystery lady's veil, he'd been able to tell that she had a slender body and a proud bearing.

It was strange how the veil made her more fascinating rather than less, a man couldn't help but wonder what lay beneath it. Something about her told him that despite her proud bearing, she was young. And frighteningly innocent. Rodrigo's lips twisted as he recalled the outrage in her tone when he'd kissed her hand. It hadn't been his finest hour. He'd kissed her to distract her; he'd kissed her out of anger.

It had been surprisingly stimulating. He was unlikely to see her again, although if he did, he would enjoy testing her with a more measured kiss. Since talking to her in that cell, he'd spent many nights with her scent twisting through his dreams. Orange blossom and woman. It had been tantalising and very frustrating.

Could the stories of three identical Nasrid

Princesses be true? Might his mystery lady be one of them? Her questions had all concerned Sultan Tariq's dead Queen, Lady Juana, so it was possible.

Guilt preyed on his mind. Rodrigo had told the truth when he'd said that he didn't know any Lady Juana. He'd never met her, though he had heard of her. All of Christendom knew of Lady Juana's scandalous abduction, and Rodrigo more than most had reason to regret it. Should he have told that girl what he knew?

He grimaced. Her questions had caught him off guard. They had opened old wounds, wounds which, despite the passing of many years, still smarted. By the time Rodrigo had himself in hand again, the girl had swept out of the cell.

I frightened her off.

Should he have told her?

Lord, no. He'd never see the girl again and what was the point of delving into the past? The best thing he could do would be to put the entire incident out of his mind.

On the other hand, her bangle had bought Inigo more treatment. She had certainly saved Inigo's leg, and possibly his life too. Which left Rodrigo with an inconvenient sense of obligation towards her. Scowling at the road ahead, Rodrigo told himself to forget the entire incident.

Doubtless, his mysterious visitor had many bangles.

Still, he felt bad that the girl had gone away with none of her questions answered. He could at least have told her that when Lady Juana disappeared she had been betrothed to Count Jaime of Almodóvar.

His nostrils flared. Doubtless, Count Jaime would be able to answer the girl's questions in more detail. Not that she was ever likely to meet him if she was indeed a Nasrid princess.

Rodrigo and Count Jaime weren't exactly on speaking terms. It wasn't that he and the lord of Almodóvar were enemies, but they certainly weren't friends. Perhaps, when Rodrigo was finally free of Al-Andalus, he'd let Lord Jaime know that someone in Salobreña Castle had been asking about Lady Juana. Perhaps.

Scowling at a stone in the road, he toed it into the ditch and marched on. What the devil was he doing thinking about Count Jaime? He'd far rather be wondering about his mystery lady. Had she been among those women in the castle tower on the day their ship had docked? Why had she singled him out for questioning? There were plenty other prisoners in Salobreña to choose from. She must have been watching him.

He felt a smile form. The thought that his mystery lady might be the dark beauty who'd leaned out of that window had a certain appeal. If she was a princess, she was his enemy's daughter.

Faith, what was he doing? It was pointless

thinking about her. He'd only allowed himself to do so because back in the prison it had been either that or dwell on the horror of Diego's death. He wasn't ready to grieve, though grief would doubtless be a dull ache he'd be carrying for years.

God willing, he'd soon be home.

Freedom. Heart aching, Rodrigo squinted up the road. Today it seemed a million lifetimes away. He hated not having command over his life; he hated not knowing how many more miles lay ahead.

Rodrigo gave Inigo an assessing glance and was relieved to see him walking as well as a man could when hobbled with chains. Thank the Lord, that wound hadn't festered. He wasn't sure how patient the guards would be if they fell behind.

A guard cantered past, bellowing orders. Choking on grit, Rodrigo found himself wishing for the man's horse. No matter that the animal had a back like a bow and an uneven gait, at least on horseback there was a chance of escaping the worst of the dust.

The guard shouted again, in Arabic. The words meant nothing to Rodrigo, but a nearby prisoner must have understood them, for he muttered under his breath and scowled back along the road. He was probably bemoaning the lack of water. Rodrigo didn't blame him, rations—even of water—were in short supply on this trudge to hell. The riverbed at the side of the road was completely dry, a scrubby patch of weeds grew in the middle where water must once have flowed. The river, like Rodrigo's throat, was bone dry.

Another shout from the direction of Salobreña caught his attention, the voice was tight and angry. The ground shook and Rodrigo turned.

A troop of horsemen was thundering towards them.

Lord, what a troop! Even in battle, Rodrigo had never faced fiercer-looking foes. The horses— black stallions—and their knights were surely giants, sprung out of some ancient Arabic fable. Silver breastplates gleamed on the knights' wide chests. Beneath their armour, the knights' tunics were black. Black turbans, black tunics, black boots, black shields. The knights' faces were hidden.

The stallions were big-boned and well muscled and their coats gleamed like jet. Envy stirred in Rodrigo's breast. A man might sell his soul for one of those horses. Dust swirled into his eyes, he blinked it away. This was an elite troop and he knew of only one man in Al-Andalus who could field knights as formidable as these. This troop answered to Sultan Tariq.

A harsh voice cracked out an order, a whip snaked out and the black horses wheeled as one, stepping purposefully forward to herd the straggling line of prisoners into the dried-up riverbed. A scimitar flashed.

Rodrigo stumbled along with the rest of them. When the prisoners were strung out among the withered weeds at the edge of the highway, there came another shout. To Rodrigo's astonishment, every man fell face down on the ground.

Almost every man. Inigo and Enrique had no clue what was happening either, the three comrades were the only ones still on their feet. Rodrigo's bemusement grew when their guards flung themselves off their horses and prostrated themselves along with the prisoners.

The nearest black horseman was screaming at Rodrigo, eyes bulging with anger. From his frantic gestures, Rodrigo understood he was expected to fall on his face like everyone else. Rodrigo didn't move. He'd be damned if he was going to put his face in the thistles for no good reason.

Hoofbeats heralded the arrival of a second, smaller, party—about a dozen knights on brown horses. The knights were armed to the teeth.

The nearest horseman continued to scream at him. Rodrigo ignored him, because something most intriguing had caught his ears.

The light tinkle of bells. Bells?

Dust puffed out from beneath the horses' hoofs, coating the shrubs and weeds. A standard fluttered. It was red and gold, the colours of the Nasrid dynasty. Those magnificent black knights did indeed answer to Sultan Tariq. If

Rodrigo was not mistaken, he was about to set eyes on the King himself.

A scimitar flashed.

Unless that brute in black killed him first.

Chapter Four

Princess Leonor sat on her grey mare, Snow-storm. Behind her veil, she was smiling, she loved riding and it was a rare privilege to be out during the day. Best of all, she and her sisters were finally leaving Salobreña Castle. They were on their way to the Alhambra Palace to live with their father.

Naturally, there were drawbacks. Owing to the length of the journey, they were riding through the heat of the day. It was hot and sticky and Leonor's veil clung to her skin. However, it wasn't often that the Princesses could see the roads and highways of their father's kingdom. Leonor was determined to make the most of it.

Excitement bubbled inside her. Change was in the air. Sultan Tariq, may blessings shower upon him, had deigned to acknowledge his daughters' existence.

The Sultan had arrived at Salobreña Castle a few days ago, and he'd practically turned it upside down when he'd announced that the Princesses were to travel with him to Granada. Apparently, a tower had been built especially for them in the Alhambra Palace. Sultan Tariq's eyes had softened when he told his daughters that the tower overlooked the surrounding countryside. There was a fine view of the mountains from one side, and from the other they could look down upon the palace gardens.

The Sultan had been smiling and charming. Uncertain as to what Inés might have told him, Leonor had been dreading seeing him again, but he had greeted his three daughters with equal warmth.

'Let me look at you. Such beauties you have become.'

Their father had seemed genuinely pleased to see them. Inés could not have told him about her unorthodox visit to the prison.

That visit haunted Leonor. She found herself chasing away the mental image of Lord Rodrigo in that narrow cell far too often. Doubtless, she couldn't stop thinking about him because conditions in the prison were so appalling. It was a place of evil, fit only for the devil. She was ashamed her father sanctioned it.

And there was that other matter. *Lord Rodrigo kissed my hand.* The first foreigner she'd ever spoken to. If her father found that out, he'd have Count Rodrigo torn apart.

The Sultan had taken pains to describe the alabaster fountain in the central court of the Princesses' new tower. He told his daughters that he'd ordered poems to be inscribed in tiles on the tower walls and that delicate arabesques adorned the arches and door frames. As Leonor watched her father's smiling face, as she listened to him describing what he'd planned for them, her anger for the years of neglect began to fade.

And her fears for her future? Hope was starting to flower. They weren't to languish in Salobreña until the end of time. Finally, she and her sisters were going to become part of their father's court. Life could change. She even dared to hope that her father might learn to be less intransigent in his dealings with his enemies.

So, here they were, riding towards the Alhambra Palace with a full escort of household knights ahead and behind them. Nothing as exciting had happened in years. True, there wasn't much to see on this stretch of road. The landscape was bleached by the sun. Scorched weeds lined the route and there were few signs of habitation. Still, Leonor wasn't going to allow that to lower her mood.

Leaning forward, she patted Snowstorm's neck. As her name implied, Snowstorm was the palest of greys. Almost white, she was an exact match to her sisters' horses. Silver bells were attached to the braids in the mares' manes, and a gentle tinkling accompanied their every step. As their party covered the miles, the dry air was filled with faint, otherworldly music.

There were restrictions on this ride to her new life. A palace eunuch was riding at Leonor's side. Ostensibly, he was there to hold a sunshade over her head. The sunshade didn't do much. She knew the eunuch was really there to keep her in line. For once, she didn't care.

It was stifling beneath her veil and she didn't care about that either. Not today, when she was out and about in her father's realm. Naturally, she wouldn't be human if she didn't resent having to look at everything through a haze of fine silk. However, today, none of that mattered. Her father had come for them. He had realised that she and her sisters had grown up and they were about to start afresh in Granada.

The previous night the royal party had taken shelter in one of her father's hunting lodges. That had been exciting too, it was the first time that the Princesses remembered sleeping anywhere except in their apartments in Salobreña Castle.

The horses slowed. There was a disturbance up ahead, which was odd. Leonor hadn't expected delays on this, the final leg of their journey. The King had sent heralds out in advance of their departure and his subjects had been ordered—on pain of death, apparently—to remain indoors as the royal party rode past. No one should be abroad to slow them down.

Privately, Leonor suspected that the real reason her father's subjects had been told to stay indoors was because Sultan Tariq didn't want anyone to see his daughters. Which was ridiculous. *We are wearing veils, and one veiled woman looks very much like another.* No one would see as much as an eyelash.

None the less, Leonor prayed that her father's people had obeyed their orders. Whilst she hadn't come up against the Sultan's temper personally, there were tales that froze the marrow in her bones. Imprisonment—well, she'd seen that for herself—but she'd also heard that whippings and starvation were commonplace. She'd even heard whispers about summary executions.

Her saddle creaked as she peered ahead. Her father's personal knights were bunched up in a knot. There was a lot of shouting. She clutched her reins and prayed that nothing dreadful was about to happen. Her father had made it clear that delays wouldn't be tolerated. Whilst he had been kind to her and her sisters, Leonor couldn't dismiss the rumours about his bloodcurdling rages.

What would happen if they stumbled across a stray peasant who hadn't heard the orders to stay indoors? Leonor's brow knotted. Her optimistic mood faded, like a flower that had stood too long in the searing sun. She held Snowstorm at a standstill under the sunshade so helpfully held over her and told herself firmly that they would be on their way soon.

An arm's length away, Alba and Constanza sat on their grey mares amid a froth of full skirts and rippling veils. Like Leonor, they were wearing circlets starred with gemstones; like her, their wrists were adorned with heavy gold bracelets.

Snowstorm tossed her head and the light chime of bells shimmered about them.

Alba guided her horse closer. 'I didn't think this journey would take so long,' she murmured. 'Are you as stiff as I am?'

'I'm a little sore, but I don't care. Father has come for us and we shall live in a tower and look out across the mountains. We shall have our own household.' Leonor tried to sound bright, even though she had a terrible feeling that something awful was about to happen. Could Alba hear the worry in her voice?

'Leonor.' Alba switched quietly to Spanish, in the way the sisters did when they wanted to converse privately. Of all the royal servants, only Inés spoke Spanish. 'Life in the Alhambra might not be quite as you expect.'

Behind her veil, Leonor's eyes went wide. She lowered her voice to a whisper. 'You also doubt Father?'

'I suspect he only came for us because Inés wrote to him after you visited the prison.'

Leonor stiffened her spine. She'd told her sisters what she had done and they had been so shocked, she regretted mentioning it. It seemed all she had achieved was to worry them. 'Alba, I won't apologise. I wanted to know about Mamá.'

Alba leaned in. 'I don't blame you. I am as curious about her as you.' She gave a small sigh. 'Inés, on the other hand, was frantic.'

Leonor didn't need reminding. 'I know, and for that I am deeply sorry.'

'I'm pretty certain she told Father we'd been watching the Spanish captives when their ship arrived at the quayside.'

Leonor's heart sank. 'You don't think she mentioned my visit to the prison?'

'I doubt it, Father has shown no signs of anger.'

'I pray you are right.'

'Be careful, Leonor. It's my belief Father came to fetch us so that he could keep an even closer eye on us. Life in the palace might not be the paradise you are hoping for.'

Leonor gripped her reins, it wasn't pleasant having Alba echo her fears. Yes, the Sultan had come to escort his daughters to the palace. The question was, what would happen after that?

The horses walked on a few paces. Craning her neck, Leonor saw what was holding them up. The Sultan's personal guard clustered around him. Nearby, a line of prisoners was lying face down in a dried-up gully by the side of the road.

Oh, no! What about Father's orders that his subjects remain indoors? The guards in charge of these men could not have been told.

Goosebumps ran down her neck. Her father's black horsemen lined the route. Even they didn't dare look at the Princesses' escort. All save one had turned to face resolutely away from the road. The lone horseman who had not turned was screaming at a prisoner. A prisoner who was on his feet. Worse, he was staring directly at the royal entourage.

Leonor's mouth dried. Didn't he understand? Her father would kill him! Leonor willed him to lie down with the other prisoners.

The prisoner stood straight and tall by the side of the road, apparently oblivious of any danger. His crimson tunic hung in rags from his broad shoulders and, even at this distance, his casual arrogance was unmistakable. It was the commander of the garrison at Córdoba, Count Rodrigo Álvarez.

Ice filled her veins. She ran her gaze along the prisoners prostrated along the highway. Apart from Lord Rodrigo, two other prisoners were also standing, a man in blue and another in green. Despite the irritation of having to see through her filmy veil, Leonor knew them for the Count's comrades. One was the knight with the injured leg, the other had helped Lord Rodrigo keep him upright on the quayside.

'The three knights,' Leonor murmured. God have mercy.

Her father, the Sultan, may he live for ever, was glaring at Count Rodrigo. With a sense of dread, she watched her father snatch out his scimitar. He was preparing to charge!

Leonor spurred forward amid a tinkling of silver bells. Dust fogged the air, blurring the expression on the Sultan's face. It was impossible to judge the level of his anger. Given his order that his subjects should remain indoors whilst the royal party rode past, he was likely in a fury and had only stayed his hand because Lord Rodrigo's effrontery had temporarily stunned him.

'Father, stop!'

The Sultan turned to her, dark eyes incredulous. 'Daughter?'

His scimitar glittered. Leonor's insides quivered. No one, *no one*, questioned Sultan Tariq, never mind gave him a direct order. She swallowed hard, desperate to avoid bloodshed. 'The prisoner doesn't understand.'

She prayed for calm, understanding instinctively that if her father sensed her agitation, he would react badly. And she dreaded to think what might happen if she inadvertently revealed that she'd spoken to the Count in person. That would surely condemn him to a slow and painful death. She prayed for the right words.

'Father, it is my guess that that man is a Spanish knight, so he won't speak our language. How can he obey an order he doesn't understand?'

Her father's eyebrows formed a heavy black line. 'You are an expert on Spanish knights, Daughter?'

Dimly, Leonor heard the light ripple of bells. Her sisters had joined her, their horses flanked hers.

'Please, Father, they won't speak our tongue,' Alba whispered.

'Father, be merciful,' Constanza added softly.

The King looked from one daughter to the other, and when his gaze returned to her, Leonor forced her lips to move. 'The foreigners mean no insult, I am sure.' Recalling her father's obsession with refilling his treasury, she paused. 'Look at their clothing, Father.'

'Rags,' the Sultan bit out. 'Filthy rags.'

'Look closer, Father, and you will see that the embroidery is most fine. These men must be especially wealthy. Kill them and you will lose much in the way of ransom.'

The Sultan glowered. 'They are arrogant dogs. They should not be looking upon you. They must be punished.'

'We are veiled, Father,' Leonor said, in a cool voice. In truth, her heart was beating wildly and she felt sick with fear. She didn't want the Spanish knights killed simply for looking their way. She gripped the reins and hoped her voice wasn't shaking. 'Make an example of them, Father, by all means. Please don't kill them because they can't speak Arabic. Be merciful, Father, I implore you.'

Alba and Constanza added their voices to hers. 'Please, Father. We beg you.'

The Sultan watched them, face inscrutable. Then he glanced at a nearby guard. 'Guard? *Guard!* Yes, you with the prisoners. Get up.'

The guard scrambled to his feet, his face as pale as parchment. He bowed so low his forehead almost touched the ground. 'Great King?'

'You are in charge of these insolent fools?' the Sultan asked, indicating the three knights.

Leonor held her breath.

'Yes, Great King,' came the wary reply.

The Sultan tapped his boot with the flat of his scimitar. 'You expect them to fetch something in the way of ransom?'

The guard kept his head down. 'Yes, Great Lord. Their families have been notified and the ransom is on its way.'

The Sultan gave a curt nod and put away his scimitar. He looked at Leonor. 'Very well, my daughter. Since you ask so prettily and your sisters have added their pleas to yours, I shall be merciful. These men shall be imprisoned in the Vermillion Towers until their ransom arrives. However, they should not have gazed upon you. For that insolence, they shall do hard labour until their release.'

He flicked his hand in a gesture of dismissal and the guard effaced himself.

Leonor drew in a relieved breath. 'Thank you, Father.'

As she spoke, a skirl of wind raced along the highway, whisking up dust as it came. It caught the edges of the Princesses' veils and, distracted as they were, their veils lifted. For a few tense moments, their faces were revealed and there were no barriers between them and the world.

Leonor saw everything very clearly. That was to say, she saw Lord Rodrigo very clearly, for she was looking at him and him alone. Her stomach lurched. Apart from that day she'd been watching the port from the pavilion, Leonor's father was the only man she had gazed on without the protection of a veil. In Salobreña, distance had been her shield. Lord Rodrigo was closer now, close enough for his dark brown eyes to catch hers and, for her life, she couldn't look away.

She could see the rise and fall of his chest. His firm mouth was crooked into a faint smile, just as it had been that day she had visited him in the prison. His hair was tousled and dusty, and a grey smudge ran across one high cheekbone. As her eyes met his, she thought she saw him dip his head. His beard was untidy, he was hung about with chains, but he held himself like a prince. A strong, well-muscled prince who stole the breath from her lungs. Despite his unkempt state, Count

Rodrigo de Córdoba was surely the most handsome knight in the world.

'Daughters, your modesty!' The Sultan's growl brought Leonor sharply back to reality. 'Cover your faces!'

Leonor wrestled her veil into submission and the moment was gone.

Realising his mouth hung open, Rodrigo closed it with a snap. Before the woman's veil had lifted, her voice had revealed her to be the girl who had given her golden bangle to pay for Inigo's treatment. His heartbeat quickened. His mystery lady was a princess, just as he had suspected.

She was a rare beauty. His most fevered imaginings could never have conjured so sweet a face. Those large dark eyes, that twist of shining black hair, that shy yet sensual tilt to her mouth—in truth, she was the most beautiful woman he had ever seen.

A twist of longing tightened inside him. Ruthlessly, he quashed it. She was his enemy's daughter, a Nasrid princess.

After talking to her in that cell, Rodrigo had thought about her more than once. In his mind, she had become Lady Merciful. He'd passed many an hour wondering what Lady Merciful looked like beneath her veil, and whether in fact she was his enemy's daughter. Now his doubts had melted away.

The guard jerked on the chains. As they bit into his wrists, Rodrigo was pulled further into the ditch. He didn't resist; the sight of the Princess had left him oddly stunned. That Princess—Lord, it wasn't right that the tyrant's daughter should be so lovely. She had her veil under control now, he could no longer see a thing. It didn't matter. A man could live off one glimpse for years. The jolt she had given him had been visceral. Her face— delicate and lovely—was unforgettable.

Covertly, he watched her gather her reins and prepare to ride on. He had no way of knowing what had passed between her and her father, but it was obvious that she had interceded on his behalf.

She had saved him. She had saved Inigo back in Salobreña and now he too was beholden to her. He grimaced. It was an uncomfortable feeling. Being beholden to his enemy's daughter made a mockery of his grief for Diego. He ought to hate her.

The royal party proceeded up the road and the horseman in him watched her critically. She rode surprisingly well, sitting straight in the saddle, her posture graceful and relaxed. Veils fluttered, bells chimed and all too soon the pretty grey mares had disappeared behind the brown stallions of the Sultan's household knights.

Were her sisters equally beautiful? Rodrigo hadn't noticed, he'd only had eyes for her. She was a brave woman, intervening with Sultan Tariq like that. Exasperated with himself, Rodrigo shook his head. He mustn't allow a pair of shining black eyes to bewitch him. Even tyrants must love their daughters. Maybe she hadn't been so brave, she must have known her father would bend to her will—he probably adored her. She was certainly impulsive, though he knew that already, for a similar impulse had driven her to visit him in the prison. It was possible that wanting to learn about Lady Juana hadn't been the only reason for her visit, curiosity must also have played a part. She probably craved a bit of excitement.

God knows what life must be like for a pampered princess. She'd be kept closer than a nun on retreat. And those veils—Rodrigo grimaced—it must be stifling under all that cloth.

Rodrigo watched the royal party go with mixed feelings. The face that had been revealed when Lady Merciful's veil had lifted had left him feeling wrong-footed. And more than a little confused. In his heart, he knew he wasn't doing her justice. And justice was something that woman cared about. Briefly, the fury in the tyrant's eyes had made it seem he was about to lash out, yes, even at his daughter, yet she'd still intervened to stop her father using that scimitar. Without hesitation, she'd drawn the Sultan's anger on herself.

Rodrigo narrowed his gaze on the Nasrid standard as the dust enveloped the crimson and gold. Gripped by a feeling of unreality, he clenched his jaw. He had now become beholden—twice—to the Sultan's daughter, to a princess who looked as though she had stepped out of another world. Everything about her was fresh and innocent. Had his mind conjured her? It must have done, that arresting beauty couldn't be real. However, the way she had confronted her father certainly was. There'd been definite tension in the air. All three Princesses had been palpably afraid of what their father might do, yet they had still confronted him.

He drew in a deep breath. So. His enemy's daughters had at least one virtue, they were brave. No, make that two virtues, they were merciful.

The dust drifted back to earth, the guards cracked their whips and the line of captives was driven back on to the highway. As Rodrigo forced his weary legs to move, he couldn't stop thinking about the way the Princess's gaze had held his. She had looked directly at him and every fibre of his being had snapped awake. He'd liked it. He'd also noticed a faint flush on her cheeks as their eyes had caught. He'd liked that too.

He trudged on, adjusting his pace to take account of the play of the chains. His feet throbbed, they had to be bleeding. There was dust in his eyes, dust in his hair and dust in his throat. Yet despite everything, he couldn't get the face of the Nasrid Princess out of his head. So lovely. His enemy's daughter. *Dios mio*, he was losing his mind.

Hardening his heart, Rodrigo pushed her from

his thoughts. He would do far better to be thinking about the revenge he would take against Sultan Tariq when his ransom was finally paid.

Chapter Five

⧼⧼⧼⧽⧽⧽

The Alhambra Palace, Granada

It should have been paradise. Instead it was a beautiful prison.

The alabaster fountain in the central court of the Princesses' tower played continually. By day, the jets of water gleamed like fire; at night, the central pool had the sheen of silver. From the top of the tower, Leonor looked down into the palace gardens. She was filled with disquiet. Sparrows flitted from myrtle to orange tree and back again to the myrtles. On moonlit evenings, nightingales sang in the lemon trees. How could she be unhappy in so lovely a place?

The Sultan lavished every luxury on his daughters. Three pairs of songbirds were brought to the Princesses' tower. The birds twittered and fluttered in golden cages, filling the top floor with song. A few days later, peacocks appeared on the palace lawns; they paraded up and down, luminescent feathers shimmering in the sun— turquoise, green, gold. Shortly after that, the Princesses were given a pet monkey. Alba adored him, named him Hunter, and took to carrying him on her shoulder.

A step away from the Princesses' tower, there was even a Romanesque bathhouse. Maidservants stood under gorgeously tiled arches, linens in hand, silently waiting on the sisters' every whim. Light filtered through fairy-tale fretwork, and the surface of the bathing pool danced and sparkled with borrowed life. There were hot rooms, and cold rooms, and a restroom for the Princesses to lie in after they had bathed. Long divans were built along the tiled walls of the restroom, and they overflowed with cushions. The silent maidservants brought iced juices, grapes, sweetmeats...

Paradise? Leonor was afraid that a snake lurked at its heart.

Her thoughts were dark. She no longer trusted her father. The look on his face when he'd confronted Lord Rodrigo had been so ugly. If she hadn't intervened, her father would have butchered him there and then.

Tucked away in Salobreña all these years, Leonor had no real grasp of the King's character. Unfortunately, she was starting to know him. His moodiness was chilling. One moment he was all benevolence, showering his daughters with gifts, and the next he behaved like a tyrant. It was wrong. Wrong, wrong, wrong.

It was also wrong that Leonor spent so much time worrying about the fate of the three Spanish knights. If her father could read her thoughts, he'd fly into a frenzy. She told herself that mind-reading was impossible and was careful to guard her tongue, particularly in front of Inés. It wasn't that she feared for herself or her sisters, what she feared was drawing her father's anger down on an innocent servant or slave. She felt unbearably edgy.

It soon became clear that Alba too was concerned. Leonor was lying on a crimson cushion threaded with gold, staring blindly into the gardens, when Alba came in, Hunter perched on her shoulder. Since they were in the privacy of their tower, the Princesses had discarded their veils.

Alba took the cushion next to Leonor. Hunter jumped from her shoulder and scampered towards a bowl of sunflower seeds, chattering happily. 'What do you think they are doing?' Alba murmured.

Leonor didn't have to be told Alba was thinking about the three Spanish knights. 'We shouldn't be thinking about them.'

Alba's mouth turned down. 'I can't help it. What did Father mean when he said they'd be put to hard labour?'

Leonor shot a guilty look at the doorway. No one was there. Constanza was playing her silver lute and the faint strains of a Spanish folk song that Inés had taught them floated up from the chamber below. Constanza's choice of song—their duenna's favourite—made it obvious that she too was dwelling on the fate of the men.

'It's dangerous to talk about them.' Leonor kept her voice low. 'Alba, we must dismiss them from our thoughts.'

Alba fiddled with her emerald ring. 'Hard labour, Father said, and one of them was wounded. You don't think they'll be worked to death?'

Firmly, Leonor shook her head. 'Ransom money is needed to fill Father's coffers. They'll be kept alive.'

'May God have mercy on them, I pray you are right.'

Leonor rose from her cushion and went to the window on the other side of the chamber. The difference in outlooks both fascinated and troubled her. From this side of the tower, the view was of an altogether wilder landscape. At the foot of the palace wall, the land fell sharply into a deep, rock-strewn crevasse where stunted shrubs struggled to find a foothold. In the distance, the snow-topped peaks of the Sierra Nevada soared towards the sky.

'Even in summer the mountains are capped with snow,' she said, sinking on to another cush-

ion as the caged birds trilled behind her. Their
song blended prettily with the sound of Constanza's lute.

'Aye.'

Several tiny dots—birds, possibly eagles—
were moving across the sky. Leonor watched
them thoughtfully. Something about the location
of their tower—so far from their father's apartments—disturbed her. 'Alba, do you think the
position of this tower is significant? Could Father
be sending us a message?'

Silk rustled as her sister came across. 'What
do you mean?'

'The view from this side is completely untamed.' Leonor pointed. The crevasse cut through
the hill like a scar and ran the entire length of
the palace wall. 'Look, you can see right down
that gully.'

Alba's brow wrinkled. 'I can see trees and
boulders and not much else.'

'Exactly. On this side of our tower, all is wild;
on the other, all is cultivated. I can't help feeling
this tower is a warning. Or a threat.'

Alba threw her a puzzled look. 'A threat?'

Despite the heat, Leonor shivered. She gestured
in the direction of the gardens and tried to explain
her disquiet. 'Inside the palace walls, everything
is civilised. We walk through gardens fragrant
with orange blossom and jasmine; we find shade
in marbled hallways where ceilings look like hon-

eycombs and must have been made by angels. Father showers every luxury on us. Outside, however, we have that wilderness. Is Father warning what might happen if we cross him?'

'You think he would banish us to the wilderness?' Alba laughed. 'Leonor, only you would say something like that. Father can be difficult, but I am sure life will be better here.'

'Will it?'

'Yes! Think about the silk Father shipped in from Constantinople. Think about those gorgeous bangles, the rings.'

'Yes, yes, the silk is very fine, but we have so much, we can't possibly use it all. Do we need songbirds in golden cages? Do we need monkeys?' Leonor stared in exasperation at the new bangle weighing heavily on her wrist. 'Father loads us with jewels unearthed from the mines of India; he gives us caskets overflowing with necklaces, bracelets and anklets. We have velvet purses bulging with golden bezants and Frankish silver and I've no idea why we've been given them, we can't spend them.'

Alba's eyes brightened. 'Leonor, that is a good idea! Let's ask Inés for an escort. We'll ride into Granada—the shopkeepers will fall over themselves in the rush to serve us.'

Leonor shook her head. 'I've already tried that. Inés refused to give us one.'

Alba's face fell. 'That can't be right, we could ride out in Salobreña.'

'At night, Alba, we were only allowed out at night.'

'Surely we will be allowed the same privilege here?'

'Inés says not. We are women now, not girls, and different rules apply.' Leonor reached for her sister's hand. 'Alba, when we set out for the palace, I hoped our lives would change for the better. I'm no longer so sure that they will.' She looked at the songbirds and heaved a sigh. 'We are caged, just like those birds.'

Vehemently, Alba shook her head. 'No, no. Father's gone to such trouble to welcome us. I'm sure he'll allow us an escort to visit the town. Inés has misunderstood.'

'You truly believe that?'

'Yes!'

Leonor nodded. 'Very well. Father has asked to see us tomorrow. I shall ask him then.' She looked at the white-capped mountain range beyond the palace walls and smiled. 'I would like to see more of the Kingdom than what lies inside these walls.'

When the sun rose the next day, a distant chipping sound could be heard somewhere in the gully. Leonor peered out of a window on the wild side of the tower. Nothing. Just a shadowy crevasse filled with rocks and choked with shrubs and brambles. The noise was a mystery.

She turned to Constanza. 'What's that chinking sound?'

'Maybe there's a quarry nearby.'

Whilst the Princesses waited for the Sultan's summons, Leonor lay on her silken cushion and stared at the mountains. The elusive tapping continued throughout the morning at random intervals. It would start, and then stop, and then start again. Leonor could still hear it when the summons came.

'My ladies, your father is ready to see you.'

Leonor and her sisters reached for their veils and followed a servant through the sunlit gardens that led to their father's apartments. Doves drank from jetting fountains; butterflies flew drunkenly through the hot air; bees buzzed in the lavender. So much beauty and it meant nothing. Leonor clenched her hands into fists and they remained clenched as she and her sisters passed through a shady antechamber and under the series of arches that opened on to the Court of the Lions. Her slippers whispered across the marbled courtyard and they were shown into one of the smaller audience chambers.

Robed in white, Sultan Tariq lay on an elaborately carved couch that was heaped with red velvet cushions. A huge ruby glittered in his turban, and several rings vied for attention with a golden sword belt.

As was the custom, the Princesses prostrated themselves before rising to kiss their father's hand. His dark eyes were sparkling and his expression benevolent. Leonor felt herself relax.

'My daughters, the sight of you gladdens my heart.' The King gestured expansively at a gilded coffer on a nearby footstool. 'Here, I have a gift, you may share it between you.'

'Thank you, Father.' Constanza stepped forward and opened the coffer.

Sugared almonds, the coffer was brimming with them. Leonor looked at the almonds and then back at her father's face as he watched Constanza take one. Constanza couldn't lift her veil, not with the King's personal guard lining the walls. She ate the almond delicately, slipping it discreetly under her veil.

The Sultan gave her an indulgent smile. 'I know you like them.'

'I like them very much, Father, thank you,' Constanza said.

Her voice was soft and quiet and very polite. Only someone who knew her intimately would understand that her response was not particularly heartfelt. Constanza didn't care for sugared almonds any more than Leonor did.

Leonor felt wretched. Sad. And horribly ungrateful. Their father's generosity was wasted. *We*

aren't dolls to be dressed up in silks and velvets.
Sweetmeats were all very well, but to be truly
happy, she and her sisters needed more. They
needed to be accepted for themselves.

Constanza and Alba felt as she did. With every
day that passed, they were becoming more and
more withdrawn. Moving to the Alhambra Palace had changed nothing.

*We cannot go on like this, something must be
done. We need to get out. We need to meet other
people. We need friends. We see Inés and our servants; we see the eunuchs and a handful of slaves;
we speak to our father. We see no one outside the
palace, we have no friends. Nothing will change
until I tell him. It's possible he doesn't understand.*

Leonor stiffened her spine and put a smile in
her voice. 'May I speak, Father?'

The Sultan waved an expansive hand. 'Of
course.'

'We've not seen much of Granada. Father, we'd
like to explore the city.'

The Sultan's eyebrows almost vanished into
his turban. 'Explore Granada? Certainly not! It's
dangerous. You are my precious daughters and
you must remain in the palace, where you can be
safely guarded.'

Leonor clasped her hands together and lowered
her head. Well schooled by Inés over the years,
she knew the King found pride in a woman re-
pulsive. Perhaps he would respond to a show of

humility. 'At Salobreña,' she persisted softly, 'we were permitted to ride out at night. With a suitable escort, naturally.'

The Sultan's eyes went as hard and as dark as obsidian. 'You were children then, that is no longer possible. From this day forth you will confine yourselves to the palace gardens, and then only with an escort.'

'But, Father—'

Sultan Tariq's face darkened. Brusquely, he gestured at one of his knights. 'Captain, escort my daughters back to their tower.'

The captain bowed. 'At once, Great King.'

Anger burning in her breast—*we need to get out, we need friends*—Leonor touched her forehead and bowed in obeisance.

Before they could blink, the Princesses found themselves back at the entrance to their tower. The guards saluted and stood back and the Princesses filed inside.

As the door shut behind them, Leonor heard the most ominous of sounds, the grate of a key in a lock. Her breath caught.

'Was that what I think it was?' Alba asked. Her cheeks were as white as milk.

Leonor lurched for the door and wrenched at the handle. She pushed and pulled. It didn't budge.

'It's locked?' Constanza asked, hand at her throat.

'Locked.' Leonor wrenched off her veil. Pushing past her sisters, she stalked for the stairs, not stopping until she reached the chamber at the top. Jaw set, she frowned at the gorgeously tiled walls, at the lacy plasterwork ceiling, at the cheeping birds in their gilded cages. Those poor birds…

Marching for the nearest birdcage, she unhooked it from its stand.

Alba came in, the monkey clinging to her shoulder. 'What are you doing?'

'Something I should have done when these poor creatures were given to us.' Gently, Leonor put the cage on the window ledge and opened the door. The songbirds fell silent. One of them hopped along the perch, head tipped to one side. 'Go on, take your chance,' Leonor murmured.

'Leonor, you mustn't!' This from Constanza. 'What about the hawks? They'll never survive.'

Leonor said nothing, she simply watched as the boldest songbird sidled to the cage door and, with a whirr of wings, took flight. The second bird swiftly followed.

'They were not created to live in cages.' Turning on her heel, she marched to the next cage.

'No!' Constanza gripped her arm. 'Those are my birds. I won't risk them to the hawks. Leave them.'

'Are you sure?'

'Yes.'

With a shrug, Leonor looked at the third cage

and raised an eyebrow at Alba. 'Alba? What about yours? Will you free them?'

Alba's brow knotted. 'I'm not sure, I'll think about it. As Constanza says, there are hawks out there. And this morning I saw an eagle.'

'Very well.' Leonor flung herself on to a cushion. Her blood was boiling. How could their father treat them like this? She was so enraged she could barely think. 'My birds must take their chances. They will survive, I am sure of it.'

Her sisters came to sit either side of her and then all three of them were frowning at the distant mountains. That mysterious chinking sound was still coming from the gully outside the palace walls.

Chink, chink. Pause. Chink, chink.

'Face it, Leonor,' Alba said, on a deep sigh. 'Father will never let us leave. We will never marry. We are prisoners just like those Spanish noblemen.' She pushed to her feet and began pacing the chamber.

'The noblemen will be free when their ransom is paid,' Leonor pointed out. 'We, on the other hand...'

She dug her nails into the silk fringe of her cushion. Their father had locked them in. She wanted to shout, she wanted to scream. Next to her, Constanza sighed, unpinned her veil and draped it across the window ledge.

Leonor twisted the cushion fringe. She wasn't

alone in her frustration. She had lost count of the times she had seen Alba stalking up and down with Hunter on her shoulder. Alba was always on the move, she prowled the tower like a caged beast. As for Constanza, drooping sadly on the cushion next to her, all life seemed to have left her. Since arriving at the Alhambra, Constanza had hardly uttered a word. She trailed about after her sisters, silver lute in hand. On a good day, she played the lute. Mostly, she stared at the enamelled tiles, silent and listless.

Inés poked her head through the door arch and smiled brightly. Either she was oblivious of the mood in the chamber or she was ignoring it. 'My ladies, we have ice fresh from the mountain. Do you care for refreshment? Chilled fruit juice?'

Inés was speaking in Spanish today, which probably meant she was missing her home. Of course, it could simply be because the Princesses had removed their veils. Leonor didn't know why, but since moving into the tower, they'd taken to speaking Spanish more than they ever did in Salobreña Castle. It was, she supposed, their small and secret rebellion, a way of preserving some part of their Spanish identity. It was no longer enough.

Their father had locked them in, drastic measures were called for.

'Ladies, some refreshment?' Inés repeated.

Leonor struggled to frame a polite response. 'Thank you, a cool drink would be lovely.' The distant chinking in the crevasse caught her attention once again. It echoed around the chamber walls, louder than ever. 'Inés, what is that noise? Is there a quarry nearby?'

Inés came to the window. 'It's prisoners, I expect. There was a great flood after the last storm, water poured off the mountain and threatened to undermine the palace walls. I'm told it happens often. Your father has ordered the gully cleared.'

'Prisoners?' Leonor couldn't help but think of Count Rodrigo. Had he and his friends been ransomed yet? For his sake, she hoped so—he didn't look the type of man to take kindly to forced labour. 'I pity them, working in this heat.'

Inés left to fetch the iced fruit juice and Constanza picked up the silver lute.

In the gully at the base of the palace wall, Rodrigo hurled another rock on to the cart with a satisfying crash. Anger burned in his chest. He'd had his fill of Granadan hospitality. Forced labour, indeed. Sultan Tariq had earned his poor reputation. Noblemen shouldn't be breaking rocks, it made a mockery of all the laws of chivalry. Not to mention that it was boring beyond belief.

Noticing the guard's attention was fixed on a group of men working with chisels further downhill, Rodrigo eased his aching back and caught

Inigo's eye. 'Heard anything concerning your ransom?'

'Shouldn't be long.' Another rock thudded on to the cart and Inigo flexed his injured leg with a grimace. 'You?'

'God alone knows, I can't get a word out of our jailers.'

'I reckon you'll be back in Córdoba within the month.'

'I'd better be.'

An ale skin swung temptingly from the side of the cart. Glancing at the distracted guard, Rodrigo reached for it, took a long draught and passed it to Inigo.

'*Gracias.* Thank you.' Inigo drank, tossed the ale skin Enrique's way and tipped his head to one side. 'Faith, listen to that. Unless I've finally lost my mind, I can hear music.'

Astonishingly, Inigo was in the right, though the music was faint. It seemed to be drifting down from a tower set high in the palace wall. 'Sounds like a lute.' Rodrigo gave a puzzled frown. It was a Spanish folk song.

'*Dios mío*, I know that tune.'

An odd thrill rushed through him. Could the Princess be in that tower? She was fluent in Spanish and her curiosity regarding her mother's background meant it was possible she would know the tune. Grief and boredom temporarily forgotten, he felt a smile form.

Inigo smiled back. 'I wouldn't expect a song like that to be floating out of the tyrant's palace. Rodrigo, you have a good singing voice, would you care to demonstrate?'

Rodrigo glanced towards the guard, cleared his throat and began to sing.

The guard, naturally, let out a shout and strode towards him, face dark with anger.

The guard's whip snaked his way and, as Rodrigo put up his arm to deflect the blow, he would swear he saw the flutter of a banner—or a silken shawl, perhaps—through the window at the top of the tower.

Leonor was humming under her breath when she heard it—a man singing along to Constanza's playing. From the direction of his voice, he was in the wilderness beyond the walls. One of the prisoners must have recognised the tune.

His voice was strong and true. To Leonor's ears it was unusually strong, for the only men she'd heard singing were palace eunuchs. And fine and well trained though the eunuchs were, they weren't half as moving. This man's voice was so deep. No eunuch, he.

A quiver went through her as Lord Rodrigo stepped into her thoughts. Which was ridiculous, it couldn't possibly be the Count of Córdoba. Unless… No. Surely her father wouldn't put a count to breaking rocks?

Resting her elbows on the wide ledge, she leaned out. At the foot of the wall stood a cart, half-filled with rubble. Three men were grouped near it, their faces upturned.

Lord Rodrigo! Her breath stopped. The Count was singing and his comrades were grinning up at her. Seized by a rebellious flash of fury—her father wasn't going to dictate her every action— she snatched up Constanza's veil and waved it like a pennon.

A few yards further down the gully, a guard was stalking towards the knights, whip in hand. Loathe to make matters worse, Leonor ducked out of sight. She heard the snap of the whip and flinched.

Constanza stopped playing. 'Leonor, whatever's the matter?'

Leonor gestured for Constanza to play on. 'Don't stop.' The idea of Count Rodrigo being whipped was deeply upsetting. An honourable man didn't deserve such ill treatment. 'Please, go on.'

Lightly, Constanza touched the strings and the Spanish folk song danced around the chamber and out into the gully. A different voice picked up the refrain.

Had that whip struck him? Leonor must not look.

She had to look. Pulled by an invisible force, she turned back to the window.

'What is it?' Alba asked.

And then Alba was leaning her elbows on the window ledge next to Leonor. She had barely stuck her head out when Constanza's playing faltered a second time. Inés was back, tray of refreshments in hand.

'Leonor! Alba!' Inés set the tray down with a bang. 'Come away from that window! Saints, how many times must I tell you? You shouldn't lean out of the windows like common street girls.'

Leonor's chin went up. 'Father has locked us in.'

Inés shook her head. 'And that justifies a flagrant disregard for his wishes?'

'He shouldn't have built this tower by the mountain if he didn't want us to look at it.'

Inés drew closer. 'Without your veils, you are half-dressed. You must wear your veils by the windows, lest you are seen.' Gently, she touched Leonor's cheek. 'You are too stubborn for your own good, my dear. The King is already in the darkest of moods; anyone would think you're asking for more punishment.'

'Inés, he locked us in!'

Inés sighed, her eyes were sad. 'And sold your horses, I know. As I say, he is most displeased.'

Leonor felt the colour drain from her face. 'What?' She must have misheard. 'Father has sold our horses?'

'He wouldn't do that,' Alba said, eyes wide.

Inés seemed to sag. 'He didn't tell you.'

Alba gripped Inés by the wrist. 'It's not true, he wouldn't. Not our horses!' Alba's voice was fierce, she loved her animals.

Guilt swamped Leonor, this was her doing. 'He's selling them because I asked if we could ride into Granada.'

'Not at all.' Suddenly, Inés looked very old and very tired. 'Your father sold your mares the day after you arrived in Granada. He didn't appreciate your interference with those Spanish knights.' Her gaze rested briefly on each of the sisters. 'He must have decided you needed punishment.'

Alba clenched her fists. 'Why didn't he tell us?'

'Must a king explain his actions? Sultan Tariq hopes that you will come to understand that his authority should never be questioned.'

Leonor's tongue turned to stone. Half of her ached to look outside to see what was happening to Lord Rodrigo; the other half was ablaze with anger. Father had sold Snowstorm! Finally, she found words. 'Even by his daughters?'

Her duenna's smile was sad. 'Especially by his daughters.'

Chapter Six

Thank the Lord, the light was fading. Rodrigo dropped the last rock on to the cart with a sigh and wondered if they would get meat that night. Meals in the Vermillion Towers were frugal, though there was usually enough to keep body and soul together. They were given basic labourers' rations—hard bread, cheese, olives. They'd had lamb once. Meat was especially welcome even if, as in this case, it had been poorly seasoned and boiled to shreds.

Rodrigo was lining up with the others, preparing to return to the cells, when the overseer caught his eye. 'You, over here.' The overseer's Spanish was strongly accented. He lobbed a sack at Rodrigo.

Rodrigo's eyebrows lifted. 'What's this?'

'Food.' The man jerked his thumb at the foot of the Princesses' tower. 'You and your comrades eat by the wall.'

Rodrigo stared, a break in routine was unheard of. Was this a trick of some kind? A trap?

'You have an hour,' the overseer said. His eyes glittered through the dusk. 'You will remain chained and you will be watched, there will be no chance for escape.'

'Who arranged this?'

'I cannot say.'

'Is everyone to be allowed this privilege?'

The man shook his head impatiently.

'Why? Why us?'

Tellingly, the overseer's hand crept to a bulging pouch on his belt. Someone must have paid for them to be allowed to rest beneath the Princesses' tower. Rodrigo tipped back his head. The tower stood stark against a purpling sky that was sprinkled with early stars. Windows were shuttered. A telltale yellow glimmered through the cracks; inside, the lamps must already be lit. Had one of the Princesses arranged this? His Princess?

'Someone has paid for us to eat outside?'

'No questions!'

Rodrigo shrugged. 'As you wish.'

There was no sense arguing and, in any case, Rodrigo wasn't sure he wanted to. Inigo was in pain, though he never complained. Inigo was also bored and exhausted, they all were. An evening resting by the wall rather than in their stinking quarters might lift them out of their malaise. And if they could attract the attention of the

Princesses, well, at the very least it might prove amusing.

Aye, an evening's flirtation with the tyrant's daughters would be most enlivening. He almost smiled. A taste of forbidden delight might be exactly what they needed.

At the top of the tower, Leonor pushed open a shutter. The mountains rose in front of her, a black silhouette beneath a canopy of stars. Wondering about the land that lay beyond the mountain range, Leonor discarded her veil and draped it over the window ledge. Wanton disobedience, maybe, but it was dark outside, no one would see. In any case, she no longer cared whether she was an obedient daughter or not. Father was impossible. How could he have sold their beloved horses? What would he do next? The questions echoed round and round. Was worse to come?

Constanza was stretched out on the cushion next to her, the silver lute abandoned at her feet, her eyes blank and her face expressionless. It was awful to see her staring up at the ceiling like a dead thing. She had lost all hope.

Leonor understood how she felt. 'Constanza, what are you thinking about?'

'Father.'

'Me too.' Leonor's chest heaved. 'Sometimes I hate him.'

Constanza gave her a pained look. 'Hush, Leonor, you must never say so.'

'I love Snowstorm, I wanted to keep her.' Leonor's eyes stung.

'That's not the point though, is it?' Constanza said. 'Our interference angered Father and we must pay.'

'I hope that whoever buys our horses will look after them properly.'

'There'd be no point in buying three beautiful mares only to mistreat them, I am sure they will be cared for.'

Leonor managed a strained smile. 'I pray that is true.'

The heavens were alive with stars and Leonor glimpsed a tiny flicker of darkness, a bat was flying past the tower. She reached for Constanza's hand and her gaze fell to their veils, sitting limply across the window ledge.

'Our small rebellion,' she murmured thoughtfully. 'Our very small rebellion.'

Constanza gave her a puzzled look. 'I beg your pardon?'

'Our veils, we are near the window and we are not wearing them,' Leonor said. 'What would Inés say?'

Constanza shrugged. 'It is night, and we need not worry, the ravine is empty.'

'Has it occurred to you that the only place

where we are granted any freedom is in this tower, where we are locked in.'

Constanza gave a tight smile. 'Ironic, isn't it?'

'I should warn you that I have had enough of small rebellions. It's time to do something a little more significant.'

Eyes wide, Constanza stared. 'What will you do?'

'I want to run away.'

'Leonor!'

Fired by a gut-wrenching mix of anger and fear, Leonor ignored the shock on Constanza's face and continued. 'If we ran away, we could find somewhere to start a new life, the three of us. Together. Think about it. There must be somewhere where we can have command of our lives.'

'We?' Constanza looked absolutely horrified. 'Leonor, you mustn't speak like this.'

'Father has destroyed my trust in him. He showers us with gifts when we please him, and when we displease him, he takes them away. He locks us up. We are Father's playthings, we only exist in so far as we please him.'

'He can't imprison us for ever.'

Leonor gave an indecorous snort. 'Can't he? Well, it makes no difference. Even if he gives us each a key to our tower door, I'll never trust him again.'

Constanza reached for her hand, her eyes

glassy with tears. 'Leonor, it does no good to speak this way.'

'I am sorry if it upsets you. I cannot live like this any more. I will not.' Leonor's chest heaved. 'Don't you wonder what Mamá's life would have been like if Father hadn't taken her captive?'

'She would have married a Spanish lord and we would never have been born.'

Leonor stared pensively at Constanza's lute. 'It's a pity Inés tells us so little. I'd like to know what Mamá would think about her daughters being locked in a harem until the end of their days.'

'I am sure Father will relent soon.'

'Constanza, you're a dreamer. If we stay here, we will never be free.'

A cat mewed outside the tower. Closer to hand, Leonor heard a clunk and the thud of heavy boots, the guards must be checking the palace boundaries. Everyday regular noises that had once brought comfort. No longer. *We are shut in. What will Father do next?*

Chink-chink.

How strange, wasn't that the sound of prisoners at work?

Chink-chink. Chink-chink.

Leonor exchanged a puzzled glance with Constanza. 'They can't be clearing the gully at this hour.'

Constanza pushed the shutter a little wider and

leaned over the window ledge. When she turned back to Leonor, her expression had lightened. 'Leonor, come and see.'

The ledge was cool to the touch. At the foot of the wall, a faint light glimmered, a lantern. There was movement in the shadows.

Chink-chink. Chink-chink.

A spark flared at the base of the tower. A flame shot skywards, and as it strengthened, the shadows reformed. Three men were crouched around a small fire.

'That noise is rhythmic,' Constanza said softly. 'Like the beat of a tune.'

Leonor could barely see a thing, yet her pulse quickened. It made no sense, and though she couldn't make out his face, she knew Rodrigo Álvarez was down there in the dark. Just then, he began to sing. Yes, that was Count Rodrigo, his voice was rich and mellow. Unforgettable.

'That's the song Inés taught me, the one I played earlier,' Constanza said.

Leonor gripped her sister's hand. 'Indeed, it is. Pick up your lute, you must accompany him.'

'Leonor, you are a wicked, wicked girl,' Constanza said, smiling.

Heart warmed by Constanza's smile, Leonor unfolded her veil, taking care to ensure that it dangled from the window like a signal. With luck, even though the sun had gone down, Count

Rodrigo would see it and understand he had an audience.

Constanza struck the first chord. A lamp flickered, and behind them, the shadows quivered.

Leonor glanced over her shoulder, Inés and Alba had entered. Resisting the urge to slam the shutter, Leonor smothered a sigh. Here it comes, she thought, and braced herself for a barrage of chastisement concerning veils and modesty and the correct behaviour expected of a Nasrid princess.

Constanza's lute fell silent.

Inés crossed the chamber and came to stand at her shoulder. 'They are there already?' she asked mildly.

'You know about this, Inés?' Something clicked into place and Leonor's eyes widened. 'You arranged it!'

'If I did, I would never admit it.'

Baffled, Leonor stared at Inés. 'You arranged it, I know. Why?'

Inés looked from one Princess to the next and her face softened. 'A duenna who loves her charges might not like to see them so unhappy. She might not like to see them lose their beloved horses. Nor would she like to see them denied the opportunity to learn about their mother's people. Those men...' Inés jerked her chin towards the window '...are Spanish, and so is that duenna. My dears, a duenna who cares for her charges might wish to distract them from the way they are kept so confined. She might also hope that distraction would help them overcome their unhappiness at losing their horses.'

Leonor gave her a straight look. 'A duenna such as that would be playing a very dangerous game,' she said quietly. 'If I were to meet her, I would thank her from the bottom of my heart. How did you do it?'

Inés shrugged. 'The overseer's wife has expensive tastes.'

'You bribed him!'

Inés smiled.

Leonor turned back to the window. 'Put out that lamp, if you please, we shall see better.'

Constanza resumed playing and Leonor's eyes adjusted to the night outside. A crescent moon hung among the stars, and the fire cast an orange glow on the stony ground. The Spanish knights were looking up at the tower, their faces ghostly in the firelight. What looked like the remains of a meal sat on a rock—a couple of flasks and a fragment of flatbread.

She gripped the windowsill. Had Count Rodrigo and his friends enough to eat? Were they hungry? To her shame, Leonor realised she knew nothing of how the prisoners put to hard labour were treated. Conditions had been appalling in Salobreña. Were they worse here? Better?

With Constanza's music floating over her head,

Leonor leaned out as far as she dared and gave a loud whisper. 'Lord Rodrigo?'

'My lady?'

'Are you and your friends hungry?'

'Always,' came the dry response.

Leonor ducked back inside. Her father had sentenced these men—her mother's people—to hard labour simply for staring at the royal caval-cade. It was folly to interfere with that decision. She set her jaw. If Inés had been brave enough to defy him, she also could be brave. These knights were Spanish. They couldn't be blamed for not understanding orders shouted to them in Arabic. If Lord Rodrigo and his companions wanted de-cent food, she could supply it. Her mother would surely have approved.

'Inés?'

'My lady?'

'My sisters and I are astonishingly hungry. We would like a large bowl of rice, some chicken in almond sauce and some fruit. Do we have sweet grapes? Dates? Honey biscuits?'

'Of course, my lady.'

'Oh, and we will need a large basket and a long rope.'

'Very good, my lady.' Inés hurried out.

Constanza finished the Spanish folk song and switched to another. By the time the food arrived in its basket, she was on the third song. Lord Rodrigo and his friends knew them all. Their voices, rich and full, overpoweringly masculine, filled the clearing. In truth, they were so loud, Leonor feared they would attract attention.

Luckily, the palace guards seemed to be occupied elsewhere.

Had Inés arranged for that too? She must have done.

Leonor sat on the wide window ledge and drew up her knees as she listened.

'I like this,' Alba said dreamily. 'They are serenading us.'

Leonor gave her a sharp look. 'Don't get carried away. You must remember they are only there because Inés bribed the overseer. They are Father's enemies.'

'They are Mother's people,' Alba said, and her sigh melted into the night. 'Don't spoil things, Leonor.'

The arrival of the food basket put paid to further singing. After it was lowered to the ground and the men had gathered around it, Lord Rodrigo turned his face up to the window and bowed. 'A thousand thanks, my lady. Your generosity overwhelms us.'

Leonor heard the irony in his tone and glanced at Alba. Her heart twisted. Poor Alba. Alba longed to be serenaded because she more than any of them wanted marriage and children. Alba wanted to be wooed.

Yet that would never happen, not whilst they

were under lock and key. This mockery of a serenade was all the wooing she and her sisters were likely to have.

The singing continued briefly after the knights had eaten. And at length, when the men had been escorted back to the Vermillion Towers, Constanza laid down her lute. 'I never realised how diverting duets could be.' Her face was soft, her mouth relaxed.

Alba smiled. Her eyes were full of dreams. 'Indeed, yes, that was marvellous.'

A moth fluttered through the window. Leonor closed the shutter. She too had enjoyed herself and not purely because of the singing. The idea that they were finally doing something that was outside their father's control was unexpectedly stimulating. She was a wicked daughter and doubly so because she didn't feel the least bit guilty. Leonor also recognised that a large part of her enjoyment came from watching her sisters' enjoyment. The singing had brought them back to life.

We have been living shadow lives, and it is not enough.

'Do you think they will return tomorrow?' Alba asked wistfully.

'I imagine that depends on the size of the bribe Inés gave to the overseer.'

Alba glanced pensively at her emerald ring. 'I would be happy to donate some jewellery, if that would help.'

Leonor laughed. Thank heaven, Alba and Constanza were finally behaving more like their old selves.

In the event, there was no need for Alba to part with any rings. The next evening, that telltale clinking summoned the Princesses to the window overlooking the shadow-filled ravine. The firelight was again playing over the dark, handsome faces of the Spanish knights.

Another basket of food was sent down. A bottle of wine.

There was more singing. As Leonor took her place on the wide ledge and Count Rodrigo's deep voice rose to the window, she couldn't help but wonder what was going through his mind.

Is he singing because he is half-starved and he knows we will feed him? Does he think of us with scorn? Or are we merely a pleasant interlude in an otherwise disastrous period of captivity?

Overhead, the stars glittered, cold and mysterious. They had no answer. The moon gleamed like a silver sickle. There was no answer there either.

The second evening flew by.

Then came the third, and the fourth. The days melted into one another, a blur of unwonted happiness. After sunset, as the moon grew progressively larger, the Spanish knights would light a small fire at the foot of the tower and serenade their enemy's daughters.

Each evening, the food basket was lowered and raised. And each evening, Leonor sat on the window ledge and listened. Sometimes she sang. Occasionally she would hug her knees and fall silent. It was then that the ideas crept up on her, ideas that were as untamed as the wilderness outside the palace walls.

Soon the Spanish knights would leave Al-Andalus, they would be free. What must she do to be free? If there was a way to go with them, should she take it?

Leonor's ideas were so wild, she kept them to herself. In truth, she tried not to think too much, as some of her thoughts were simply too alarming. It wasn't easy.

When the sun blazed overhead, she looked forward to moonrise. Her sisters did too, Constanza would bring her lute up to the top chamber and Alba would sit by the window, fingering the latch on the shutter. Waiting.

What would they do when the men had gone?

Was there a way to go with them? Was there?

Surely there was no reason for Lord Rodrigo to help them, they were his enemy's daughters. Unless…

Might he be convinced to help them steal away as a form of revenge against their father? Might that work?

We could return to Mamá's homeland. Of course, the three of them knew nothing about life outside the palace, they would face untold dangers. But it didn't matter, they would be together, and together they could face anything.

All Leonor had to do was persuade the knights to escort them out of their father's kingdom.

After that, well, their jewels had value. They could surely survive until they found their mother's family. *Our family.*

There was one huge drawback. Could she trust Lord Rodrigo?

Night after night as the moon grew fat and Leonor pondered on what she might do, the Spanish noblemen and the Princesses played duets. They sang to each other. It was a pleasant game with a slight frisson—in short, it was a most engaging interlude.

Then came the moment that Leonor had dreaded. It was night once more, and she was alone with Constanza, Alba was in the chamber below, talking to Inés.

The moon was almost at the full and its pale light washed over the stones surrounding the knights' fire. Only there were no cheerful yellow flames tonight, only a charred log left over from the previous night. Save for a small animal rustling through the undergrowth, the ravine was silent.

'Where are they?' Constanza asked, a pleat in her brow.

'Perhaps they're working in another part of the gully.'

Constanza's shoulders slumped. 'Their ransom has come and so they have gone.'

Leonor frowned. 'No, no, they can't have gone, not yet.' She stared frantically out into the gully. It was ominously quiet.

Had she left it too late? She'd been waiting for the right moment to ask Lord Rodrigo if he and his friends would escort her and her sisters out of Al-Andalus. She'd been waiting for what? Courage? A sign that these men—her father's enemies, after all—would treat her and her sisters honourably? She had little experience of men and her confidence had failed her.

A wave of nausea swept through her. She'd waited too long. If the knights' ransom had been paid and they'd been released, she'd missed her chance.

Her heart clenched and she forced herself to face the truth. There was more to it than that, she'd been looking forward to seeing the flare of the fire. She wanted to hear that strong, male laughter again. *Count Rodrigo, where are you? Have you gone home?*

The gully remained dark. It was filled with night sounds—the whisper of dry grass at the foot of the tower, the screech of an owl. Surely the Count was still there?

A lamp flickered, shadows trembled. Outside,

the stars slowly turned, silver specks set in a deep, velvet blackness. A bat flitted by, vanishing into the rocky crevasse that ran alongside the palace wall.

'Leonor?' Constanza whispered.

'Mmm?'

'Do you think Father has found us out?'

A chill ran through her. 'I pray not.' Leonor leaned on her elbow and peered into the night. Nothing.

Quick footsteps sounded on the stairs and Alba swept in, her mouth was pinched. 'It's no use, Leonor,' she said. 'There are no lights. There will be no more serenades. Our knights are not there.'

Leonor gave Alba a searching glance and her heart filled with dread. She had to clear her throat to speak. 'You are certain?' *I will never see Count Rodrigo again.*

'Their families have paid the ransom,' Alba said, in a dull voice. 'Inés tells me they were freed today.'

Chapter Seven

His massage over, Rodrigo was reluctant to peel himself from the bathhouse couch. The wear and tear of the past few months had been kneaded and soothed into oblivion by the best body servant Granada had to offer. Rodrigo felt reborn, in truth, he was so relaxed he could barely move.

His squire stepped forward and laid a fresh set of clothes on the couch.

'My thanks, Miguel.' The sweet scent of almond oil still in his nostrils, Rodrigo stretched luxuriously. 'Holy Mother, I never thought to feel clean again.'

'Will you be wearing armour tonight, my lord?' Miguel asked. 'I've brought it with me.'

Rodrigo grimaced. The sun had set almost an hour since and the streets and alleys of Granada hoarded the heat. It was sweltering here in the city, far hotter than it had been higher up the valley, and Rodrigo had no wish to abrade his abused body with heavy armour. 'Thank you, Miguel, but no. This place is hotter than Hades.'

Miguel's eyebrow shot up. 'Is it cooler by the Vermillion Towers, my lord?'

'Aye, the towers sit on higher ground. The air is fresher there,' Rodrigo said, with a wry smile. 'That is why the Sultans of Al-Andalus built their palace nearby.'

A pair of dark, kohl-lined eyes took shape in his mind's eye. Eyes that were as beautiful as they were mysterious. Eyes that he should never have seen because they belonged to a Nasrid princess.

Rodrigo didn't know her name and probably never would, but he had fantasised about her often. He'd always remember those extraordinary evenings by the palace wall. His Lady Merciful had given him something other than Diego to think about and for that he was grateful. In an odd way, the Princess had given him heart. He'd only seen her face a handful of times, and on each occasion, it had been the briefest of glimpses.

Despite that, whenever the Sultan's three daughters had appeared at the top of that tower, silhouetted by lamp and candlelight, Lady Merciful had been easy to identify. Her voice, husky and sensual, was unforgettable. The pity was that the Princesses' tower was too high and the light too poor for him to see her properly.

The Sultan kept his daughters tucked well away from curious eyes, and from the little he had seen of Lady Merciful, Rodrigo understood why. Her beauty stole his breath. She had large black eyes and a mouth a man would kill to kiss. The tales of Helen of Troy's beauty launching a thousand ships had always struck him as a ludicrous exaggeration, no woman could be that beautiful. However, after seeing the Sultan's daughter, Rodrigo was no longer so sure. During his days in that rock-choked gully, Rodrigo had lost count of the times he had imagined drawing her close to give her a real kiss.

An angry, grieving man needed something to distract him from his sorrows, and sight of the beautiful Princess had sparked a thousand fantasies. It made a pleasant contrast to the drudgery of heaving boulders on to a cart.

One fantasy had led to another. Rodrigo hadn't stopped at a kiss and the fact that the Princess was his enemy's daughter had added spice to his imaginings. Meeting her had been so unexpected. Forbidden. Delicious. Rodrigo had imagined peeling away the Princess's exotic silks; he'd caressed perfumed skin that was smooth as satin.

He was grateful to her. Diego's death had been the most bitter blow and the presence of the Nasrid Princess had stopped him from dwelling on it to the point of obsession. Without her to distract him, Rodrigo would have been stewing in grief and misery. The knowledge that he might catch sight of Lady Merciful each night had helped him through the bleakest of days.

In the normal course of events, the Count of Córdoba would never meet a Nasrid princess. A chasm lay between them. It had made no difference. Even this evening, mere memory of his imaginings brought a smile to his lips.

No more, Rodrigo told himself firmly, he must push her from his mind. The Princess's father was the tyrant who had held him captive. His ransom had been paid. He was going home. A free man had no need of fantasies.

'Tonight, we're celebrating with Inigo,' Rodrigo said. He didn't know what Enrique had planned and, frankly, he didn't care. What Diego had seen in his cousin would always be a mystery. Relation or not, Enrique was a grave disappointment. Rodrigo would be happy if he never saw him again.

Miguel looked at him. 'Here in the city?'

'Why not?'

'Is it safe, my lord? Granada's crawling with the Sultan's men.'

Rodrigo's squire Miguel was of Arab descent and his original name had been Hakim. Rodrigo had virtually adopted him. He'd found the lad hurt and dazed, after a particularly unpleasant border skirmish. Hakim had been little more than a child. Appalled that someone so young had been caught up in the fighting, Rodrigo had taken him back to Castle Álvarez and seen to it that his wounds had been healed.

Having lost his family, Hakim rewarded Rodrigo with unswerving loyalty. He learned Spanish and pestered Rodrigo to make him his squire. He even changed his name from Hakim to Miguel. Over the years, they'd become close.

Rodrigo shook out his tunic. 'The captain of the guard knows we'll be on our way at first light.'

'He gave you a safe conduct?'

'Aye, we've been given leave to explore and I intend to find the best tavern in town. It's been a lifetime since we had a decent meal and some palatable wine.'

'Yes, my lord.'

'Be a good lad and ask the way to that tavern, will you?'

'At once, my lord.'

The filthy rags which Rodrigo had been wearing lay in a heap on the floor, Miguel nudged them with his toe. 'What shall I do with these, my lord?'

'Burn them.'

When they left the bathhouse to head for the stable, the sky was dotted with stars. Miguel had discovered that the best tavern lay slightly outside the town. Inigo had gone on ahead and they would meet him there.

Rodrigo tossed a coin at the stable-boy and

mounted his horse. 'It's good to be in the saddle again,' he said. 'I'm glad you brought Eagle, we ride with the wind tomorrow.'

They spurred down the road and Miguel glanced his way. 'Your lady mother will be glad to see you.'

'And I her. How has she been since Diego's body came home?'

'Lady Isabel is brave, my lord,' Miguel's tone was sombre. 'No one has seen her shed so much as a tear, not even her maid. She withdrew to the chapel and arranged a vigil that went on for days. She has been fasting.'

Rodrigo nodded, he had expected as much. 'She will be weeping inside.'

'Assuredly. My lord, what happened to Khan? Was he killed in battle?'

Khan was Rodrigo's warhorse and, up until the moment of Rodrigo's capture by the Sultan's men, a prized possession.

'Khan lives, thank God.' Rodrigo's voice took on a hard edge as he remembered.

There was much to lay at Enrique's door. Diego's death. Rodrigo and Inigo's capture and subsequent imprisonment. And to make matters worse, Enrique's rashness had lost Rodrigo the best warhorse in Spain. Rodrigo tamped down his anger, reminding himself that Enrique was his aunt's son. He was family. Yet Rodrigo was finding it nigh on impossible to forgive him. He reminded himself that his captivity was ended, he could surely arrange matters now so that he need never see Enrique again.

He looked bleakly at Miguel. 'The warlord who captured us took Khan as booty. He refused to let me buy him back.'

Miguel didn't reply and they rode on in silence. The lanterns of the town fell back and the night closed in. All was silver, grey and black. The highway was pale in the moonlight, stars shimmered overhead, and bats flitted in and out of the orange trees. Cicadas sang.

After a space, a new light gleamed, they had reached the tavern. The stable proved to be simply a paddock by the side of the road, guarded by a couple of greybeards. Inigo's squire, Guillen, was sitting with them, devouring a piece of bread.

As Rodrigo rode up, Guillen shoved the bread in his pouch and hurried over.

'Lord Rodrigo, thank God.'

'Guillen?'

Guillen fiddled with the strap of his belt. 'Lord Inigo has asked that you wait for him here.'

Rodrigo's eyebrows lifted. 'Outside?'

'Yes, my lord.'

'What the devil's happened?'

'Lord Inigo will explain.' Guillen sprinted into the inn.

Rodrigo's stomach growled. Heavens, would

he never eat again? He exchanged glances with Miguel. 'This had better not take long. I'm starved.'

'Yes, my lord.'

The inn door flew open, spilling light across the yard. Inigo marched towards them, Guillen at his heels.

'Take this,' Inigo said, shoving a bundle into Rodrigo's hand. 'Save it for later.'

'Later?' Rodrigo's nostrils twitched, the bundle contained food. At a guess, roast fowl of some kind. 'Inigo, what in hell is going on?'

'Enrique's in trouble again,' Inigo said curtly. He hauled himself on to his horse.

Guillen handed Miguel a similar bundle to Rodrigo's and then he too mounted.

'*Madre mía*, this must stop.' Rodrigo leaned on his saddlebow. 'Last time we rushed to Enrique's rescue, Diego died. Cousin or no, I've no wish to see him again.'

Inigo spoke through gritted teeth. 'We have no choice.'

'Don't we? Enrique never learns; as far as I'm concerned, he can stew in his own juice.'

'Not this time.'

'What's he done?'

'He's drunk.'

Rodrigo felt himself relax. 'Is that all? Good grief, given the conditions we've endured, you can hardly blame him for that.' He glanced pointedly at the tavern. 'I wouldn't mind a drink myself.'

Inigo's eyes glittered. 'If only it were as simple as that.' He dug in his spurs and his horse sprang forward, on to the road that led back to the Alhambra Palace.

The Alhambra Palace? Rodrigo's spine prickled. He kicked Eagle's flanks and urged him level with Inigo. 'Slow down, man. What's going on?'

Inigo reined back to a walk. 'Enrique's been muttering about revenge all day. Wants to make the Sultan pay for treating us like slaves.'

Rodrigo swore under his breath. 'There's no way he can get to Sultan Tariq, the palace is a fortress and he rarely leaves it. Not to mention that entire battalions answer to the Sultan's command and we are in his heartlands. Leave it, Inigo. My cousin can get himself out of the mire this time.'

Inigo grimaced. 'You wouldn't be so sanguine if you knew what he was planning.'

'Surprise me.'

'He's going to abduct the Sultan's daughters.'

'What? That's insane.'

'I assure you, it's true. Enrique's going to lure them out of that tower.'

Rodrigo saw the gleam of dark, kohl-lined eyes; he heard the chink of golden bracelets. 'They'd never leave the palace.'

Even as he spoke, Rodrigo found himself wondering if that were true. The first time he'd seen the three Princesses, at the port of Salobreña, his Lady Merciful had shown signs of rebelliousness—she hadn't been wearing her veil. Given the Sultan's insistence that no one as much as looked as his daughters, it had been a serious breach of etiquette. There'd been other proof of her rebelliousness—her visit to the prison; that incident when she'd intervened on the road to Granada; the food baskets.

Rodrigo's stomach tightened. Saints, all three Princesses had been involved on that occasion. And if that weren't bad enough, the nightly lute-playing surely proved they were all capable of flouting the rules.

Dios mío, there was no doubt of it. As the weeks had passed, the Sultan's daughters had broken rule after rule. Who could say what they might do next?

'No, they'd surely never leave the palace,' he muttered again, but even he could hear the doubt in his voice.

Inigo's brow was furrowed. 'Rodrigo, hear me out. Enrique's made contact with someone inside the palace: a maidservant or duenna of some kind, I believe. It's already arranged. The Princesses want to run away. They're to meet your cousin tonight.'

'What?' Rodrigo couldn't believe his ears. 'We've only been released a day, how on earth has Enrique managed to organise it in that time?'

'He didn't give me any more details.'

It hardly seemed possible. Enrique had conspired to steal the Princesses from the palace? Rodrigo narrowed his gaze on the Sultan's highway. Bleached white in the moonlight, it wound up into the hills ahead of them, apparently empty of traffic.

Checking that Miguel and Guillen were bringing up the rear, Rodrigo raised his voice to carry over the thud of the horses' hoofs. 'You're certain it's tonight?'

'That's what he said. Rodrigo, your cousin's a madman when the drink is in him.'

Rodrigo grunted in acknowledgement. 'Unfortunately, he's a madman with a will of iron.'

'Well, he's after vengeance tonight, and he's decided the Sultan's daughters will give it to him. I've never seen him quite so set on anything.'

Rodrigo stared bleakly at Inigo. 'I'll thrash him when I see him. Those Princesses are very young. Sheltered.' Tension balled in Rodrigo's gut. 'What do you reckon he's after, ransom? You don't think he'd harm them?'

Inigo let out a short laugh. 'His reputation with women is not good.'

'He's a married man.'

Inigo snorted. 'Don't make the mistake of judging your cousin by your standards. Enrique is roaring drunk and he wants revenge.'

A pulse ticked in Rodrigo's jaw. Inigo was right, this could get very ugly. 'If my cousin carries off just one of the Sultan's daughters, he could set off a minor war. And I'm not just referring to here in Al-Andalus. If Enrique's father-in-law believes my cousin has slighted his daughter by carrying off a Nasrid princess, he will never forgive him. Enrique must be stopped. When did he set out?'

'He'd already gone when I got here. The innkeeper says he left about an hour ago.'

'I take it he took his squire with him?'

'Aye.'

Swearing under his breath, Rodrigo gave Eagle the spur. Doubtless he should be worrying about the insult this would represent to Enrique's wife, Lady Berenguela, and her family. Enrique could set all Spain in a ferment. The uneasy truce with Al-Andalus would be put in jeopardy.

Yet he couldn't stop worrying about the sort of vengeance Enrique might wreak on three Princesses foolish enough to leave their father's protection. His stomach growled and he barely noticed. All he could think about was whether the young woman he'd been dreaming about from dawn to dusk was walking blindly towards disaster.

Rodrigo and Inigo left the horses with their squires some way from the palace and crept up the ravine on foot. The Princesses' tower was dark, a wall of blackness reaching to the sky. On previous nights, it had looked like a lantern with the shutters at the top flung wide and light streaming into the night. Tonight, the entire palace seemed to be deep in slumber. Most importantly, there was no sign of Enrique.

Relief flooding through him, Rodrigo turned to Inigo. 'He must have changed his mind.'

'If he has, then I'm surprised.' Inigo scratched his head. 'I've never seen him quite so determined.'

'Well, he's not here. No one is. Come, dinner awaits.'

The wind was getting up. Rodrigo gave the tower a last look. Was his Princess asleep? How soon would it be before she forgot about the foreign knights who had serenaded her and her sisters? Impatient with himself—the beautiful young woman he had met so unexpectedly was certainly not his—Rodrigo turned away. Leaving the palace to its sleep, he and Inigo headed back for the horses.

A cloud blotted out the moon. The path grew progressively more challenging as one by one the stars winked out and the dark edged in. The atmosphere was so stifling you could cut it with a knife. In the distance, Rodrigo heard a rumble of thunder.

'Storm on its way,' Inigo muttered.

They found Miguel and Guillen and swung back on to their horses.

An owl screeched as they approached the road

which led back to the tavern and, through the scrub on their left hand, a light flared. Rodrigo glimpsed a long section of wall and the unmistakeable gleam of a guard's helmet. This must be another part of the palace. He'd heard it was vast. He signalled for silence.

On their right, the owl screeched a second time, it was suspiciously close. Briefly, Rodrigo shut his eyes. Enrique was in the habit of using the cry of an owl as a signal, this wouldn't be the first time he'd used it to draw their attention. He shot a glance at Inigo and, sure enough, the screech sounded again, slicing through the hot air. When it came a fourth time, Inigo's horse tossed his head.

'Holy hell, that's Enrique,' Inigo breathed, peering towards the right.

Swallowing an oath, Rodrigo guided his horse off the track and plunged deeper into the scrub. His devil of a cousin was nearby, planning Lord knew what. He had to be stopped.

Leonor reached the rusty iron gate at the entrance to the underground passageway and, as Inés had promised, it was open.

'Where's Constanza?' she whispered to Alba. 'We can't leave without her.'

'She's just behind, stop fretting. She'll follow us, she always does.' Alba gave Leonor a gentle shove. 'Hurry, for pity's sake, Father's guards are everywhere.'

Heart in her mouth, Leonor hugged her cloak tightly about her and peered down the tunnel. Inés seemed to have arranged everything. A few yards in, a torch was jammed into a bracket. Below the torch, a heavy key hung on a hook. The key looked every bit as rusty and ancient as the gate. The torch flickered—it was spitting and hissing like a basket of snakes.

Stepping into the tunnel, Leonor snatched up the key and thrust it at Alba. 'Take this, I'll take the torch.'

Gripping the torch with one hand and keeping her cloak out of the way with the other, Leonor plunged on. She'd hidden a pouch of money and jewels beneath her clothes and it banged against her thigh with every step.

The tunnel was narrow. Inés said it was an ancient sally-port, long disused. It was horrible. Rough, unfinished walls cut through rock and earth alike. The ground was uneven. In places, crudely cut timbers held back the earth. Shadows fell back as Leonor advanced, but even so, she couldn't see the end of it. Her heart thumped like a drum and her hand was shaking so much the torchlight wavered all over the walls.

Out of the corner of her eye, she saw a quiver of movement. A rat? A snake? She had no idea.

If she weren't so desperate, she'd refuse to take another step.

We must get out. A chance like this will never come again.

Leonor had heard about the subterranean tunnels, of course. The servants and slaves in the Alhambra each had a different tale to tell about the secret corridors that wormed this way and that beneath the palace. There were said to be escape routes, constructed by earlier sultans in case they needed to flee for their lives. There were said to be sally-ports, like this one. There were underground chambers where the Sultan's enemies were left to moulder. There was rumoured to be an entire city down here, a city of demons.

Until tonight, Leonor hadn't believed the stories, she certainly never expected to use a tunnel herself.

The air smelt strongly of earth. It was cool. Grisly thoughts of being buried alive jumped into her mind. To distract herself, Leonor wondered which part of the palace lay just over their heads. The orange grove? The Court of the Lions? Ahead, a dark shadow shifted. The floor sloped downward, ever downward. Would it never end?

The walls pressed in, the roof was getting far too low—she had to duck her head to continue. Merciful God, if it got any lower, they'd be crawling.

The torch sputtered again. Leonor looked over

her shoulder and Alba almost walked into her. 'I can't see the end,' she said. 'Is Constanza behind us?'

'I think I can hear her. Keep going,' Alba said, in a tight, suffocated voice. Alba didn't like confined spaces.

Leonor gripped the torch and forced herself on. Her chest was tight with anxiety, and she was finding it hard to breathe herself. As the roof became ever lower, it was more of a struggle to keep her veil clear of the torch. The money pouch weighed heavily against her leg.

We will never see Father again.

I don't care.

Father never trusted us.

If he catches us, he will kill us.

He won't catch us.

There was a slight shifting in the air. A draught. And then she was blinking at a door so ancient it was scarcely distinguishable from the tunnel walls.

She swallowed. 'We've reached the end.'

Panting slightly, Alba reached past her and fitted the key to the lock.

Chapter Eight

The ground fell sharply away. In a scrubby hollow in front of Rodrigo, a grey blur took on the shape of a horse. His cousin's warhorse. Enrique must have been there a while because a lantern stood on a rock, the yellow glow revealing that Enrique was standing—or rather swaying—in a small clearing.

Enrique waved a wineskin in greeting. '*Hola*. Thought it would be you.' His voice was slurred. In truth, he was so drunk he was barely keeping upright. 'Pray join me.'

Rodrigo dismounted in silence and gestured for Inigo and the squires to do the same. They led their horses into the hollow. Twigs cracked. A peacock screamed—the palace grounds were too close for comfort. They would have to keep quiet.

'Here.' Enrique tossed the wineskin across with a grin. 'You look as though you need it.'

Rodrigo caught the wineskin, checked the

cork was secure and looped the strap over his saddlebow.

The grin fell from Enrique's face. 'Damn it, Rodrigo, if you're not thirsty, you can hand that back.'

'Later.' Rodrigo was fighting an acid mix of anger and scorn. He had a pretty low opinion of Enrique, but even so, it was hard to credit that his cousin was planning to avenge himself on the Sultan by taking it out on his daughters. Enrique was a barbarian, and the list of his sins was growing by the day. He kept his voice down. 'Enrique, what the devil are you doing?'

'This…' Enrique waved his arms in a dramatic gesture '…is the night I teach Sultan Tariq a lesson. The Princesses are coming home with me.'

Rodrigo made a swift negative gesture. 'You can't take your anger out on innocent women.'

'Innocent? *Dios mío*, what are you talking about? You saw them. They've stepped straight out of a harem.'

'They are princesses, Enrique. They will be as pure and chaste as nuns.'

'Pure?' His cousin let out an unpleasant laugh. 'Not for much longer.'

'Enrique, you can't do this. Believe me, I understand your fury, but this will achieve nothing.'

'I want those Princesses.'

'There are three of them.' Pointedly, Rodrigo eyed Enrique and his squire, who was shifting uneasily in the background. 'You plan on riding off with all three when you and your squire have but two horses? This should be interesting.'

'Holy hell, Rodrigo, one Princess will do.'

Rodrigo narrowed his eyes and leaned in. 'What will you do with her?'

Enrique made a crude gesture. 'What do you think?'

Rodrigo didn't bother to hide his disgust. 'That is ugly beyond belief. What about your wife? What will Lady Berenguela say about this? Have you forgotten you are married?'

'Berenguela doesn't need to know.'

'Enrique, be reasonable, you can't do this. You will break your mother's heart. Such an act would dishonour you; it would dishonour our family. Not to mention that Berenguela's father, Count Yague, will never forgive you.'

'It's none of anyone's damn business but mine.' Enrique's face twisted. 'I want a princess and I will have one. I will teach the tyrant a lesson. He was within his rights to keep us captive until our ransom arrived; he was not within his rights to put us to hard labour.'

'Oh, I don't know.' Rodrigo kept his voice light, he didn't want his cousin working himself into even more of a frenzy. This drunk, he was capable of anything. Not for the first time Rodrigo regretted his kinship with him. Enrique's foolhardiness had caused his brother's untimely death, and tonight's little jaunt could get them all, including their squires, executed. He gave a casual smile. 'It wasn't all bad, we got to serenade the Sultan's daughters.'

'I intend to do more than serenade them.' Again, Enrique made that vulgar gesture. 'And mark my words, I will. This very night.'

'Enrique, the Princesses are innocent.'

Enrique's lip curled. 'Innocent be damned. We're talking about the tyrant's daughters.' He swayed and fell against his horse's flank, clutching a stirrup to steady himself. 'How can they possibly be innocent? The Sultan has been using them to torment us. He tempted us with sight of their faces on the road to Granada, and when we got here, he tempted us again by allowing us to take our evening meal beneath their tower. *Dios mío*, he must have ordered his guards to turn a deaf ear whilst we were serenading them.'

Rodrigo shook his head. 'That isn't how it happened. On the day of our release, I had it from the overseer that the Princesses were dispirited. Their duenna used bribes to get the overseer to allow us to rest at the foot of their tower.' He made his voice dry. 'We were the entertainment. Nothing more, nothing less.'

Enrique swore. 'You're delusional. Rodrigo, you saw them on the road to Granada—the silks, the jewels, the pretty grey mares. The Sultan's daughters live in luxury humble mortals like us cannot imagine. What do they have to be dispirited about?'

'Their father guards them closely—they rarely go out.'

Enrique gave a derisive snort. 'Don't be ridiculous.'

'It's true, apparently. They were so cast down that their duenna struck on the idea of using us to lift their spirits. But don't tell me that Sultan Tariq knew what was happening. He didn't.' He made his voice hard. 'If he'd known, the Sultan would have flayed us alive.'

'You're a fool.'

'At least I'm not suicidal, which you seem to be. Come on, Enrique, Berenguela and your mother want you home in one piece. Let's get back to the tavern.'

Enrique's gaze flickered to something just past Rodrigo's shoulder and his eyes glinted. 'It's too late for that.'

Rodrigo turned to see what at first glance appeared to be a cave in the side of the hill. No, not a cave, behind a curtain of ivy he saw the faintest of lights. He could hear the distinct thud and scrape of a reluctantly opening door. A sally-port? If so, the thickness of the ivy suggested it was decades old. The grating noise told him that it hadn't been opened in years.

There came a hollow thud, then another. The door groaned, the chink opened and the light brightened. Rodrigo gripped the hilt of his sword. Another thud and the chink became a crack.

The ivy parted and a veiled woman appeared, hissing torch in hand. Her cloak had the richness of velvet, and her veil floated about her in the way that only the finest silk could float. A bangle sparkled on her wrist and an elusive fragrance accompanied her, sweet and heady. Orange blossom. Rodrigo's innards tightened. He couldn't make out her face because of the veil, but he knew her. This was Lady Merciful.

Beneath the cloak, her body was long and slender. Rodrigo took a deep breath and drew her scent into his nostrils. In that instant he knew he would do anything to prevent Enrique from harming her or her sisters.

Enrique squeezed past Rodrigo and managed a bow. 'Princess, I am honoured.' He straightened, not too successfully, and held out his hand.

Rodrigo caught Enrique's arm and manhandled him to one side. 'I think not.' If Rodrigo was honest, in the dark reaches of the night there had been times when Rodrigo had thought of revenge, but this—Enrique's desire to coldly and deliberately despoil an innocent woman—his soul revolted against it.

A second woman slipped past the ivy. More jewels glittered, a veritable constellation had been sewn on to her veil. Behind her in the shadowy depths of the sally-port, a third woman hung back.

She seemed to be watching, waiting for something. She must be nervous. Something about her struck Rodrigo as odd, but he couldn't quite grasp it.

He felt as though he'd been knifed.

The three Princesses. God help us, we're going to die.

How Enrique had done it, Rodrigo had no idea, but somehow, his cousin had prised the Sultan's daughters out of their tower. His gaze swung back to Lady Merciful as Enrique sidled round him and made a grab for her wrist. Her torch wavered. There was no time for niceties.

'No, you don't.' Rodrigo shoved Enrique to the ground. Drunk as he was, it wasn't hard.

Enrique swore. In the distance, a dog barked. A heartbeat later an entire pack of hounds joined in.

The Princess's torch wobbled and the shadows jumped. 'My lord, I am glad to see you. When your friend came to the tower alone, I feared you would not come.'

Rodrigo blinked. 'Oh?'

'Please help us.' Her whisper—in Spanish— was urgent. Desperate. 'Our father, the Sultan, will kill us if he finds us. Please, Lord Rodrigo, help us.'

She remembered his name. She was glad to see him. Facts that distracted Rodrigo even as he was thinking that she must be wrong about the Sultan. 'Your father won't kill you, my lady,' he said. 'But he will kill me and my comrades, if he catches us.'

'I fear you may be right. I am sorry, my lord.' Jewels caught the flare of the torch—ruby, emerald, topaz.

Rodrigo gave her a curt nod. Stepping back to the ivy-hung sally-port, he looked at the third woman and prayed she spoke Spanish too. 'If you value your virtue, stay here.' He jerked his head at Enrique, who was sitting on the ground, watching proceedings with a befuddled grin on his face. 'On no account let that man touch you. Do you hear?'

'Yes, Great Lord.' The woman's hand shot out and she clutched his sleeve. Rodrigo blinked, it was a very wrinkled hand for a young woman and she was wearing a plain silver ring, there wasn't a gemstone in sight. Something about this woman was definitely wrong. Who was she?

'Great Lord.' The woman's voice was dry and little more than a whisper. 'Hurry, I beg you. When you are safely away, tell my ladies that Constanza stayed behind. They need to know she wouldn't leave the tower.'

Constanza? Who the devil was Constanza? The third Princess? Rodrigo opened his mouth to ask, but a series of bloodcurdling howls cut him off.

'Go, Great Lord. Go!'

Rodrigo put his shoulder to the door of the

sally-port, sealing the woman in the tunnel, where, hopefully, she'd be safe from Enrique.

The dogs bayed. Full-throated and loud, they were closing in. God willing, they were still in the palace grounds. If not, it would be a matter of moments before they picked up the Princesses' scent. They must leave at once.

'Father's hunting dogs.' Lady Merciful's breath hitched. 'We are discovered. Please, my lord, help us.'

Rodrigo's mind raced. He couldn't abandon the Princess to Enrique, and though she clearly belonged in the palace, she seemed genuinely afraid of her father. One thing was clear, if he didn't get away—fast—he'd be joining Diego in the hereafter. He'd worry about the details later.

He held out his hand and his stomach twisted into a thousand knots when her small fingers touched his. If the Sultan's guards caught them, it was unlikely any of them would survive the night.

'I will do my utmost to assist you.' He grasped her torch, upended it and thrust it into the earth. The flames died and the clearing dimmed, leaving only the glimmer of Enrique's lantern.

It was then that he felt the first splash of rain. The moon and stars had vanished. God save them. It was raining; Enrique was blind drunk; and two Nasrid Princesses were looking to him and Inigo for help. Not to mention that the Sultan's guard had set the palace hounds on their trail.

He ushered Lady Merciful towards Eagle, relieved to see that Inigo didn't need telling to keep the other Princess away from Enrique. He was already bowing over her beringed fingers. 'My lady, I believe you can ride?'

The second Princess nodded. 'Certainly, my lord.'

Inigo smiled. 'This way, if you please. You must ride astride, I'm afraid.'

By the time Inigo had helped the other Princess to his horse, Rodrigo had tossed her sister into his own saddle and was seated behind her. He kicked his heels, trusting Eagle to find his footing in the gloom-filled gully. Miguel and Guillen followed.

It had been a long time since Rodrigo had held a woman in his arms. Having his arms about the Princess—her body was slight and lithe—had an immediate effect on his concentration. It was a struggle to keep wholly focused.

We must find the best way to escape her father's men.

And all the while his baser self was wondering what the Princesses had in mind when they had crept into that sally-port. Were they really running away? Or had this entire incident been cooked up as a means of attracting their father's attention?

Rodrigo kept one hand on the Princess's waist, the other on the reins. He was a tall man and she fitted neatly beneath his chin. She was shaking like a leaf. Terrified. Probably only now was the enormity of what she had done sinking in. She had indeed rebelled against her father. Did she realise that she and her sister had put Inigo and himself in mortal danger? Did she even care?

The Princess twisted to look round at him. She was probably also realising that she had put herself in the hands of a total stranger, no wonder she was afraid.

Her veil fluttered over his hands. Stomach muscles clenching, Rodrigo cleared his throat. 'It's too late for regrets, my lady.'

'I know.' Her voice was soft and slightly husky. Beguiling. 'My lord?'

Again, her veil teased the back of his hand. How she managed to wear the blasted thing was beyond him, it would drive him mad. 'Aye?'

'Where will you take us, my lord?'

Through the veil, he imagined the glimmer of large black eyes. He ached to see her full face again. This was the girl who had filled his dreams during the long nights of his imprisonment. Was she as beautiful as his memory had made her?

He managed a laugh. 'Anywhere away from here. Would you tell me your name?'

'Princess Leonor.'

'Leonor? You have a Spanish name?'

'My mother was Spanish, my lord.'

'Of course, the Lady Juana you mentioned at Salobreña.'

'Aye.'

He heard the dogs again, closer this time.

'I am honoured to meet you, Princess Leonor. Hold fast.'

He dug in his heels and Eagle sprang into the night.

As Lord Rodrigo's horse carried them down the slope, Leonor prayed he didn't notice how jumpy she was. Anger against her father was a dark flame in her heart. And then there was fear—she was walking into the unknown and it was terrifying.

Leonor was fluent in Arabic and Spanish, she could sing and play the lute, in short, she was a highly educated woman, but she understood her limitations. She had never stepped outside the small world of a Nasrid princess. Her entire life she'd been surrounded by slaves, servants and eunuchs. Inés had always been within calling distance. And as for her sisters, well, the three of them were inseparable.

And here she was, sharing a saddle with a Spanish nobleman. She was practically in the man's lap, and all she knew about him was his name and that he was the commander of the Spanish King's garrison in Córdoba.

Rodrigo Álvarez, Count of Córdoba.

She gripped the pommel of the saddle and told herself that she didn't need to know more about him. As far as she was concerned, he was little more than a means of escape. Could she persuade him to accompany her and her sisters beyond the borders of Al-Andalus? She hoped so.

With luck, he'd set them on the road to finding their Spanish relatives. Among the Count of Córdoba's noble connections, there must be someone with information about her mother. If she and her sisters found their mother's family, they would have somewhere to settle, somewhere they could live, free of their father's influence. They could lead their own lives.

The Count's hand tightened on her waist and doubts began to circle, like crows over a corpse. This was a foreign knight with whom she and her sisters had conducted a forbidden flirtation from the top of their tower. His body was presently pressed against her in the most shameful of ways. She could feel his strength. She, who had never been allowed in the company of a real man, was leaning against a total stranger. One who was, undoubtedly, all man. Could she trust him? Was he honourable?

This warrior, her father's enemy, felt so strong. With a sense of surprise, Leonor realised she didn't fear him. He was—the word 'dependable' leaped into her head—Lord Rodrigo was dependable.

Where on earth had that come from? She snorted. Dependable? What was she thinking?

Lord Rodrigo was just another man. Like her father, he probably had feet of clay.

Thunder rolled across the darkened skies and Leonor told herself to be realistic. The best she could hope for would be that Lord Rodrigo wouldn't hold her father's sins against her. Now she thought about it, there were several incongruities concerning his capture in battle. He had the build of a powerful warrior, so how on earth had he been defeated?

Raindrops pattered on to her veil. And there, muffled by thunder and drumming hoofbeats, she caught once more the baying of her father's hounds.

She tightened her hold on Lord Rodrigo's saddle and prayed that she and her sisters—and their Spanish knights—would survive the night.

She tried to look back and Lord Rodrigo's grip tightened.

'Hold still,' he said, and urged his horse on.

Leonor's pulse raced, she had never ridden so fast in her life. Through dark, through rain. She prayed the horse wouldn't stumble and that her father's hunting dogs wouldn't catch them. Most of all she prayed she'd never have to face her father's fury.

We must outrun Father's anger. He'll surely kill us if he catches us.

The rain poured steadily down. Trees shot past in a blur. Undergrowth rustled and hoofs pounded.

Through the chaos, another sound reached her, a light rushing sound, higher pitched than thunder or hoofbeats. Leonor recognised it instantly.

Water. Every muscle went rigid, Inés had told her about this.

May God preserve us!

She stared at the ground rushing past them, and a faint glimmer in the bed of the normally dried-up river confirmed her fear. Water. Her duenna's words came back to her. The reason the three knights and the other prisoners had been put to work in the gully had been because it was prone to flooding after storms.

The rain. The months of searing heat. The parched earth. That sudden, heavy downpour up in the mountains. The riverbed was filling, fast. Lightning flickered and there was an immense crash of thunder. The storm was directly over-head.

Heart thumping every bit as loudly as the horse's hoofs, Leonor put her hand on Lord Rodrigo's. 'My lord, the river!'

He sleeved rain from his face. 'My lady?'

'Water is pouring off the mountains. Much water.'

The pace slackened. There was no hesitation, which she found surprising, the Count simply took her at her word. She felt him turn to examine the empty riverbed. He looked towards the mountains and then back at her. Lightning rippled above them.

'The terrain here is similar to the gully where we cleared rocks?' he asked, not sounding the least bit perturbed.

'Yes, Lord Rodrigo, it is exactly like that.'

White teeth flashed in the dark. 'Thank you, Princess Leonor, that is most interesting.'

He reined in and his friend, the nobleman who had taken Alba, drew up. Two other young men trailed behind them, presumably the knights' squires.

Leonor peered past the squires, searching in vain for a third pair of riders. Nothing. She frowned. Where was Constanza? Had she got lost?

Before she could ask about her youngest sister, Lord Rodrigo turned to the nobleman riding with Alba. 'The riverbed is prone to flash floods.' He gestured at the water swirling around the horses' hoofs. 'We'll use that in our favour. Get the river between us and the palace. With luck, it'll confuse the dogs.'

'Good idea,' the other knight said, settling Alba more comfortably before him.

Leonor touched her sister's elbow. 'Alba, is Constanza behind us?'

'I don't know, I haven't seen her.'

Leonor glanced at the squires. 'And you, sirs, have you seen my other sister?'

'No, my lady.'

Leonor gripped the pommel and stared back the way they had come. There was still no sign of the third knight and Constanza. She looked at Count Rodrigo. 'My lord?'

He held up his hand. 'A moment, if you please. Inigo, our chances of escape will be better if we separate. I'll head south-west. They won't be expecting that.'

Lord Rodrigo's friend nodded. 'Understood.'

'God willing, I'll be in Córdoba in a week.'

'Very well. I'll meet you there.'

Lord Rodrigo beckoned at a squire. 'Miguel, you're with me.'

'Very good, my lord.'

Leonor's eyes fixed on Lord Inigo as he urged his horse up the riverbank with Alba clinging to his saddle like a burr. Then he and his squire galloped into a curtain of rain and were lost from sight.

The downpour had plastered Leonor's veil to her face. Her stomach twisted. Where was Constanza? They couldn't leave without her.

'My lord, about Constanza—?'

She was interrupted by a dull roaring sound. Behind her, Lord Rodrigo tensed. His horse jibbed.

'My lord, the river!'

Lord Rodrigo clapped his heels to his horse's

flanks and they tore up the riverbank as though the devil himself was at their heels.

They rode for hours, long after the sounds of pursuit had faded. Rodrigo drove Eagle to the point where he risked laming or exhausting him. The storm moved on and the stars reappeared, guiding Rodrigo south-west. They passed villages and farms and crossed miles of scrubland.

Princess Leonor gripped Eagle's mane and occasionally shifted in the saddle. She made no complaint. The Princess, it would seem, was stronger than she appeared.

As they rode, the scent of orange blossom teased his nostrils. By this time, Rodrigo had had plenty of time to think, plenty of time to realise that, in giving in to the impulse to help her, he had made a seriously grave error in judgement. This little escapade could cause a major diplomatic incident and relations between the Kingdom of Castile and the Emirate of Al-Andalus were already strained to breaking point. The consequences could be disastrous.

What the devil was he to do? She was a Nasrid princess, for pity's sake. Sultan Tariq would surely move heaven and earth to get her back.

It was tempting to pay Sultan Tariq back in his own coin by asking for a ransom for his daughter's safe return—no, the idea left him with a bitter taste in his mouth. Yes, Rodrigo had wanted revenge. And with the Sultan's daughter land-ing—quite literally—in his lap, he had the per-fect tool by which to get it.

Except he couldn't use her in that way. First, there was that bangle she'd given him in prison to help Inigo. Then there was the way she'd flown to his defence on the road to Granada. A Nasrid princess had saved his life. She'd saved them all. There was no way he could use her to avenge him-self on her father. She must be sent back home.

The Sultan's daughter. Lord help him, what a dilemma. Princess Leonor had asked for help to get away. Yet she would clearly be safest back in the palace.

She would be furious. Well, so be it. There was too much at stake, and he couldn't answer for the consequences if she stayed in Spain. Princess Leonor had to be sent back to where she belonged. A girl like her—dangerously naive, cossetted and impossibly beautiful—wouldn't last a week out-side her father's palace.

As soon as he was certain they'd shaken off the pursuit, he would send Miguel back to arrange for her safe return.

Rodrigo frowned over Leonor's head and tried to ignore the scent of orange blossom. He shifted in the saddle. Why did the idea of sending her back to her father make him so uncomfortable? What else could he do with her? He certainly couldn't keep her. Sending her home made political sense. It was the honourable thing to do.

Light was strengthening in the east when Rodrigo judged they had put enough distance between them and the Sultan's hounds. He slowed the horse and bent to murmur in the Princess's ear. 'There is an inn a mile or two ahead, we'll stop to rest and refresh ourselves.'

She nodded.

Allowing the question of what he was going to do with her to settle in his mind—he would return her to her father as soon as he could—Rodrigo spent the rest of the ride justifying his decision.

Likely a fit of pique had driven Princess Leonor to flee the safety of the Alhambra Palace. Perhaps there had been a family argument. No matter, the reason for her escape was irrelevant. Life was dangerous outside the palace. To avoid a major diplomatic wrangle, as well as for her own safety, Princess Leonor must be returned.

Chapter Nine

They reached the inn in the grey light of dawn. After Leonor dismounted, she stood by a water trough and eased her aching legs. Her veil itched, it was slightly damp. Grimacing, she tugged at the fabric, managing to draw it away from her skin without removing it.

Count Rodrigo was taller than she remembered. Merciful heavens, he was incredibly well built. Even without his armour, he would dwarf her father's guards.

The Count handed his horse to his exhausted-looking squire. 'Rub him down well, Miguel. We rode hard and he'll be thirsty, but don't let him have too much at once.'

'Of course, my lord.'

Lord Rodrigo looked her over top to toe, and Leonor received the distinct impression that something about her amused him. Then he shrugged and crooked his arm at her. 'My lady?'

His hair was dark, dishevelled from their ride, and his eyes were even darker. A quiver ran through her as she placed her hand on his arm. Close to, this man was more than a little alarming. Mercifully, he had shown no sign of violence or ill will towards her.

After the restrictions of the palace, Leonor was uneasy touching a man in so familiar a fashion. It was extremely disturbing. Unsettling. However, there was nothing in the Count's face to suggest that the offer of his arm was anything but commonplace. She would simply have to get used to it, the last thing she wanted was to cause offence.

She needed a man who was brash and bold and strong, someone who could protect her from her father's wrath. The commander of the garrison at Córdoba was just such a man and Leonor would use any means to persuade him to help her. Any means. She had won her freedom and she intended to keep it, even though it meant never seeing her father again.

'My lord, I was thankful to see you at the sally-port,' she said, putting a smile in her voice, despite her fatigue. 'When your friend arranged to meet us, I wasn't sure you would join him.'

His lip twitched. 'You were happy to see me.'

'Yes, of course.' And that was the truth, she realised, with a jolt. This was more than mere flattery to win him over, she truly had been glad to see him.

'I nearly didn't come.'

Leonor felt her face fall. 'Oh?'

'Inigo and I didn't discover what Enrique was up to until the last moment.'

'Well, I'm thankful you came. Your friend seemed to be a little—how shall I put it?—excitable.'

'Enrique's a liability.'

'He'd had much wine, I think.'

'He was totally drunk.'

'Is he capable of riding in such a state?' Leonor asked. It would be too dreadful if Constanza hadn't got away because the knight named Enrique had had too much wine.

The Count gave a short laugh. 'Riding when drunk is a skill my cousin mastered years ago.'

Beneath her veil, her eyebrows lifted. 'That knight is your cousin?'

'Aye.' The Count's dark eyes were slightly narrowed as he looked down at her. Doubtless, he was trying to read her expression through her veil. This man had seen her face more than once— when he'd arrived at Salobreña, on the road to Granada and again at the tower. Did he find her attractive?

Leonor hoped so, because if Lord Rodrigo liked the look of her, he might be more inclined to help. Unfortunately, her only experience of the way a man's mind worked was based on her dealings with her father. Her father responded well to flattery, and he liked his daughters to agree with him. Her father's word was law. Count Rodrigo was an unknown, she couldn't be certain how he would react.

What did he think of her? What must she do to keep this man on her side? If she was going to make a life for herself outside her father's kingdom, she would need all the support he could give, particularly at the outset.

The Count had arranged to meet Lord Inigo in Córdoba, and if she and Alba were to be reunited quickly, it was essential that he help her that far. He was also likely to know where his cousin was likely to take Constanza.

They were proceeding towards the inn when it struck her that she had no idea whether they had even left her father's kingdom.

'Are we still in Al-Andalus, my lord?'

'Aye, why?'

She dug in her heels and took her hand from his arm. 'My lord, we can't stop yet, my father's men will hunt us down.'

Firmly, he shook his head. 'We need rest. We are quite safe here, my lady.'

'You don't understand, Father will find us. He will never stop looking, never. We must go on.'

A warm hand took her elbow and Leonor was steered towards the tavern door. The Count's boldness startled her and she went with him, meek as a lamb. And in so doing, she discovered that his touch didn't trouble her. It felt reassuring rather than threatening.

'I will not permit anyone to harm you, my lady,' he said, drawing her across the yard. 'The innkeeper is loyal to my family. He will post a man on the road to alert us if your father's men appear. I shall secure us a private chamber. We have much to discuss.'

A private chamber? That did sound ominous, and tired though she was, Leonor's mind began to race. Was the innkeeper as trustworthy as Lord Rodrigo believed? Her father rarely spoke about the people living near his borders and she had no way of judging. Everything Leonor knew was gleaned from Inés. And, love Inés though she did, Leonor would be the first to admit that many of her duenna's stories were too fanciful to be true.

What she did know was that her father's kingdom had in ancient times been ruled by the Visigoths. Boundaries had been fluid for centuries and battles such as the one in which Lord Rodrigo had been captured were often fought purely to fill the royal treasury.

The irony wasn't lost on her. In order to keep the peace, her father owed tribute to Castile, and to get it he was in the habit of capturing Spanish knights simply for their ransom.

Leonor sighed, she was well out of her depth and it seemed that her best course was to follow the Count's lead. Warily. She would remain watchful. Above all, she must keep him sweet if she was to bend him to her will. That had worked with her father. Sometimes.

The inn was small and unremarkable. Built almost entirely of wood, the outside was largely bare of ornamentation. There was no carving on the walls, indeed, the only image Leonor could see was three golden swirls on a signboard.

The main chamber inside smelt of woodsmoke and fresh bread. The floor was devoid of coloured tiles. Goodness, surely it wasn't beaten earth? Yes, she rather thought it was.

Through what she guessed must be a serving hatch, she could see an open fire with a complicated arrangement of metalwork hanging over it. A boy was slowly turning a spit. Several cauldrons hung on chains over the flames and a woman was flipping flatbread on an iron griddle.

Curiosity pulled Leonor closer. Never having set foot in the palace kitchens, this was the first time she'd seen anyone cooking. A young girl with a white cloth tied about her waist was chopping onions at a worn table. The girl's gown was practical and modest, though the fabric looked a trifle heavy. Recalling Inés telling her that most people spun the cloth to make their own clothes, Leonor wondered if the fabric was homespun. It seemed likely. The girl murmured to the woman before crossing to the fire to stir something in one of the pots.

Leonor could feel the heat from the fire on her cheeks, it must be stifling work.

Conscious of a heavy silence behind her, she turned. Lord Rodrigo was waiting for her, a quizzical expression on his face. He gestured towards the main room.

'My lady, if you please.'

Cursing her naivety, Leonor lifted her chin and followed him to a bench in a darkened corner. Doubtless, seeing food being prepared was an everyday experience for most people. Her stomach churned, she felt very vulnerable. Knowing so little of life outside the palace, she was bound to give herself away at every turn. And it made it worse somehow that she wasn't sure what was making her more nervous, Lord Rodrigo de Córdoba or the fact that she'd escaped her father.

For the first time in her life, she had only herself to rely on. She had won her freedom by hurling herself into a world about which she knew next to nothing. And she was in the company of a Spanish lord who was virtually a stranger.

She gave him a sidelong glance. It would be easier if she didn't find his dark looks so attractive. Of course, she'd realised he attracted her long before she'd allowed him to toss her on to his horse's back. What she hadn't bargained for was the fact that close proximity would have her tingling whenever she looked at him. It unnerved her.

Not that that mattered. What did matter was that Lord Rodrigo had already suffered at her father's hands. She felt guilty that in rescuing her he risked her father's wrath yet again. Sultan Tariq wouldn't let his daughters go without a fight. They'd made a fool of him and his rage would know no bounds. Their father would be vengeful. He'd want his daughters punished, and to that end, many troops would be sent in search of them. Lord Rodrigo might have to pay a heavy penalty for carrying her away.

Was the Count honourable? Was he a patient man, or was he cast in the same mould as her father? In short, was he a tyrant? Until Leonor learned more about Lord Rodrigo's character, she must hide her vulnerabilities. She must keep her ignorance of the ways of the world to herself.

It was fortunate that she wouldn't have to be reliant on him for long. When she met up with her sisters, she'd have no further need of him.

'My lady, your cloak will be damp, allow me to have it dried for you.'

He wanted her cloak? 'My lord?'

His mouth went up at the corner. 'Relax, I'm not about to ravish you.'

Ravish. The word was not one that Inés had taught her, but something in the Count's smile conveyed its meaning and her cheeks scorched. She clutched her cloak to her and looked pointedly towards the girl in the cookhouse.

The girl's sensible homespun gown wasn't half as revealing as hers. Women had more freedom outside the palace, just as Inés had said, but none the less, Leonor's gown with its heavily ornamented belt and airy fabrics would probably cause a scandal.

'My clothes are not suitable. My lord, they are not practical.'

Lord Rodrigo seated himself next to her on the bench. His eyes danced. 'You mean,' he said softly, for her ears alone, 'you look like someone who has just walked out of a harem.'

There was a heat in those dark eyes that Leonor had never seen before. 'Certainly, my gowns are not suitable for life outside the palace. They will draw attention to us.' She shrugged. 'We left in a hurry. Besides, all my clothes are like this, I have no sensible gowns.'

'I see.' Lord Rodrigo leaned back, a disturbing smile playing about his mouth. 'My lady, I should think your gown is the least of your worries.'

'Oh?'

'Your veil draws the eye. Spanish ladies wear veils, of course, but in the main they show their faces. If you want to look inconspicuous, you must wear your veil in the Spanish fashion. You might even try doing without one.'

'Everyone will see me!'

'Exactly.'

'My lord, I am not accustomed to showing my face. People will stare.'

'I can assure you they will stare far more when you hide your face completely. It is unusual and the unusual arouses curiosity.' He shrugged. 'Without a veil, you will look like that girl over there. By that I mean you will look like an ordinary woman. No one will give you a second glance. I am sure you will soon become accustomed to being seen.'

She bit her lip. 'I shall think about it.'

'Very well.' The Count gestured the girl to their table and went about ordering breakfast.

Leonor's jaw dropped. Count Rodrigo could easily have forced her to remove her veil, yet he hadn't. He could easily have relieved her of her cloak and he hadn't done that either. She frowned as she studied him. She wasn't used to forbearance in a man and his calm reaction was worrying. Ought she to brace herself for an explosion of anger?

Her father always insisted that she and her sisters did exactly as they were told. Count Rodrigo—heavens, she had just disagreed with him and he didn't seem to mind. And earlier, when she had warned him about the flash flood, he had listened to what she was saying. This man had taken her advice without a murmur. It made her uneasy and she knew it couldn't last. Didn't he have a temper? Didn't he hate it when a woman knew more than he did?

Dimly, Leonor heard him asking for a private chamber where they might rest and refresh themselves. She scarcely heard the answers, she was too busy wondering what it would be like when he finally lost patience. It was rather like waiting for another storm to break, she knew it would happen, it was just a matter of when.

It wouldn't be pretty—a man's anger was never pretty. Clearly, she must find a way to keep him calm. She was going to have to charm him, she was going to have to remove her veil.

Taking a deep breath, Leonor lifted the hem of her veil and casually pushed it back over her head.

Two things happened. The first was that Lord Rodrigo turned to look at her. His dark features lighted in a smile so warm Leonor felt it in her toes. She forgot to breathe. Apart from her father, she had never been this close to a man without the protection of a veil. Her throat dried. It was too much, the Count was too much, his eyes seemed to hold her hostage and she couldn't look away.

In that instant, her entire body understood why her father insisted that she and her sisters wore veils. The veils were not there to keep the world at arm's length, they were there for their protection. *Men are predators.*

The excited churning in her stomach warned her that it wasn't simply that she needed protection against Count Rodrigo. Astonishingly, it seemed that Leonor might need protecting against herself. This man—handsome, alarming, a stranger from another world—attracted her. Fiercely. Her father had been right, all along.

The second thing was that the serving girl noticed her for the first time and dipped into a curtsy. 'Good day, my lady, welcome.'

'Thank you.'

Leonor's cheeks were on fire, without her veil, she felt naked. Her hands were trembling, so she folded them carefully on her lap and clasped them. She was doing the sensible thing, she told herself firmly. If her father's men succeeded in tracking her here, they'd be looking for a woman—how had the Count put it?—a woman who had walked out of a harem.

'Well done,' Lord Rodrigo murmured.

His gaze held hers, moved over her entire face and stopped at her mouth. Truth be told, though he flustered her, it wasn't an unpleasant feeling.

The serving girl, having glanced her way, didn't seem to have noticed anything unusual, and her attention was back on the Count, who was asking about payment.

'My lord, there is no need to pay us straight away.' The girl smiled. 'We are honoured by your custom and your word is good here.'

Leonor frowned, there was a problem over payment? Surely Lord Rodrigo wasn't short of money? His ransom had been paid, his people must have sent him spare coin.

She had assumed the garrison commander of Córdoba was a wealthy man, though she knew very little about him. Perhaps she'd been mistaken, perhaps his family was poor.

'My lord?' Beneath the cover of the table, Leonor felt for the purse hidden beneath her clothes and extracted a pendant necklace. She pressed it discreetly into his hand. 'Take this, please. I would not wish you to be short on my account.'

He took the necklace, fingering the ruby centrepiece with a bleak expression, and tucked it into his scrip. 'My thanks.' He pushed to his feet and held out his hand.

Leonor blinked at his hand. 'We're leaving?'

'Certainly not. I can't speak for you, my lady, but I need food and rest before we go any further. Come, we have use of a private chamber.'

'You swear we are safe here?'

'Absolutely.' He met her gaze straight on and his eyes were sombre. 'I have a number of questions. As I mentioned, we have much to discuss and it's best done in private.'

Once in the chamber, the Princess allowed Rodrigo to remove her damp cloak.

Rodrigo tried not to look too closely at her clothes. As he suspected, they shrieked that she had just walked out of a harem. Fashioned from silks that were as light as gossamer, they had surely been designed to reveal rather than conceal. He tried not to notice her body either, but that was impossible. She was as slender and neat as he had guessed. Infinitely desirable. Lord, what a lovely woman.

Princess Leonor was perfect. Her face was almost too beautiful to look at. Dark eyebrows emphasised black eyes that were flecked with grey and carefully outlined with kohl. They looked as though they held a thousand secrets. Her eyelashes were long and thick. Her skin was smooth and her mouth rosy and sweet-looking. Her father was no fool, to keep this daughter hidden from men. Her body was so perfect she would tempt a monk to break his vows of chastity.

Rodrigo had brought her with him in the heat of the moment. The idea that Enrique might get his drunken, lecherous hands on her was not to be thought of. And with the Sultan's hunting dogs baying for blood, it had been the only thing to do. In the cold light of day, however, he was certain he'd made a grave mistake.

Politically, the Princesses' escape was bound to have consequences, the alliance between the Kingdom of Al-Andalus and that of Castile was as fragile and complicated as a spider's web. Sadly, conflict along the borders was almost an everyday occurrence. Both sides were to blame. There were plenty of Spanish noblemen of the same ilk as his cousin, troublemakers out for personal gain. And then there was Sultan Tariq himself, urging his troops to make forays into Castilian territory in the hope of capturing knights for the ransom they would bring him.

An incident such as this—removing Princess Leonor from the palace—was bound to be misunderstood.

Sultan Tariq would never accept that Rodrigo had saved the Princess from his lecherous cousin. The Sultan knew that his soldiers had killed Diego, he'd be sure to conclude that Leonor's disappearance was down to Rodrigo taking a bizarre form of revenge against him. Furthermore, knowing the Sultan, the entire incident would be twisted out of all proportion. Rodrigo would probably be accused of plotting to subvert the Kingdom of Al-Andalus.

Dios mío, the repercussions could destroy the delicate diplomatic balance. Years of painstaking work would be lost. He must contact the Sultan with all speed.

He stared down at her, so beautiful, so innocent and open, and was gripped with a feeling of deep melancholy. This woman was utterly unlike her father. The longer Rodrigo spent with her, the more he realised that he'd like nothing better than to spend time uncovering her secrets one by one. That was impossible. And irresponsible in the extreme. Only a madman would act on the attraction he felt for a Nasrid princess.

She needed to go home, where she would be safe. And the peace between their peoples, shaky though it was, would be preserved.

'My lady, you do realise you must return to the palace.'

Her eyes filled with horror. 'My lord?'

'You have to go home.'

'No. *No.*' She backed away, took a tiny step back towards him and retreated again. 'No, my lord, I cannot.'

'My lady, you must. You belong in Al-Andalus.'

Hand at her throat, she shook her head. 'I can't go back. My lord, please understand, I won't go back.'

'What happened? Did you and your father have an argument?' After a few moments, Rodrigo realised she wasn't going to answer. He sighed. 'Did he find out about your visit to the prison in Salobreña? Or the singing, perhaps?'

She shook her head. 'Father knows nothing about either of those things.'

'Well, whatever has caused this breach between you, you must return and mend it.'

'No.'

'Princess.' Rodrigo kept his voice low and

even. Her head was high and her mouth was set in stubborn lines, yet her fear was palpable. He couldn't understand it, her father wouldn't hurt her, not his daughter. 'Your father will be worried about you. He will want to know you are safe.'

'I'm not going back.' She held out her hand. 'Please, my lord, take me with you to Córdoba.'

Rodrigo frowned, she'd lost all colour. Was she so afraid? It made no sense. 'Princess, you must return to the Alhambra.'

'I cannot go home. Father will kill me.'

'My lady, you're overwrought, your father won't kill you.'

'I am not overwrought. It is the truth.'

Several thoughts flashed through Rodrigo's mind as he took her hand and enfolded it in his. The Sultan wouldn't kill his daughter! Still, there was no way he could abandon her to be found by his troops, she was too unworldly to be left to her own devices.

God help him, the last thing he wanted was to act as nursemaid to a spoilt princess. Unfortunately, for the moment, he had no choice. He would keep her safe until he could arrange for her to be sent home. But home she would assuredly go.

In the meantime, if he didn't want her kicking and screaming every step of the way, he must play along with her. She really wasn't fit to be left on her own.

'Very well, my lady. Will you accompany me to Córdoba?'

Her face softened. 'Yes, my lord, I will. Thank you.'

Releasing her hand, he absently touched his scrip. That little misunderstanding over paying the innkeeper had been a godsend. He could send Princess Leonor's ruby pendant back to her father as proof he had her safe. Once the Sultan knew that his daughter was unharmed, he would doubtless send a suitable escort to take her back to Granada.

God willing, the Sultan would accept Rodrigo's account of events without quibbling. With a little luck, returning the Princess might pave the way to a new understanding between their peoples. Diego's death wouldn't have been in vain if the Sultan learned that peaceful co-operation was possible. What a coup that would be. Rodrigo recognised he was being optimistic, but stranger things had happened.

In the meantime, his task was to guard Princess Leonor. This was a golden opportunity to teach the Sultan that Spanish noblemen could behave with honour. The Princess was as innocent as a newborn babe, and until she went home, it was incumbent on Rodrigo to keep her that way. He must protect her.

No one would touch so much as a hair on her head.

And the other Princess? The one who had ridden off with Inigo?

Rodrigo would sort that out with Inigo when they got back to Córdoba.

In the meantime, Rodrigo was in no doubt that Inigo would also treat Lady Leonor's sister with all honour. She too would be sent back to the palace and the three Princesses would be reunited.

Rodrigo made a play of examining the chamber. Apart from the bed, there wasn't much. A jug and wash basin sat on a coffer. There was also a platter of bread, cheese and grapes; and two cups and a flagon of ale.

He waved in the general direction of the food. 'My lady, you may wish to refresh yourself before resting. If you'll excuse me, I need to speak to my squire.'

She sent him a sharp look and bit her lip in a way that told him she was more nervous than he had supposed.

'You will return, my lord?'

'Aye.' Rodrigo was unable to meet her eyes. Guilt. He didn't like the idea of sending Miguel back to her father to negotiate her safe return whilst she clearly imagined she had escaped the palace. It left him with a bad taste in his mouth.

Yet what could he do? His only course was to send her back. She was so vulnerable. She knew nothing about life outside the harem. Without doubt, the best place for a Nasrid princess was in her father's care.

He ought to tell her his intentions, and he would. Eventually. First, though, he would reach an understanding with her father, then he would arrange for a suitable escort to return her—and her sister—back to the Alhambra. There was no point upsetting her before then. She wouldn't be used to having her will denied, there was no saying what she might do.

Rodrigo had his fill of problems and he didn't need another. His mother would be grief-stricken after Diego's loss, and he was already behind with his affairs—both at the garrison at Córdoba and on his estate. The last thing he needed was having to deal with a spoilt, hysterical princess.

Princess Leonor went to the ewer and stared at it. Was she waiting for him to pour the water for her? Dear heaven, what next? He suppressed a sigh and reminded himself that, until today, she had never seen a kitchen. This woman had been waited on hand and foot from birth, doubtless she'd never had to pour her own water.

The jug was chunky earthenware, and it did look heavy. Rodrigo leaned past her, reaching for the handle at the same time as she did. The contact sent a faint frisson shooting to his groin, a definite tug of attraction. He frowned. *Ignore it.*

She snatched back her hand and those black eyes met his. Her eyelashes fluttered, dark crescents against perfect olive skin. 'My apologies, my lord. I can manage.'

Rodrigo bowed and cleared his throat. 'If you are sure, please excuse me, my lady, I really do need to speak to my squire.'

Whilst she was occupied with the washcloth and water, he slipped from the chamber and went to find Miguel.

Chapter Ten

'You understand your orders, Miguel?' Rodrigo asked in a low voice. He and his squire were sharing a jug of ale in the main room, and whilst no one was near enough to hear them, one couldn't be too careful.

'Yes, my lord. I'm to rest for a couple of hours before taking this to Granada.' Discreetly, Miguel patted his scrip—the Princess's ruby necklace was tucked inside. 'I have memorised your message.'

'Excellent. Miguel, understand that you are not to approach the palace in person, I value your hide far too much. You are *not* to take risks. Speak to Sa'id at the bathhouse. He has relatives in the palace guard and will know who to approach.'

'I understand.'

'Good lad. I'll see you back in Córdoba. The Sultan can contact me there.' Rodrigo pushed back the bench and got up. 'I regret not giving you longer to sleep.'

'My lord, I'm honoured to help, after everything you have done for me, I owe you a thousand thanks. The loss of a night's sleep is nothing.'

Rodrigo knocked on the door of the private chamber.

'Enter.'

The Princess was sitting on the bed, toying with the folds of her flimsy gown. Her eyes were huge and her face strained, she looked alarmingly vulnerable. The food and drink on the side-table didn't appear to have been touched, and he walked towards it. 'Are you thirsty, my lady?'

'I had some ale, thank you.'

Rodrigo lifted his eyebrows. 'You drink ale?'

Some of the tension left her expression and she smiled. 'I admit, we're not usually offered it.'

'I find it refreshing, some wines are very cloying.'

'Indeed.'

'Would you like more?'

'If you please.'

Rodrigo poured two measures of ale.

'Thank you.'

She shifted to take the ale and he noticed she'd removed her riding boots. Her feet were long-boned and delicate, and her toes neat. Sweet Mary, she was wearing golden anklets. Rodrigo's gut clenched. He'd never seen a woman wearing anklets before, and it was hard not to stare. He found them extraordinarily arousing. Belatedly, he became aware she was talking and tore his gaze from the anklets.

'My lord, I should like to ask about your conversation with my sister.'

'I didn't speak to your sister.'

She gazed over her ale cup, a faint crease in her brow. 'Yes, you did, back at the sally-port. You were talking to Constanza and then you shut the door on her.'

'Constanza is your other sister?'

'Yes, she was the last to leave the tower. What happened?'

Rodrigo tapped his finger on the side of his ale cup. 'My lady, you are mistaken about Princess Constanza leaving the tower.'

'That can't be right, I heard her in the tunnel. Behind Alba.'

'My lady, the woman I spoke to definitely wasn't your sister.' He felt his lips twitch. 'She was far too old and was dressed most severely.'

'Inés?' she said in a puzzled tone. At his enquiring look, she added. 'Inés is our duenna.'

'Well, whoever she was, she asked me to tell you that your sister stayed in the tower.'

Princess Leonor clutched her cup. 'That can't be. Constanza must have come with us, I am sure she was just a little way behind.' Her voice became small.

'I am sorry, my lady, your duenna was most

clear on that point. Princess Constanza stayed behind.'

The Princess's eyes brimmed with tears. 'What will happen to her alone in the palace? Father will kill her.'

Rodrigo drew his head back, frowning. 'My lady, surely you exaggerate.'

She released a shuddering sigh. 'Father can be cruel. Although it's just possible that he'll be pleased with Constanza for choosing to remain.' She was clenching the ale cup very tightly—her fingers were bone white. 'My lord, you cannot comprehend what our life has been like. We're never allowed out. In the main, we're forced to keep to the tower. Father even locks us in.'

Rodrigo stared at her downbent head. It was hard to accept the Princesses weren't given the run of the palace. What about those three grey mares he'd seen on the road to Granada, bedecked with silver bells? However, he would be the first to admit that he knew nothing of the life of a Nasrid princess.

'My lady, you were allowed to play and sing with us.'

A tear trembled on the end of her eyelashes. She dashed it away. 'I told you, we kept that secret.'

He laughed. 'We made so much noise, I should think half the palace knew.'

'Not so. Our tower is across the gardens. It is

some way from Father's state apartments. And Inés kept watch for us.'

Rodrigo poured himself another cup of ale, he wasn't sure what to believe. He had no way of knowing the layout of the palace, and if what the Princess was telling him might be true. As for her claims that her father confined his daughters to the tower, the man was known to be a tyrant, but to imprison his daughters like that?

'Constanza is very shy, my lord,' she said sadly. 'I was certain she would come with us, as she usually follows my lead.'

'Clearly not this time.'

'I can't bear to think of her stuck there for ever.' Her voice shook. 'That tower is a gilded cage.'

'A gilded cage has to be better than a real prison,' Rodrigo said drily. 'In any case, siblings are often separated.'

She blinked. 'What do you mean?'

Diego. The pain knifing through his guts, deep and visceral, came out of nowhere. *Diego.* Fists clenched, he turned sharply away.

'My lord?'

Her voice was closer. She'd crossed the chamber and was standing behind him. A light touch— her fingers on his knuckle—brought him away from his pain and his fists uncurled.

'What is it, my lord?'

He shrugged. Forced a smile. 'Siblings are bound to separate at some point. They marry and move away. They enter the church. They go on pilgrimage and never return.'

She drew back, suddenly pale. 'You've lost someone.'

'Haven't we all?' Rodrigo lightened his tone and tried another smile, but it felt as forced as the previous one. 'My lady, there's no law that guarantees that siblings should prosper equally, never mind that they should stay together for ever.'

'What happened? Who have you lost?'

'Forget it.'

'My lord, please. You've lost a brother, haven't you?' Her breath caught. 'You lost him in the recent conflict.'

He could see from her expression that denials were pointless. 'Aye. My younger brother, Diego.'

She drew a shuddering breath. 'My lord, I am so sorry, I had no idea.' She swallowed, her eyes were no longer meeting his. 'Please accept my heartfelt sympathies, I cannot imagine how you must feel. To lose a brother...'

'My lady, politics are to blame for my brother's death, not you.'

'I don't know how you bear to look at me. Th-thank you for treating me so kindly.' Her black eyes lifted, they were brimming with sympathy and something else. Hearing about Diego had made her wary of him. 'My lord, please, I know you will want revenge on the Sultan, but I beg you, do not send me home. My father is not a kind man.'

Revenge? Rodrigo didn't know how she did it, but when he looked at this Princess, revenge was the last thing on his mind.

He couldn't work her out. There she stood, a perfumed, exotic beauty, glittering with gems and wearing those distracting golden anklets. And she claimed her father mistreated her?

White teeth were worrying her bottom lip. Hearing about Diego had truly upset her and she seemed genuinely sympathetic to learn that he was grieving. How could that be? They barely knew each other.

A pretty foot shifted, an anklet glittered and a bolt of pure want shot through him. Lord, this woman was dangerous, she was simply too beautiful. She was also oddly convincing, and he was tempted to believe her.

Well, there was no going back now. He'd already sent his message to her father. She was going home and all he had to do was guard her until her father's men came to Córdoba to collect her.

'My lord?' Huge black eyes were watching him. 'Please understand, my sisters and I are inseparable, we are not used to being apart.'

'I see that,' Rodrigo said carefully. He was beginning to feel that he had wandered into a quagmire.

'The three of us belong together. My lord, I am sorry about your brother, but if fate allows, my sisters and I would like to be reunited. To that end, I must send a message to Constanza. I also need to speak to my other sister, Alba.'

'Later.' Rodrigo set his cup down on the table with a click. 'I am beyond weary and you must be too. My lady, as you no doubt heard, it is my intention to meet up with Inigo at Córdoba. You may see Princess Alba there. Any discussion regarding Princess Constanza must wait until then.'

Hopefully, he would shortly receive word from her father. Princess Leonor must have exaggerated the Sultan's likely response to her actions. Even though he was harsh as a ruler, as a father he would surely be out of his mind with worry to discover that two of his daughters had gone missing.

All I have to do, Rodrigo thought, turning his gaze from the beautiful body that lay beneath the diaphanous silks and satins, *is keep the Princess safe until the Sultan's escort reaches Córdoba. At all costs, Princess Leonor must be protected.*

Rodrigo felt a twinge of doubt. He had been through testing times, yet it was beginning to dawn on him that perhaps his time with Princess Leonor might prove the most testing of all. She was far too distracting for his peace of mind.

'Very well.' She gave a delicate yawn and a dark eyebrow arch upward. 'I confess I am tired. Where will you sleep, my lord?'

He gestured at the door. 'I shall be just out-side. Should you need anything, all you have to do is call.' He bowed. 'My lady, I am at your command.'

'Thank you, Lord Rodrigo, you are most kind.'

It took an age for Leonor to fall asleep, her belly felt as though it was full of stones. Lord Rodrigo's brother had been killed by her father's men. Leonor knew that men on both sides had died in the fighting and her visit to the prison had given her an inkling of what some of them had suffered. But Count Rodrigo's brother had died. Died.

How he must hate her. Her father, with his greed for ransom money, was largely responsi-ble for Diego's death.

Miraculously, despite the guilt that twisted through her, Leonor eventually found rest, of a sort. She dreamed she was fumbling about in the dark labyrinth of corridors beneath the Alhambra Palace. She was certain the way out was close, but she never got there. The passages ran on for ever, and she was lost and utterly alone.

It was a relief to be dragged back to reality by a brisk knocking.

'My lady, may I come in?'

That deep voice was unmistakable.

'Lord Rodrigo?' Leonor heard the faint clack of the latch being lifted. Sitting bolt upright, she held the covers tightly under her chin and glared at him. 'My lord, you said I could rest.'

Eyes impenetrable, he walked fully into the chamber and tossed a bundle on to the bed. 'You've had three hours. We've lingered long enough. It's possible the palace guard might pick up our trail, so the sooner we leave Al-Andalus, the better. If I must meet your father's men, I prefer to do so on home ground.' He gestured at the bundle, his smile wry. 'The innkeeper's daughter has gone to some lengths to find clothes and boots for you.'

Leonor stared at the boots. They were brown and were without question the ugliest she had ever seen. Heavy and extremely large, they looked sturdy rather than comfortable. Her own boots—soft red kidskin embossed with gold—were sitting side by side next to the wall. She couldn't help but give them a regretful glance.

He followed her gaze and, stalking over to the red boots, picked them up. 'These will have to be burned.'

'Burned!'

'They're too showy for you to wear and we can't leave them here. There must be no traces of our visit.' He jerked his chin at the brown boots. 'Those might not be what you are used to, but they won't attract any attention. Be so good as to put them on. And hurry, we're leaving as soon as you are ready.'

The door shut smartly behind him, leaving Leonor to blink at the clothes on the bed. Her head was muzzy with fatigue. Lord Rodrigo had said she'd been asleep for three hours, but it felt like only moments. And what did he mean by saying that if he must meet with her father's men, he would do so on home ground? Yesterday he seemed certain they had escaped the palace guard.

She dragged the clothes towards her. There was a fine linen garment she took for a shift, a plain green gown in a more serviceable weave and a veil. Rising, she padded to the ewer when it occurred to her that though she had been affronted that Count Rodrigo had interrupted her sleep and entered her bedchamber, it hadn't occurred to her to be afraid. Somehow in the night, she seemed to have decided that he was unlikely to hurt her. Yes, he'd lost his brother fighting against her father, but he would never avenge himself on her.

What a blessing he had been the one to take her up on his horse. She could only pray that Alba had been equally fortunate in Count Inigo. Lord Rodrigo had assured her that Lord Inigo was a man of honour and that Alba would be safe, Leonor could only trust he was right. Thus far Lord Rodrigo had been most chivalrous, surely his friends would share his ideals.

Except that the third knight—Lord Rodrigo's cousin—had been horribly drunk. Perhaps it would be wise to reserve judgement on the characters of Lord Rodrigo and his comrades until she knew more about them.

After a hasty wash, Leonor pulled on the clothes, making sure her purse was safely hidden beneath the linen shift. Next came a brief tussle with gown lacings and the unfamiliar veil. She shook out the skirts and looked down at herself with critical eyes. The boots absolutely swamped her, her feet looked enormous.

The boots aside, the innkeeper's daughter had found her the clothes of a Castilian lady. Well, perhaps not a lady exactly, the green gown was too plain for that. There was no gold thread, no beading or embroidery of any kind. Leonor smiled, she rather liked the simplicity. If she was going to reveal her face to all and sundry, it was surely better to be a sparrow than a peacock. In this gown, no one would give her more than a passing glance.

Had Lord Rodrigo asked the innkeeper's daughter to find these unremarkable clothes? Had he understood how ill at ease she felt revealing herself to the world in her Princess's clothing? Or was it simply that these were all the girl had to hand?

Impatient with herself—Lord Rodrigo's motives should be of no interest to her—she lifted the latch and tramped through to the main room of the inn. The boots felt so heavy they might have been fashioned from lead.

The Count was sitting at the table in front of a plate of bread and sliced meat. A bowl of olives sat at his elbow. He rose at her approach and his dark eyes took her in, head to toe. His mouth went up at the corner when he got to the boots.

'You look very well, my lady.' He gestured at the bread and meat. 'It might be a while before we find an inn as welcoming as this. If you are hungry, please eat.'

Leonor seated herself and broke off some bread as he finished eating. Lord Rodrigo remained an enigma, but she was coming to see that when he said something, he meant it. He would leave when he was ready and she really didn't care to be left behind.

'After last night, Eagle is winded,' he said, pushing to his feet and looking to the door. 'I won't risk laming him. I've hired a couple of fresh horses to take us to the border. Please hurry. You have until I have seen to the horses.'

She was too edgy to be hungry, but with a nod, she forced down a fig. Her brief sleep hadn't refreshed her and she ached in every bone. Yet she understood the need for haste. They must go on, she had no wish to be caught by the palace guard, and not simply because she had no wish to return home.

What would they do to Lord Rodrigo if they were caught?

Goosebumps rose on her skin. The Count hadn't

asked to be burdened with her company, he had only carried her away because the hounds had been loosed and he'd had no wish to be caught so close to the palace. If he were found in the company of the Sultan's daughter, he would be given a long and painful death. It was a sickening thought. Shakily, she reached for an ale cup and had a quick drink. Taking up a chunk of bread, she left the tavern.

He was in the yard holding the reins of two very ordinary-looking horses—a bony brown mare with a grey muzzle and a sway back, and a solidly built black gelding.

Realising the brown mare would never carry Count Rodrigo, Leonor approached the mare, allowed her to take her scent and patted her neck.

'This animal is not young,' she observed. 'She doesn't look strong enough to make it to those trees on that hill, never mind manage a journey to Córdoba.'

Lord Rodrigo grunted. 'That's why you're riding her. Best I could do, I'm afraid.' He put his head to one side. 'Can you cope with that saddle? You will have to ride astride.'

'That is fine,' Leonor said, thanking the stars for the riding lessons she had had whilst she and her sisters had been living at Castle Salobreña.

Handing the bread to the Count, she took the reins and mounted. Riding astride in a Castilian gown wasn't something she'd done before and the skirts rode up, almost to her knees. Her cheeks burned. As a princess, she had either ridden in a litter or in a voluminous divided skirt.

Calmly, Lord Rodrigo tugged her skirts down as far as he could. His expression was solemn, but his eyes glinted, and she had the distinct impression he was trying not to laugh.

'My lady, I realise none of this is what you are used to. If it means anything, you are managing admirably. I'll put the bread in my saddlebag, unless you want to eat it now.'

'Thank you, my lord, I thought we might need it later.'

'Very good.'

As they set the spurs to the horses, Leonor felt a flicker of unease. What had happened to Lord Rodrigo's squire? She drew up sharply and twisted in the saddle to look back at the inn.

'My lady?'

'Where's your squire?'

'Miguel?' His expression was blank, all traces of amusement wiped away. 'He'll be joining us in Córdoba when Eagle has rested. Come, we must be on our way.'

He rode on, leaving Leonor to frown at his broad back and wonder at his tone, it had been so dismissive. Something about that studied blankness didn't fit with what she knew of him. Thus far Count Rodrigo had been extraordinarily open-handed and fair. He had not let his grief touch his dealings with her. He had treated her as though she were his equal, and that brusque tone struck a distinctly jarring note.

Shaking her head, she spurred after him. What did she expect? He was a man.

Earlier, he had surprised her by listening to her when she'd warned him how the gully flooded after heavy rain. And that hadn't been the only time he'd surprised her. When they'd reached the inn, he hadn't forced her to remove her veil, he had only suggested she do so. Further, he'd persuaded the innkeeper's daughter to find more suitable clothes for her.

In short, she'd been given a tantalising glimpse of a world where men and women might listen to each other and treat each other with respect.

His forbearance earlier must have been an aberration. Doubtless he'd been so happy to be free that he'd treated her kindly. That was why he had been patient with her. Plainly his patience was at an end.

Leonor rode on with a heavy heart. She had been mad to think, even for a moment, that when she had walked away from the palace she had stepped into a new world. Lord Rodrigo was simply a means of escaping the tower and she must never forget it.

Rodrigo kept the pace as hard as he dared and braced himself for a litany of complaints, a Nasrid princess certainly wouldn't be used to spending an entire day in the saddle.

Their road rose inexorably into scrubby foothills. Rodrigo wasn't familiar with the route and the sun was unrelenting. After three hours' riding, he called a halt and they rested beneath the awning of an inn for an hour. Somehow, when his back was turned for a few moments, the Princess managed to acquire a fan from one of the serving girls. Sensible woman.

Then came three more hours of riding, followed by brief rest and a change of horses. He pushed relentlessly on.

By the time the sun was sinking behind the mountains, Rodrigo had gone beyond simply being impressed. Princess Leonor hadn't complained once. Given that she must have spent her entire life languishing in one palace or another with a bevy of servants catering to her every whim, it seemed nothing short of miraculous.

During the ride, Rodrigo had plenty of time to think. First sight of her in that simple Castilian gown had stolen his power of speech. If she'd been lovely in her exotic palace silks, that plain gown had somehow turned her into a goddess. In it, she was utterly beautiful. Ravishing.

It didn't make sense that a plain gown made her even lovelier. Yet so it was. Was it that she seemed more approachable in it? Her eyes glowed. The glimpses he had of the glossy dark hair tucked beneath a less concealing veil made him long to unbind it. He had an idea that it reached far below her waist and he spent far too much time wondering about it.

When the Sultan's daughter wasn't looking his way, he watched her constantly. He told himself he was keeping an eye on her to make sure she could keep up. When she went back to the palace, her father would want her to be as healthy as when she left it.

He was lying to himself. Her bright eyes gleamed with interest. It was a joy to watch the way she took everything in. She studied the shepherd's huts they passed on the way and stared at the sheep; she gazed with unfeigned fascination at the tiny villages and irrigation channels built by the farmers. She watched sparrows darting from bush to bush; and when she saw the eagles floating high above the far mountains, her pretty mouth curved. Her whole face shone with delight and pleasure.

After a while Rodrigo found himself wondering if she understood how much danger he was in. Did she think this race to the borders of her father's realm was just a game?

He continued to observe her and his mood darkened as reality hit home. This was far more than a game. If the Sultan's men caught them, the danger for Rodrigo was dire. If they were caught near the frontier of her father's realm, there would be no negotiating. For him, it would be a death sentence.

Grimly, he urged his mount on. He kept up the pace all day, he was determined to reach a tavern known as The Forge. When they got there, they could rest. The afternoon heat built and the Princess's shoulders drooped. Her smile dimmed and every now and then she shifted in the saddle. She dragged at her veil and glanced his way.

'Not long before we can find some shade,' Rodrigo said.

She gave him a tired smile. 'That's good to hear.'

'I'm aiming to reach the frontier.'

She glanced up the road, a slight pleat in her brow. 'How will we know when we get there?'

'You may have noticed we're using a back road. I've not come this way before and I'm hoping the border won't be manned. It's possible we might have crossed it already.'

Finally, on a small rise, he saw the battered inn sign and let out a sigh of relief.

'We've definitely crossed the border. My lady, you have left your father's kingdom.'

The Forge was rundown and smaller than Rodrigo had expected. It appeared deserted, but a line of smoke was rising from somewhere behind it, so someone must be about. Rodrigo tethered the horses and led Princess Leonor to a rickety table in the shade of a pine tree.

Dark eyes met his. 'We're to remain outside?'

'Only until I have spoken to the landlord. Be so good as to wait here.'

The Princess nodded and Rodrigo went into the inn.

'Landlord?'

There was a slight scuffle and a man emerged from the gloom, wiping his hands on his tunic. 'You want food, sir?'

'And a private chamber, if you please.'

The innkeeper gave him a blank look. 'We only have the common room. If you need food, I can serve you inside.' He peered doubtfully through the door at Leonor. 'Or outside if you and your lady prefer.'

'We need somewhere to rest.' And, Rodrigo thought, somewhere they could stay out of sight, just in case they'd been followed. Since they'd crossed the border, the worst of the danger was past. However, there was no sense courting trouble.

The inn seemed safe enough. A couple of dozy-looking shepherds—their crooks propped against a table—were the only other patrons.

The landlord gestured at a pile of pallets at the far end of the chamber. 'I could let down the curtain in the sleeping area. You can rest there.'

'Thank you, landlord, we'll eat inside.'

An hour later, with his belly pleasantly full of bean soup and bread, Rodrigo was seated at a table next to the curtain that screened off the tables from the pallets. With a wine jug in front of him as cover, he was actually on guard. Behind the curtain, the Princess was sleeping. Or at least he hoped she was. She hadn't wanted to rest. Despite the shadows under her eyes, she'd put her pretty nose in the air and insisted she wasn't tired.

What an astonishing woman she was proving to be. Hardy. Clever. And she truly seemed to have turned her back on her father. Rodrigo had an unpleasant feeling that her urge to escape was what had kept her going, and he wasn't looking forward to her finding out that he intended to send her home.

Whatever else he did, he must keep her from discovering he'd sent a message to her father until after they'd reached Córdoba. He would have to watch his tongue. She had a quick mind and her grasp of Castilian wasn't simply good, she spoke it like a native. Her duenna, he supposed.

When he heard the hoofbeats, Rodrigo was on his feet before he'd had time to think.

Had the Sultan's men caught up with them? He gripped the hilt of his sword and stalked to the door, the landlord at his heels.

Chapter Eleven

Two riders were approaching, their horses' fetlocks dull with dust. It was Enrique and his squire, Pedro. As they dismounted, Rodrigo relaxed his grip on his sword and nodded a greeting.

'Enrique.'

Enrique's smile was sour. 'Might have known you'd beat me to it,' he said, handing his horse to a stable lad. 'Where is she? What have you done with her?'

Wondering if Enrique could have been followed, Rodrigo leaned against the doorpost and glanced back down the road. No one else was in sight.

'Where is she?' Enrique repeated, wiping the sweat from his brow with his sleeve.

'Who?'

'The wench you stole from me. What have you done with her?'

When his cousin made to pass through the tavern door, Rodrigo barred the way. Enrique wasn't going anywhere near Princess Leonor.

'The *lady* is resting. She's not to be disturbed, we can talk over there.' Rodrigo gestured at the sagging table in the shade of the pine tree and caught the landlord's eye. 'More ale, if you please. And doubtless my comrades will want food too.'

'Very good, my lord.'

As Pedro accompanied the landlord into the inn, Rodrigo slung an arm about Enrique's shoulders and steered him firmly towards the table. A lizard scuttled up the trunk of the pine tree.

'I've no idea what you were trying to do back at the palace, Enrique, but I'm relieved you're still in one piece. Those dogs were pretty close, I wasn't sure you'd get away.'

'No thanks to you, you devil,' Enrique muttered. 'You stole my Princess.'

'Your Princess? Don't be ridiculous. If you had a speck of honour, you'd be ashamed of yourself.' A mulish expression crossed his cousin's face, Rodrigo ignored it. 'What happened?'

The landlord appeared with the ale and Enrique snatched a cup and drank deep.

'Lord, I needed that.' He wiped his mouth with the back of his hand and that sour smile reappeared. 'You're a dog, Rodrigo, you have all the luck. I got the other woman.'

The other woman? For a moment Rodrigo couldn't think who his cousin was talking about.

Then he realised he must be referring to the older woman Rodrigo had shut in the sally-port, the Princesses' duenna, Inés. His jaw dropped. 'The woman in the tunnel?'

'Aye. Mistook her for the third Princess. Took her up with me.'

Rodrigo felt ill, it seemed there were no depths to which his cousin would not sink. 'You abducted an old woman? Saints, Enrique, you're a married man, what you were planning was sickening anyway, but to snatch an elderly—'

'Wasn't my fault. She climbed up behind me willingly enough. I had no idea who she was. In truth, she urged me on.' He laughed. 'She was desperate to get away. It's hard to believe a crone like that would have had so much life in her. She spoke Spanish, you know.'

Why was Enrique using the past tense when referring to Inés? Rodrigo felt a chill wash over him. 'What did you do to her?'

'Faith, man, my taste doesn't run to old women. I did nothing.'

Rodrigo glanced pointedly down the empty road. 'Then where the devil is she?'

'Somewhere in the middle of nowhere.'

'Explain.'

'She—er—she fell off somewhere in Al-Andalus.'

Rodrigo's jaw sagged. 'You went on without her?'

His cousin gave a careless shrug. 'What was I

to do? I couldn't go back for her. Jesu, Rodrigo, a pack of hell hounds was yapping at my heels. Anyhow, it wasn't my fault the hag was too weak to hold on.'

Something in Enrique's tone told Rodrigo his cousin was lying. Had Enrique—as soon as he realised he was riding with Inés rather than one of the Princesses—pushed Inés from his horse? It seemed all too plausible.

'Too weak, eh?' Rodrigo clenched his jaw, he felt like strangling the man, but that would achieve nothing. 'Have you no heart? That "crone" as you name her, is the Princesses' beloved companion and she is as Spanish as you and me.'

'That explains it.'

'What?'

'Before she fell, the blasted woman never stopped talking, drove me mad for an age—nag, nag, nag. Wanted me to catch up with you and Inigo. Was pretty anxious to reach the border. I only let her run on because I thought she was the Sultan's daughter.'

Rodrigo leaned back and crossed his arms. 'I am surprised you didn't realise from the first.'

'She was sitting behind me. I didn't see her face until we were almost at the border.'

Aye, with the dogs closing in, you were probably too terrified—and too drunk—to notice, Rodrigo thought grimly. 'Where exactly did you leave her?'

'God knows. As I said, somewhere near the border.'

'Did you trouble to look back? Did she survive the fall?'

'I'm not sure. Why does it even matter? She's an old woman, Rodrigo. She's nothing.'

It matters, Rodrigo thought, gritting his teeth. 'So, you left her in the wilderness near the border, and you don't know if she survived the fall.'

'That's the sum of it.'

Rodrigo rubbed his brow and wished Enrique was more reliable. Inés could be anywhere. It was obvious that Princess Leonor was fond of her, and she would be distraught when she discovered what had happened. 'Enrique, you have to do better than that. Do you think she might have continued on foot?'

'Truthfully, Cousin, I've no idea.'

Rodrigo stared bleakly at Enrique as it dawned on him that as soon as he got Princess Leonor to the safety of Córdoba, he would have to send scouts back along their route to try to discover what had happened to her duenna.

Inés might not be alive, but if she was…well, a Spanish duenna who had betrayed Sultan Tariq by helping his daughters to escape had signed her own death warrant. She wouldn't be treated kindly if the palace guard caught up with her. Rodrigo's men would have to travel incognito, if they were to venture inside Al-Andalus. There were risks, but they would find her, wherever she was.

Out of the corner of his eye, Rodrigo saw the inn door open. The Princess stepped out and walked determinedly towards them.

Enrique's eyes widened. 'That's the Princess? Whatever is she wearing?'

Rodrigo scowled at his cousin. 'If you value your hide, you will be respectful.' He lowered his voice. 'Furthermore, you will say nothing, not a single word, about the duenna. I should warn you, the Princess speaks Spanish like a native.'

Enrique's eyebrows shot up. 'Who the devil taught her?'

'The woman you abandoned.' Rising, Rodrigo held out a hand in a gesture of welcome. 'My lady, this is my cousin Sir Enrique de Murcia. Do you care to join us?'

'Please.'

As Princess Leonor seated herself beside him on the bench, Rodrigo noted that her bearing was unusually stiff. She looked coolly at Enrique, her eyes were full of suspicion and what looked very much like fury.

'Something troubles you, my lady?' Rodrigo asked, his heart shifting in his chest.

She knows. She's found out that Enrique abandoned her duenna in the wilderness.

She ignored his question and focused on Enrique. 'Where is Inés, sir?'

Her voice was cold and her tone imperious. It rang with the arrogance of generations of Nasrid kings who knew their every command would be obeyed. Her chin lifted. 'Your squire tells me that my duenna rode with you. What have you done with her?'

Enrique looked helplessly at Rodrigo and back at the Princess. 'You spoke to Pedro, my lady?'

'Haven't I said so?' Her expression was icy. 'Your man came into the tavern for something to eat, and when I saw you conversing with Lord Rodrigo, I recognised you as the knight who arrived first at the palace. Your man says you set Inés down *inside* Al-Andalus. Is that true?'

'Yes, my lady.'

The Princess leaned forward, her gaze pinned Enrique to the spot. 'Did you leave her near the border?'

Enrique flushed, he looked slightly stunned and Rodrigo couldn't blame him. He had no idea that the Princess could command such presence. It was rather stimulating. Not to mention that it was good to see Enrique squirm.

'I am not sure, my lady,' Enrique said. 'It...it was dark, you understand. I don't think the border was far away.'

The Princess turned to Rodrigo. 'My lord, Inés is not young. She has little money. We have to go back for her.'

Rodrigo nodded. 'I had already come to the same conclusion.'

And just like that, Princess Leonor's fierceness was gone. She took his hand and kissed it. 'Thank you. My lord, I won't forget this.'

Enrique lifted his eyebrows. 'You're going back for the old—for the other woman? Why? Surely she can return to the palace?'

Princess Leonor gripped Rodrigo's hand. 'Sir, I think you have lost your wits. My father will kill her for aiding in our escape. Lord Rodrigo, we must find her—and quickly.'

'I agree your duenna must be found, but circumspection is called for.'

She bit her lip. 'Circumspection?'

'If we retrace our steps today, there's a strong chance we'll run into your father's men.'

Enrique nodded. 'Aye. Suicide.'

'Thank you, Cousin. Suffice it to say, we would be grossly outnumbered and possibly captured. My lady, I've already had the pleasure of your father's hospitality and I'm not anxious to renew the experience.'

Enrique shoved his hand through his hair. 'I couldn't agree more. I'm for home, and the sooner, the better.' He looked down the road and shuddered. 'We may have reached the borderlands, but your father has a long reach. I'm for joining Pedro inside.' Nodding briefly at the Princess, he went into the inn.

The Princess watched him go, a pleat in her brow. 'That man is your cousin?'

'Aye.'

'I cannot like him.' She glanced down at her hand, realised it still rested on his and, blushing rosily, released him. 'My apologies. My lord, are you certain we must desert Inés?'

'For the time being. Once we reach Córdoba, I shall send scouts in search of her.'

'Thank you.'

'I seem to recall you telling me that Inés came to Granada with your mother.'

'Yes, she did. Why?'

Rodrigo held up his hand. 'Bear with me. Would you say your duenna was a resourceful woman?'

A faint smile appeared. 'There's no doubt of that.'

'And would you say she intended to return to your mother's family?'

'It's possible, though I don't see how that will help us. Inés refused to give us the name of Mamá's family, so I've no idea where she came from.'

Thoughtfully, Rodrigo drummed his fingers on the table. He had an idea as to how they might discover where the Princess's mother had been born, but he didn't like to think about it because it involved Lord Jaime de Almodóvar. Lord Jaime was a neighbour and, despite the closeness of their estates, Rodrigo was in the habit of forgetting his very existence.

He stared at the Princess and wrestled with the idea of mentioning him. Lord Jaime would undoubtedly know where Lady Juana had been born. Would he be willing to help?

Lord Jaime had a good reputation. It made sense to ask him. Rodrigo rubbed his chin. Even after all this time the idea of meeting Lord Jaime wasn't pleasant. Perhaps a letter would suffice. He opened his mouth to mention the connection, when it occurred to him that they might find the Princess's duenna before that became necessary.

He cleared his throat. 'When we arrive at Córdoba, you have my word that scouts will be sent to find your duenna.'

Yes, that must serve. His scouts would surely find Inés, and Lord Jaime could be left in peace.

By the time they reached the outskirts of Córdoba, Leonor was almost falling off her horse with fatigue. Her legs had gone numb and her eyes felt as though they were full of sand.

'We can rest shortly,' Count Rodrigo said, as they came to a long many-arched bridge. 'The city gates are on the other side of the river. The bridge is Roman. It was built long before your people came to Córdoba.'

Uncertain as to whether his tone held censure, Leonor shot him a sidelong glance. She learned nothing, his face was a mask. Still, it was a relief to know they were almost at journey's end. She roused herself to take note of her surroundings.

Midstream, a watermill was slowly turning. Other mills lined the riverbank, although with the river reduced to a narrow trickle along the middle, it was far too low for the bankside mills to be working. The hot summer, she supposed. When they passed through the city gates, their horses' hoofbeats faded, the streets of Córdoba were strewn with straw. There were palm trees everywhere.

'The large building on the right is the cathedral,' Lord Rodrigo told her. 'It was once an ancient mosque.'

A cathedral that had once been a mosque? The architecture was reminiscent of parts of the Alhambra and traces of Arabic were visible on the outer walls. Leonor felt very ignorant about life here and, not for the first time, wished that her father had allowed her to learn more about the world at large.

They plunged down a narrow street and under several arches. A pair of wrought-iron gates was flanked with crimson-clad guards. Clattering past the guards, the Count drew rein in a sunny courtyard.

'Welcome to my town house, my lady.'

His town house? Lord Rodrigo was a garrison

commander. Surely the garrison was quartered inside the Spanish King's palace, the Alcázar?

'We're not going to the palace?'

'The palace is full of prying eyes, you'll be more comfortable as my personal guest.'

Leonor dismounted. The walls around the courtyard were so white, it hurt to look at them. She was vaguely aware of vines tumbling through trellises, of terracotta pots overflowing with purple blooms. The house was larger than it looked from the street.

How strange, she hadn't expected Lord Rodrigo to have a house like this. Ever since he'd taken her necklace to pay the landlord at the first inn, she'd visualised him living in cramped quarters in the Spanish King's garrison.

'My lord!' A smiling groom ran up to lead the horses away. 'We heard your ransom had been paid. Welcome back.' The groom clicked his fingers and another groom stepped forward. 'Gaspar, alert Sir Arnau, tell him Lord Rodrigo is home.'

The grooms' tunics were emblazoned with a red shield. Leonor realised the device on it—a black horse—must be the Count's insignia. Heavens, the tunics were particularly fine. They were fashioned from what looked like Granadan silk and the black horses were most cunningly worked.

'The black horse, it is your device, my lord?'

'Aye.'

Several other people converged on the courtyard, all smiling from ear to ear. Lord Rodrigo was clearly much liked and respected.

Leonor's puzzlement grew. Everyone here was clearly well fed and well disciplined, indeed, they looked as though they were the retainers of a very wealthy lord. Yet if Lord Rodrigo was wealthy, why had he taken her pendant?

She shook out her skirts and found more to puzzle over. There was a tinkling fountain in the centre of the courtyard; there were tiled archways leading in all directions. The place was full of well-dressed servants rushing hither and yon. She would be the first to admit she knew nothing of the life of an impoverished Spanish knight, but this house surely resembled the home of an incredibly successful merchant.

He offered her his arm. 'You will want refreshment, my lady.'

'Thank you.' She met his gaze. 'My lord, I admit I am startled. I did not expect you to have a house like this.'

His lips twitched. 'Castle Álvarez lies at the heart of my estate, a few miles to the north, this is simply my town house. I thought you would appreciate a rest before we continue.'

This was simply his town house? And it was filled with a bevy of servants? Had she completely misjudged him?

Mind spinning, Leonor rested her hand on his arm and went with him into a cool chamber. He led her to a gilded couch and she sank on to a plump cushion with a sigh of relief.

'We will rest here for an hour, my lady. It will give you the chance to recover before we arrive at the castle.'

'You are most considerate, my lord.'

A servant appeared with a silver tray. Silver. Leonor was offered wine or pomegranate and orange juice. Choosing the fruit juice, Leonor cradled her cup in her hands and stared at Lord Rodrigo through her eyelashes.

This man was wealthy, a count with acres to his name. He had deliberately misled her over his need for money to pay the innkeeper, he had let her assume he was short of funds. Why?

He was keeping something from her.

She opened her mouth to ask what it might be, when he forestalled her.

'My lady, there's something I should mention before we continue to the castle. My mother, Lady Isabel, lives there. The two of you are bound to meet.' His mouth tightened. 'I need to ask for your discretion when we first arrive. I shall show you to your chamber and it would be best if you remained there for a while.'

Leonor clutched the cup of fruit juice. 'You will make me a prisoner?'

His eyebrows lifted. 'Certainly not, I am merely warning you. My mother is likely to be distressed and meeting you too soon may make matters worse.'

Her heart dropped, he was talking about Diego. 'My lord, Lady Isabel will loathe the very sight of me.' Rising, she set down her cup and came to stand before him. 'I think I would prefer to be lodged at the Alcázar.'

Lord Rodrigo shook his head. 'That is out of the question, you will be safer on my land.'

'Very well.' Here in Córdoba, Leonor was well out of her depth, what else could she do but agree with him? She sighed. 'You must hate me too.'

'What I feel for you, my lady, is complicated. I am in your debt for helping Inigo in prison. And for intervening on the road to Granada. For that I am certain I owe you my life. I thank you.' Gravely, he bowed. 'The three of us owe you a debt of gratitude, and I will not forget it. I will guard you with my life.' He paused, studying her face with a peculiar intensity that brought heat to her cheeks. He seemed to take this as a signal, for his face relaxed and that slow, attractive smile appeared. 'Rest assured, my lady, I don't hate you, I am coming to see that would be impossible.'

Leonor's cheeks burned. Why was he staring at her mouth? It was extremely unsettling, it made her nervous and shaky. Impossible though it seemed, she had the impression that he was thinking about kissing her. As she looked up at him, her impression deepened into certainty. He wanted to kiss her.

'My lady, I beg leave to tell you that I admire you. Greatly. For a moment, I crave your indulgence.'

'My lord?'

He dipped his head and kissed her.

And Leonor allowed it. His lips were warm. Soft. In a heartbeat, she was kissing him back, she could do little else. Strong fingers gripped her shoulders, they were gentle and firm and her skin warmed to his touch. Constraint wasn't necessary. Curious at the whirl of sensations he unleashed inside her, Leonor angled her body closer to his.

Lord Rodrigo's body heat spoke of comfort, his height of protection. His smell—a beguiling combination of man, woodsmoke and soap—told her that he would never harm her. Her head swam. Her limbs weakened. This man was a sorcerer and his touch was intoxicating, parts of her body that had slept her entire life sprang joyfully into wakefulness.

And all the while his mouth moved gently on hers. It was as though he was silently demanding that she open her mouth. He was simply irresistible.

She couldn't help herself, she relaxed her jaw and his tongue swept in. His tongue! She could barely stand. This man had the knack of making her body believe it had been waiting her whole life for just this moment.

This was most certainly seduction. And Lord Rodrigo was very good at it. Before she knew it, she was lying on the couch with him on his knees on the floor beside her. He pushed her veil aside and pressed a string of kisses down one cheek and around her neck.

Footsteps hurried to the doorway. A man stood there, clearing his throat.

'My lord?'

'Sir Arnau.' A final kiss was pressed to her cheek. With a crooked smile, Lord Rodrigo rose and gestured his man forward. 'You have messages for me?'

'Just so.' Sir Arnau smiled. 'My lord, first let me say we are most thankful to have you back in one piece. You suffered no hurts?'

'I am well, I thank you.'

Sir Arnau's gaze flickered briefly to Leonor, sitting hot-cheeked and flustered on the couch, hastily straightening her clothes and tucking her hair beneath her veil. 'Your mother is most anxious to see you.'

'Thank you, Arnau, I am aware of that. Princess Leonor and I had a wearying journey. We shall proceed to the castle when we have had an hour to recover.'

'*Princess* Leonor?' Lord Rodrigo's knight drew back sharply as his gaze swung back to Leonor.

He looked as though he had been struck in the face. 'My lord, who exactly is this lady?'

'That is not your concern. We shall require fresh horses in an hour. Alert Captain Vidal and inform him that I will require an escort of half a dozen knights. That will be all.'

'Very good, my lord.' Sending a final, suspicious look at Leonor, Sir Arnau bowed himself out.

Leonor gnawed at her lower lip as it dawned on her that the next few days were going to be far more awkward than she had anticipated. The death of Lord Rodrigo's brother practically guaranteed that she would run the gauntlet of hate and prejudice every step of the way. And Lady Isabel lived at the castle! If Sir Arnau spread word that she was the Sultan's daughter, Lady Isabel wouldn't be the only one to hate her, the entire castle would be out for her blood.

'Your man has worked out who I am, and he doesn't like it,' she said. 'What will he do?'

Lord Rodrigo's smile was reassuring. 'Arnau's my steward. He is the most discreet man alive, he will say nothing.'

Leonor wasn't so sure. The expression on Sir Arnau's face spoke of generations of mistrust. It wouldn't be overturned in a day. 'My lord, perhaps we should alter our plans. There must be somewhere else I might stay. Would you grant me an escort to visit your friend Lord Inigo? I need to see Alba. My sister and I would like to set up our own household. The sooner we learn to live independently, the better.'

Lord Rodrigo's face darkened. 'As yet, I have no idea whether Lord Inigo has reached Córdoba. And until I hear from him, you are coming with me to Castle Álvarez. We leave in an hour.'

'But, my lord…'

'One hour, my lady, you have one hour.'

Rodrigo's late father, Lord Gregorio, had thought it prudent to maintain a small troop of knights at his Córdoban town house, and Rodrigo had seen no reason to change the tradition.

He left Leonor with a maidservant washing away the worst of the journey and marched straight to the guardroom. Sir Arnau's reaction to Princess Leonor concerned him, although following Diego's death, it was understandable. He grimaced. At heart, Arnau was a fair and generous man, he must realise that the Princess wasn't responsible for the actions of her father and his soldiers. All of Spain knew that the women in the Sultan's harem were kept ignorant of what went on outside the palace walls. However, it was one thing to know it intellectually and another to accept it emotionally.

As far as Rodrigo's retainers were concerned, the Princess would be guilty by association. His mother would want nothing to do with her; his retainers might shun her.

Briefly, he closed his eyes. He hadn't planned on kissing her. He'd ventured on to forbidden ground there, though in truth he couldn't regret it. Her response had been so sweet—the innocence, the startled gasp of surprise. Mingled with the taste of oranges and pomegranates, he'd tasted freshness and welcome. Welcome such as he'd never felt since he'd been a youth and had fallen hard and fast for his first—and only—love.

He mustn't kiss her again. Princess Leonor came from another world and it was his duty to return her to her father in as pure a state as when she left him.

That innocence and purity of spirit was devastatingly attractive, and he'd been drawn to her from that first meeting in the prison. She had been so swift to help Inigo. Of course, she'd had her motives for doing so. And yet...

Sweet Mary, the Princess's trusting, innocent kisses had him so befuddled with longing that he'd entirely forgotten himself when Arnau walked in. He should never have referred to her as a princess. That would not happen again.

Princess Leonor's reaction to Arnau was almost as troubling as Arnau's reaction to her. If she took it into her head that all she would meet in Castle Álvarez was hatred, she was quite capable of taking off on her own. And that he could not allow. If necessary, he'd force his protection on her until Sultan Tariq sent his guard to take her home.

I will keep her safe.

When the Sultan's envoy arrived at the castle, she must be in residence. Otherwise, all hell would break loose. More lives would be put at risk.

All of which meant that Rodrigo must speak to his captain personally. He didn't think Leonor would attempt to flee his protection, but he had to be sure.

I will protect her.

He pushed through the guardhouse door, his captain was standing before a trestle table examining an array of bits and stirrups.

'Captain Vidal?'

'Welcome back, my lord. We are all relieved to see you.'

'*Muchas gracias.* Captain, I shall be returning to the castle in a little under an hour.'

'Yes, my lord, Sir Arnau has already informed me.'

'Good. Were you also told that I am travelling with a lady who is at present in my charge?'

'No, my lord, Sir Arnau mentioned no lady.'

Captain Vidal's expression was blank. Too blank. It was entirely possible that he thought the lady was Rodrigo's mistress. Rodrigo held down a sigh, perhaps that was inevitable. After his broken betrothal to Lady Sancha, Rodrigo had had his share of mistresses, although he had never thought to take one to Castle Álvarez. To do so would be to insult his mother. However, in this case, it was probably better the captain thought Princess Leonor was his mistress than he discovered who she really was.

'The lady must be carefully watched,' Rodrigo said. 'She is not to leave our party, for any reason.'

Captain Vidal's eyebrows rose. 'Very good, my lord.'

'Where was Sir Arnau headed?'

'I believe he went to the stables, my lord.'

'*Gracias.* I'll see you in an hour, Captain.'

Captain Vidal saluted and Rodrigo went to find his steward. Sir Arnau was obviously being discreet about Princess Leonor. Rodrigo wanted his word that that would not change.

Chapter Twelve

Lord Rodrigo was riding right beside her, keeping so close, their knees were bumping. This was undoubtedly why Leonor couldn't stop thinking about the way he had kissed her and whether it was significant. He was a few years older than her, he was bound to be experienced. What might it mean that a man like that—an experienced, worldly man—should kiss her?

Life in the harem had kept Leonor innocent, although she wasn't entirely naive. Inés had, in her way, tried to redress the balance. Was this the lust that Inés had warned her of? Lust sounded unpleasant, even repugnant. Leonor hadn't found Lord Rodrigo's kiss the least bit repugnant. On the contrary…

Leonor turned in the saddle and pushed the kiss from her mind. Through their dust trail, the walls of Córdoba appeared to melt into the horizon. She managed not to think about the kiss when Lord Rodrigo's knights closed in around them, riding so tightly there was barely a hand-span between them. She could see the curiosity in the knights' eyes as they glanced her way.

Father would consider that Lord Rodrigo's touch had defiled her but, God help her, she had enjoyed it. What did that make her? And why was the Count glued to her side?

She would *not* think about that kiss.

The knights' spurs chinked. The sound conjured a bittersweet memory—Snowstorm. As the ghost of her beautiful grey mare pranced delicately through her mind, silver bells a-chime, her eyes prickled.

'My lady?' Lord Rodrigo's brown eyes were full of concern. 'Are you well?'

And there it was again. That kiss. She could see it at the back of his eyes and in the slight lift of his lips.

The light was failing by the time they walked across the courtyard at Castle Álvarez and Leonor was none the wiser about the Count's motive for kissing her. Perhaps it meant nothing. Since it had been her very first kiss, she had no way of knowing.

Fortunately, there was much to distract her in the castle bailey. She hadn't been sure what to expect. On the surface, Castle Álvarez was remarkably familiar. The line of sentries posted at the gates and at intervals along the castle walls was reminiscent of Castle Salobreña as well as the Alhambra Palace. She recognised the sweet smell of straw coming from a cart near the stables, the bright clatter of hoofs and the ring of hammer on anvil.

There was also much that was unfamiliar. The atmosphere, though ordered, was entirely outside Leonor's experience. A woman was leading two goats under the portcullis. She was unaccompanied and Leonor watched in amazement as she exchanged pleasantries quite freely with one of the guards. There were other women too, three girls were flirting with one of the men on the castle walls. Guards were talking and laughing among themselves. Life in Lord Rodrigo's castle was clearly very different to life under her father. Faces were smiling and open. Happy.

People fell over themselves to greet their lord. 'My lord! Thank God you are home.'

'Welcome back, Lord Rodrigo, welcome indeed.'

Something shifted inside her. It was as though the ground had tilted. Long ago Leonor had realised that her father ruled with an iron hand. Sultan Tariq ruled by fear and she'd imagined that men could be governed no other way.

But here? Bemused, Leonor took in the smiling guards with their glittering spears, the neatly dressed women and the well-swept courtyard.

How did Lord Rodrigo keep order, if not through fear? How did he ensure loyalty among his retainers?

Doves cooed in a nearby dovecote. To one side of the main keep was a building with a cross on it. The chapel. Curious, for Inés had taught the Princesses about their mother's faith, Leonor stared. The door was open, and through it she saw shadows and the pale glimmer of a candle, which was briefly blotted out as someone had passed before it.

The keep loomed over them. Pausing at the bottom of a flight of stairs leading towards a vast double doorway, Leonor gathered up her skirts.

Lord Rodrigo stood at her elbow. 'Allow me to assist you, my lady.'

'Thank you.' Part of her was relieved he was so solicitous. His face—already so familiar—was reassuring in this bustling castle. Part of her was afraid. The atmosphere, so warm and friendly with its casual discipline, felt completely alien. Worse, the knot in her stomach warned that the warmth would not last. As soon as the Count's people learned who she was, they would hate her. And where was his mother?

Leonor had her answer soon enough. An elderly woman slipped down the stairs, smiling a greeting as she passed.

'Welcome home, Lord Rodrigo.' The woman nodded pleasantly at Leonor before her gaze returned to that of the Count. 'Lady Isabel is in the chapel, she will be overjoyed to learn you have returned safely.'

Rodrigo hustled Leonor into a tower bedchamber. She gazed about in apparent puzzlement and turned to him, her dark eyes full of curiosity as she fingered a silken bedcover and gazed in what seemed like astonishment at a fine English wallhanging and a brightly enamelled Limoges ewer.

'This chamber will suit you, my lady?'

'Thank you, it is very fine.' Her gaze flickered towards the enamelled ewer and her eyes filled with questions. 'My lord, your castle has the feel of a palace.'

'Why, thank you, my lady.'

Rodrigo found himself wondering what she'd expected, before he remembered he'd accepted her pendant under the pretence of paying for their lodgings. His lips twisted. She was an intelligent woman, any moment now she'd be demanding why he'd taken it.

As her mouth opened, he bowed himself out. This wasn't the moment to confess he'd sent the pendant to her father as proof the Princess Leonor was safely in his care.

'Please, excuse me, my mother awaits.'

Her face clouded. 'She needs to know how your brother died.'

'Aye.' Shoving his hand through his hair, Rodrigo indicated the bell on the side-table. 'My lady, should you need anything, anything at all, that bell will summon a maidservant.'

Count Rodrigo's footsteps retreated down the stairs.

Leonor wrapped her arms about her waist. For the first time in her life she felt utterly alone. And utterly confused. To say that Lord Rodrigo must dislike offering her hospitality when her father's men were responsible for his brother's death had to be an understatement. Thankfully, he didn't seem to blame her, which she found remarkable. Back in his Córdoban town house, he'd told her it would be impossible to hate her. Then he'd kissed her.

She fingered her lips. Why had he brought her here? Particularly when he himself admitted that his mother's reaction might be hostile.

She frowned at a golden bird on a wall-hanging. She missed Alba and Constanza. Being separated from them made her feel as though she'd lost part of herself. It would be a comfort to talk to them, although if Constanza had never left the palace, she was unlikely to see her again. As for Alba—was she safe with Lord Inigo? Had they reached Córdoba?

Leonor squared her shoulders. When she next saw Lord Rodrigo, she would ask, no, she would demand that he tell her the instant he heard from

Inigo. She must see Alba soon, they needed to decide how best to find their Spanish relatives. Their future in Spain—far from their father—beckoned.

Pensively, she watched a lozenge of light slant slowly across the floor. Sultan Tariq's reaction to losing his two older daughters was easy to guess at—she and Alba would be disowned. Constanza's situation was less clear. Her youngest sister, with her winning ways and agreeable temperament, had long been their father's favourite. With luck, she'd be well cared for.

Brightening, Leonor stared at the bell on the side-table. Mercifully, Lord Rodrigo hadn't locked her in, because there was much she needed to know, not least of which was the whereabouts of Lord Inigo's residence in Córdoba. The maidservant might be in a talkative mood.

She reached for the bell and reminded herself to tread warily, she would get the best response if she said nothing about her identity. A Nasrid princess wouldn't be greeted with open arms.

Rodrigo went down the twisting stairs, haunted by the look in Leonor's eyes. She'd been trying to put on a brave face, but standing there in shabby, borrowed clothes that didn't quite fit and those ridiculous boots, she looked small and very much at sea. What must it be like for her, alone in a foreign land with only a stranger to watch out for her?

He hoped that she'd learned to trust him.

Whilst she was in his care, no one would harm as much as a hair on her head. Did she understand that? He would protect her. He would feed her and clothe her and…

Clothe her! Of course, that was the answer. The making of new clothes would distract her and keep her occupied. Women loved clothes.

With a sound of exasperation, he altered course, heading for the solar. The idea of leaving Leonor friendless, even for a short time, didn't sit well with him. His mother's maid, Ana, would know what to do.

As he expected, Ana was sewing in the solar with two other maids. The instant she saw him, her face lit up. She dropped her work and hurried across.

'My lord, thank God you are home in one piece.' Never one to stand on ceremony, Ana gripped his hand and lifted it to her lips in a gesture which was an echo of the time when Leonor had done that exact same thing. 'We have been praying for you, my lord, and it is a great blessing to see our prayers answered.'

'You are very kind. Ana, I have a favour to ask.' Quietly, he drew her to one side, away from the other women.

'My lord?'

Rodrigo jerked his head at Ana's stitchery. 'It is a task most suited to your capabilities.' He lowered his voice. 'I have brought a guest with

me back from Al-Andalus, and she is currently
lodged in the White Tower.'

'She?'

'Her name is Lady Leonor.' Rodrigo didn't like
lying, particularly not to Ana, who had known
him all his life. However, it wasn't in Leonor's
interests for him to be completely frank about
her background. He would keep as close to the
truth as he dared. 'Lady Leonor had suffered a
series of mishaps, but happily, I was at hand to
lend her aid.'

Ana clasped her hands below her breasts, eyes
sparkling. 'You rescued her.'

Rodrigo held in a sigh as Ana's eyes softened,
it was obvious she believed she had stumbled on
a great romance. Ever since he was a boy and his
betrothal with Sancha had come to an end, he'd
been the subject of much romantic speculation.
He hated it, he would marry when he was ready
and not a day before. He looked repressively at
his mother's maid. 'Ana, I merely helped Lady
Leonor in her hour of need. I shall need your discretion, there is to be no gossiping.'

'Of course not, my lord.'

He kept his voice brisk. 'Lady Leonor needs
several gowns, a cloak, some shoes and slippers—
in brief, she needs a complete wardrobe. Please be
so good as to attend to her in the White Tower.'

'At once, my lord.'

He felt his face relax. 'Thank you. Allow her

to choose the fabrics for herself. Let her take her time over it, I need her to be fully occupied for the next couple of days.' That way, there would be no danger of Leonor running into his mother before he got his reply from the Sultan. 'Ana, give Lady Leonor a free rein, she is to have the very best.'

'Very good, my lord.'

Rodrigo strode towards the door, thinking about Princess Leonor and the way she had reacted at the first inn. Despite the ordeal of leaving the palace, she'd peered into that kitchen with great interest. Indeed, the Princess seemed curious about everything that came her way. She thought deeply about what she saw, and if she came across an injustice, she didn't hesitate to act. Witness her visiting the prison in Salobreña to find out about her mother; witness her donating that bangle to pay for Inigo's treatment.

If the Princess's sheltered upbringing had been designed to curb her natural intelligence, it had completely failed. All of which meant that she would no doubt be desperate to explore the castle; she would want to talk to everyone and she wouldn't be able to stop herself. She was the most singular of women.

It is too soon for Princess Leonor to meet my mother. My mother's wound will be too raw, and if she discovers we have a Nasrid under our roof, I cannot be answerable for the consequences.

Rodrigo swung back and caught the seamstress's gaze. 'Ana, one further point.'

'My lord?'

'Lady Leonor may express a desire to explore the castle, but on no account is she to leave that chamber, she must wait for my company. As soon as I am free, I will escort her myself. Is that clear?'

Ana curtsied. 'Perfectly, my lord.'

An entire day slipped by without Leonor catching so much of a glimpse of Lord Rodrigo. She understood that he had much to attend to—his mother, problems arising from his brother's untimely death, not to mention a myriad of other demands that a great lord must face on return from battle. None the less, his absence rankled.

He is avoiding me. Worse, I miss him. What is he doing?

Leonor thought about him most of the time. It wasn't that she had nothing to do—between the maid Catalina, who had answered her summons when she'd rung the bell, and the seamstress Ana, whom Lord Rodrigo had apparently sent to help her choose fabric for some gowns, she was fully occupied.

The maid and the seamstress couldn't agree on anything.

'My lady, the golden silk favours your complexion beautifully. It comes from Byzantium and there is none better. Please choose this one,' Catalina would say.

Ana would shake her head. 'No, no, no, Catalina. Gold is far too vulgar for Lady Leonor. Something with a little subtlety will suit her far better. My lady, how about the blue damask?'

Head whirling, Leonor stared blindly at the array of fabrics draped across the bed. There was a lump in her throat the size of an egg and she couldn't fathom it. Absently, she fingered the blue damask. Silk. Almost everything here was silk. A king's ransom was spread across her bed and she hated it. Was history about to repeat itself?

Her heart sank. Her father had used gifts as a means of bending her to his will, was Lord Rodrigo doing the same? Was he trying to fence her in?

Leonor understood that there would be difficulties should she run into Lady Isabel, but she hadn't fled one prison to walk into another. She looked longingly at the door. 'I shall decide about fabrics later. I need to stretch my legs. Ana, please accompany me.'

Ana's face fell. 'Oh, no, my lady, I cannot do that.'

She stiffened. 'I am a prisoner?'

'Heavens, no. My lady, you are my lord's honoured guest.'

Leonor looked sadly at the fabrics. An honoured guest. 'I need to speak to Lord Rodrigo.'

'He is occupied with estate business today, my lady.' Fabric rustled as the blue damask was pushed into her hand. 'Feel, my lady, the quality is exceptional. You will look like a queen in this gown.'

For an instant, something flickered at the back of Ana's eyes and Leonor wondered how much Lord Rodrigo had told her. She fingered the fabric, which was indeed pretty. 'It is silk.'

'Yes, my lady. The yarn came from the east, although it was woven in Granada.'

Leonor dropped the fabric as though it burned. 'I really must see Count Rodrigo.'

Ana's eyes softened. 'Later, my lady. My lord has much on his mind today. However, he has told me he intends to show you around the castle personally as soon as he may.'

'He has?'

'Yes, my lady. In the meantime, we shall make you a new gown, and when it is finished, I am sure you will look enchanting. You can wear it when you see Lord Rodrigo.'

Ana seemed a nice enough woman, but Leonor wanted her to understand that she didn't intend to moulder away in a tower. She narrowed her eyes. 'Can it be finished by tomorrow, then? I shall certainly need it tomorrow.'

'My lady, I am sure Lord Rodrigo will come as soon as he is free.'

Ana had better be correct, because if she were

not, Leonor would simply do her exploring on her own.

I will not be shut in. I will not be shut away. Never again.

For two days, Rodrigo was swamped with cares and responsibilities. His heart was heavy, though he had to hide his grief over Diego's death and comfort his mother. He paid his respects at his brother's grave; he supported Lady Isabel at a memorial service; he made her promise to eat.

Rodrigo didn't forget Princess Leonor—that would have been impossible—but his hands were too full for him to see her. None the less, she crept into his every thought. After listening to his steward's report, Rodrigo sent an envoy to Inigo's house in Córdoba. He wanted Inigo to contact him as soon as he rode in. Princess Leonor needed to know her sister was well.

He spoke to his captain at arms and ordered that a troop of scouts be sent into Al-Andalus to search for Princess Leonor's duenna. He warned his captain that discretion was essential. The men were to stick to the borderlands and conceal their Spanish loyalties. Fortunately, a number of Rodrigo's men had Moorish blood, so there would be no language difficulties.

And when Rodrigo went back to the chapel for another vigil with his mother, he found himself praying most earnestly that his men find Inés. For if they did not, the only other avenue was for him to visit Lord Jaime and request a meeting. And meeting Lord Jaime—the man who had stolen Sancha from him—was the last thing Rodrigo wanted to do. Apparently, Sancha never left the man's side, so if he went to Almodóvar, he'd be bound to see her.

Rodrigo wasn't sure why he was reluctant to see her again. Their love—if indeed that was what it had been—had died years ago. It had been boyish and naive. And so gut-wrenchingly painful when it had ended that he'd sworn never to feel that way again. Fortunately, none of his mistresses had come close to inspiring half the devotion he'd felt for Sancha.

Princess Leonor on the other hand…

No, no, no. The political situation was impossible. If he wasn't careful, he'd have a minor war on his hands. Not to mention that his mother would never speak to him again. Princess Leonor had to go home.

The Princess's summons—and 'summons' was the only word for it—came on the afternoon of the third day.

Ana ran breathlessly into the chamber he used as an office and dipped into a curtsy.

'My lord?'

'Ana?'

'Forgive me for interrupting, but I have a message from Lady Leonor. She requests your presence in the tower chamber.'

Despite his cares, Rodrigo felt a smile form. Three days. She'd waited three days. It was more than he'd expected. 'She *requests*, does she?'

Ana's cheeks darkened, which told its own story. Rodrigo suspected that more had been said, much more, and that Ana was too embarrassed to repeat it. He rose, walked round the desk and leaned against it. 'Ana, I'm curious, what did she really say?'

Ana pursed her lips. 'Lady Leonor said to tell you that she appreciates there are difficulties with her staying here as your guest. She mentioned Lady Isabel. Lady Leonor is insistent that you go to her at once, she says she needs a story to explain her presence here. My lord, she is anxious for exercise.' Ana gazed at him with the frankness of an old and trusted retainer, and added softly, 'It is in my mind that she fears, well, imprisonment.'

Guilt shivered through him. Lord, he should have thought of this, and if he hadn't been so anxious to comfort his mother, he would have done. He swore under his breath.

'Do you think it would help if I allowed her to see the rest of the castle?'

'Yes, my lord.' Ana hesitated. 'What happened to Lady Leonor? Why did you bring her to Castle Álvarez?'

Rodrigo's smile froze. 'Tread carefully, Ana. You are in danger of overstepping the bounds.'

'That may be, my lord, but Lady Leonor is kind and surprisingly innocent, I like her. Do you intend to make her your mistress?'

Ana's blunt question conjured a vision of Leonor lying languidly in Rodrigo's bed. He could see, all too clearly, the lissom limbs that had been so barely concealed by her flimsy harem silks. He could see the soft shine of a golden anklet. And the gentle curve of her breast and waist. Leonor's dark eyes were melting with passion and her hand was outstretched towards him. On her mouth was a smile of welcome and acceptance. Rodrigo had never seen such a smile, not even on Sancha. Of course, he and Sancha had been so young. But now...

Desire, hot and dark, swept through him. He didn't want it. Never mind the diplomatic ramifications, he didn't want Leonor, he couldn't want her. She was going home.

Dismissing the vision with a shake of his head, he had to clear his throat to speak. 'I have Lady Leonor's interests at heart.'

Ana studied him closely and what she saw must have reassured her, for her mouth relaxed and she nodded. 'Lady Leonor is eager to see the rest of the castle, my lord.'

'Very well, Ana. You may tell her I shall join her before the hour is out.'

* * *

'This way, my lady.' Rodrigo gestured across the bailey in the direction of the stables.

Having shown Princess Leonor the castle from battlements to cellars, they were going for a ride. The Princess, he was learning, had boundless energy and she shared his passion for horses. The ride was his way of apologising for inflicting confinement on her. He hoped it would restore him to her favour, he wanted her to think well of him.

Why, he had no idea. Her opinion of him shouldn't matter, particularly since she wasn't going to be with him for long. He was certain he would hear from her father very soon, and then she'd be gone.

The thought was disquieting. He pushed it aside.

Princess Leonor was wearing a diaphanous blue veil and a damask gown with a full skirt that swirled as she walked. No cloak, the sun was too fierce for that, but she was using her veil to simulate one, wrapping it around her throat and shoulders in a way that protected her modesty. All in all, her new clothes were less revealing than the ones she'd been wearing when she'd fled the palace—those glimpses of scarcely covered skin had been tantalising beyond belief. Today, there were no hints at the flesh beneath the gown, only her shape was revealed. Rodrigo's lips curved appreciatively. It was a very nice shape. No, it was more than that, it was perfect. Her waist was tiny, her breasts high. The blue gown emphasised her femininity, and when she moved, her natural grace came to the fore. The sway of her hips was incredibly alluring. Rodrigo wasn't the only man to notice, several of his sentries were also looking at her.

He smothered a sigh. He'd known that guarding a Nasrid princess, particularly one who was so lovely, wouldn't be easy. That was why he'd brought her here. His men were hand-picked, he trusted every one. Even so, it was inevitable they would be intrigued by the mysterious beauty he'd brought back from Granada.

In truth, as far as Princess Leonor was concerned, his mother was more of a threat than his men. However, he didn't want the Princess embarrassed by the staring. She'd spent most of her life behind a veil, it must make her ill at ease. At the next roll call, he would be sure to remind his men of the importance of focus and discipline.

'Did Ana sew your gown?' he asked. 'It is most becoming.'

'Ana's a marvel with a needle, she did most of the work,' she replied. 'Catalina and I helped. I embroidered the swirl along the edge of the veil.'

Rodrigo's brows lifted. The Princess sewed? He hadn't really thought about it, but he'd imagined that the Sultan's daughters had never had to lift a finger.

She had noticed the eyebrow. 'I like sewing.' A touch of defensiveness crept into her voice. 'Usually I stick to embroidery. It was most instructive learning how to make a Spanish gown.'

One of the grooms came out of the stables, spotted the Princess, stumbled and stared at her, mouth agape.

Rodrigo shook his head. 'Steady, Albert.'

Albert's face flamed and he looked swiftly away. It was obvious that he assumed that Leonor was his mistress. Never mind that Rodrigo wouldn't dream of bringing a mistress—even a favoured one—under the same roof as his mother. Rodrigo felt a twinge of regret, he hadn't thought Leonor would be here long enough for this to become an issue.

Fortunately, Leonor hadn't noticed Albert, she was taking in her surroundings with her usual bright-eyed interest. Her gaze flickered over the bailey and wall walk, and came to rest on the cross on the chapel roof. Her eyes narrowed and she changed direction, heading directly for the chapel.

Hell burn it, she would want to see in there, the one place he hadn't taken her.

Rodrigo strode to intercept her. Lady Isabel was a God-fearing woman, she would probably be in the chapel, praying for Diego's soul. At the best of times, his mother was the most forthright of women. And now, with her nerves raw with grief...

Rodrigo didn't like to think what she might say if she came face-to-face with the strange lady gossip was naming his mistress. And should the Princess let fall her identity...

'My lady!' He caught her elbow.

Leonor—when had she become Leonor in his mind?—looked down at his hand and lifted an eyebrow. 'My lord?'

He smiled. 'The horses are in dire need of exercise.'

'I haven't see the chapel. My lord, my mother was Christian and I've never been inside a church. I'd like to see it.'

'The chapel can wait, your palfrey can't.' Ignoring her slight gasp of surprise, he guided her firmly back to the stable. 'The palfrey is chestnut, my lady, not grey like the marc I saw on the road to Granada.'

A shadow crossed her face and her dark eyes met his. 'You remember Snowstorm?'

'I'm a knight; how could I forget her?' He kept his voice light. 'She's a wonderful animal. I've never seen three mares so beautifully matched.'

Her mouth turned down. 'Father sold them.' Her voice cracked.

Thinking he must have misheard, Rodrigo stared. 'Why on earth would he do that? Those mares were perfect for the three of you. He'll never find their like again.'

'No, he won't,' she said on a sigh. 'Not that it matters any longer, with only one Princess left at the palace.'

She averted her face, although not before he'd seen the bright sheen of tears in her eyes. He covered her hand with his. 'I am sorry, my lady, it's never easy to lose a fine horse.'

'No.'

She looked so mournful, Rodrigo's chest ached. Lord, the more he heard about her father, the more of an ogre he became. It scarcely seemed possible that Leonor—so sweet and warm—should be his daughter.

His conscience pricked him, he'd acted with the best of intentions when he'd sent word to her father with a view to sending her home. Had he made a terrible mistake?

To the people outside Al-Andalus, the Sultan's reputation was that of a tyrant. He was capricious and ruthless with prisoners. The poorer prisoners were killed, whilst noblemen with large coffers were kept for ransom. That said, Rodrigo was a realist, Sultan Tariq wasn't the only king to behave in this way. The kings of Castile also used ransom as a weapon of war; they too used it to fill their treasuries.

Rodrigo had been confident that the Sultan of Al-Andalus would treat his daughters with more care. He'd seen for himself the luxury Leonor was used to—the golden bangles and anklets, the harem silks, the grey mares with their silver bells—and he'd assumed that she and Princess Alba must have crossed him in some petty argument. That they'd run away to spite him.

Had he completely misjudged her?

Thoughts in turmoil, he steered her gently into the stable. 'The mare's in the end stall. Her name is Amber.'

'Amber.' Leonor brushed away a tear and found him a smile. 'That's pretty.'

He watched as she introduced herself to the mare, carefully allowing the animal to take her scent before she petted her. This woman was no spoilt princess. She was a sweetheart. And in alerting her father to her whereabouts, Rodrigo suspected he might have made the most ghastly error of judgement. If he sent her back to the palace, would her father punish her severely? What would he do?

Something niggled at the back of his mind, something Leonor had said shortly after fleeing the palace. She'd told him she couldn't go back and she had been very definite about that.

Father will kill me.

Rodrigo's blood chilled. Could that really be true?

I can't send her back. If I do, I would be just as much an ogre as her father.

'My lady?'

She looked across, still petting the mare. 'My lord?'

'Are you happy to ride her?'

'Very happy.'

He gave a brief bow. 'I'll send a groom in to saddle her, and allow you and Amber to become better acquainted. I'll wait in the bailey.'

Outside, Rodrigo leaned against a sun-warmed wall and returned to his dark thoughts. His instincts were beginning to tell him that he shouldn't send Leonor back to the palace and that she would be far better off remaining in Castile. But supposing he was wrong?

Leonor had been brought up in a different culture. He'd be the first to admit that he didn't know anything about the protocols a Granadan princess must follow. Did he have the right to make judgements? What he did know was that he'd come to like and trust her. Leonor was no liar, when she said she didn't want to go home, she truly meant it. As to her belief that her father would kill her if she went home—Lord, what a coil.

If Leonor didn't return to the palace, ill feeling would surely build up between Castile and Al-Andalus. It could cause more fighting at the frontiers, fighting that could escalate into all-out war.

Rodrigo shoved his hand through his hair and stared bleakly at the chapel door. He had the men and the allies to deal with further conflict, the pity was that what both kingdoms sorely needed was peace.

The sharp clip of iron-shod hoofs drew his attention to the gatehouse, where a horseman was exchanging greetings with the guards. Rodrigo didn't recognise the horse, but he knew the man. Miguel was back. Rodrigo pushed away from the wall.

Miguel dismounted with a creak of leather and a grunt that spoke of hours in the saddle.

'Well met, Miguel,' Rodrigo said. 'You made excellent time.'

'Thank you, my lord.' Miguel reached into his tunic and brought out a scroll that was covered in red and gold seals, and tied with black ribbon.

The Sultan's reply had arrived.

Chapter Thirteen

Rodrigo took the scroll with a heavy heart and glanced swiftly at the stable door. There was no sign of Leonor, she must still be petting Amber. He looked past the gatehouse, to the highway. The road was empty. He frowned. 'Where's my lady's escort?'

'My lord?'

'Didn't Lady Leonor's escort accompany you?'

His squire wrenched off his helmet. 'There's no escort, my lord.'

'What did her father say?'

'As you instructed, I didn't speak to the Sultan myself. His scribe told me the letter would clarify matters.'

'Very well. My thanks, Miguel. Did you sleep last night?'

Miguel grinned. 'Not much.'

'Away with you. Go and refresh yourself.'

Conscious that Leonor would emerge at any

moment, and praying he wouldn't have to hunt out an interpreter, Rodrigo made for the bench set against the chapel wall. He cracked the seal and the scent of saffron filled the air, the letter was perfumed. Crucially, the Sultan had done him the courtesy of getting the scribe to pen it in Spanish.

Scarcely breathing, Rodrigo skimmed past the usual salutations.

The most powerful King of Al-Andalus, Lord of Granada, sends greetings of peace and prosperity to Rodrigo Álvarez, Count of Córdoba, et cetera...et cetera.

Lord Rodrigo, after your emissaries had negotiated your release I expected no further contact between us. The missive your squire delivered came as a great surprise.

Rodrigo's brow creased. The red and gold seals swung to and fro.

Great Lord, your message spoke of my daughter Princess Leonor. I beg to inform you that I have no daughter named Leonor. I have but one daughter; she lives with me in the palace. Her name is Zorahaida and she is most beloved.

If I had another daughter and she had the temerity to run off with an infidel, I tell you she would be dead to me. To have lowered herself to such an extent she would be disparaged beyond repair.

Such a daughter, a disobedient daughter who had no care for her father's feelings, must know that she has placed herself so far beyond the bounds of filial devotion that she may expect nothing from me. Nothing.

In short, she is not my daughter. I repudiate her utterly.

I should like to point out that I have at my command many men who are loyal to the Nasrid house. If such a daughter were ever to set foot in my lands again, they would not take kindly to her disobedience and would judge her in need of serious punishment. I leave that to them. The so-called daughter you claim to have on your hands is not my concern.

I trust this is clear, and that this will be an end to our correspondence.

Powerful Lord, may God's blessings rain upon you and yours.
Sultan Tariq, King of Al-Andalus, et cetera... et cetera.

There followed the usual closing remarks.

Anger burned in Rodrigo's chest. Was the Sultan truly repudiating Leonor? He read the letter again. And again. It was hard to believe. Rodrigo stared at the sentence referring to men loyal to the Nasrid house. Who were they? Assassins?

The opening and closing phrases, so effusive and flowery, made a grim contrast with Leonor's callous rejection. Incredibly, her father had banished her from Al-Andalus. But would it end there? Did the Sultan's influence reach Córdoba? Rodrigo thought it unlikely. None the less, he wouldn't be taking any chances. Not with Leonor. He swore under his breath.

'My lord?' A groom, Felipe, was looking questioningly at him from across the bailey. 'Do you need anything?'

'No, thank you, Felipe.'

Dios mío, he'd have to double the guard on the castle gates. He'd sent word to Córdoba too; the city gates must be closely watched. And if Leonor set as much as a toe outside his bailey, she must take an escort.

Allowing the letter to curl back into a scroll, Rodrigo stared briefly at the beribboned seals before tucking it away in his tunic. He had seldom felt as conflicted. Amazingly, anger was no longer the predominant emotion. Relief was coming to the fore, his recent realisation concerning Leonor was sound. She hadn't been exaggerating when she'd spoken of her father's harsh treatment, nor had she been lying when she'd told him that her father would kill her if she returned to the palace. She was telling the truth, about everything.

The Sultan, may he rot in hell, didn't want her back. The sense of relief he felt was truly astonishing, a great swell of it flooded him, mind and body. He didn't have to send her away, if she wished, she could stay in Castile.

The question was, what should he say to her? What was he to do?

He glanced towards the stable and her face took shape in his mind's eye. He could hear her gentle voice; he could see those dark eyes and that sweet smile. He wanted to help her and he wasn't sure where to start. He leaned back against the chapel wall, conscious that this was a problem of an altogether different order. This was a problem he could enjoy solving.

How best to help Leonor settle into her new life in Castile?

Marry her.

The words echoed round his brain.

Marry her.

He was startled by a pang of genuine regret. Marrying Princess Leonor wasn't practical. In truth, it was impossible. Decades of mistrust lay between their peoples. There were grim and bloody events which couldn't be swept into a corner and forgotten and far too much personal grief. His mother, for one, would never forgive him if he married a Nasrid princess.

Lady Isabel had long been anxious for Rodrigo to marry. Ever since his betrothal to Sancha had come to nothing, she'd paraded Spanish ladies before him and sung their praises to the heavens. Spanish ladies. There was no way she would countenance his marrying Leonor. Such an alliance was unthinkable.

Footsteps drew his attention to the stable doorway and Leonor emerged.

Rodrigo came to his feet, gripped by a strange sense that his life was about to take a wrong turn. Now that Diego had died, the pressure for him to marry and produce an heir would undoubtedly intensify. Presently, his mother was lost in grief, but a new campaign would surely begin soon. The Spanish ladies would return. Rodrigo wasn't interested. In truth, Leonor was the first woman who'd held his interest since Sancha had married Lord Jaime. The pity was that there was no way he could choose Leonor.

He could help her though. He could keep her safe from the unnamed men who supported her father. He could help her find her relatives and ensure she reached them without incident.

'Ready to try Amber, my lady?' Rodrigo attempted cheerfulness.

'Something is wrong, my lord?'

'No, no. All is fine.'

As Rodrigo helped Leonor into the saddle and called for his own horse, his mind was still scrambling to catch up with the Sultan's rejection of her. Sultan Tariq didn't want Leonor back, he consid-

ered her disparaged. Worse, he had banished her
and given his men leave to punish her. Whatever
that meant. Was her sister Princess Alba also at
risk? He must warn Inigo without delay. Saints,
what a mess.

He studied Leonor's profile as she gathered
the reins and smiled her thanks at him. She was
so poised. So beautiful. Any man's heart would
ache, simply to look at her.

How could the Sultan wash his hands of her?

'My lady, will you be content to give me a moment?'

'You've been called away?'

'No, no. I have an urgent message for my captain, it shouldn't take long.'

'I'll wait here.'

Rodrigo strode to the guardhouse and issued
new instructions to his men regarding guard duty
and armed escorts for Lady Leonor should she
ever leave the castle. He asked his captain to carry
further orders to the Córdoban garrison and, finally, he sent a strongly worded warning to Inigo's town house.

By the time he was back in the bailey, his horse
was waiting by the water trough. He swung into
the saddle.

Leonor's face was alight with pleasure as she
kicked Amber into a trot. Her love of riding was
obviously undimmed by the gruelling journey
from the Alhambra. The Princess was a delight,

she was so lovely, so full of life. As Rodrigo watched her, his mind settled.

She wants to settle in Castile. I shall help her.

He would do everything in his power to protect her. Everything. And if that meant writing to Lord Jaime of Almodóvar to determine the whereabouts of the Princess's Spanish family, then that was what he'd do.

Her bravery and her innocence had captivated him. He couldn't simply abandon her to her own devices.

They rode along the riverbank with Leonor's bright eyes gazing eagerly every which way.

The watermill soon caught her attention. 'That is your mill, my lord?'

'It belongs to the village, I help with the upkeep.' Rodrigo spoke absently, half of his mind was still mulling over the ramifications of the Sultan's letter.

'Oh?' Her expression was open. Interested. 'Inés told us that mills outside Al-Andalus usually belong to the lords, who are paid whenever they are used.'

'That is often the case. However, I granted this mill to my tenants some years ago.'

'You had no loss of revenue?'

'Not to speak of.'

Her face creased in bafflement. 'My father would never have done such a thing.'

'I am not your father,' he said flatly.

Leonor didn't answer at first. Did she judge all men by her father's measure? The thought was dispiriting.

'I imagine the villagers are happy about the mill, my lord.'

'Aye, it gives them a measure of independence, and as long as they remember to give the Church the tithes it is owed, all is well.'

'Tithes.' Her brow furrowed. 'The word is unfamiliar—no, I remember—the Church is entitled to a proportion of the harvest. Is that not so?'

'Exactly.'

When some of the light left her eyes, Rodrigo realised that Inés must have taught her about the tithes due to the Church and that Leonor was once more thinking about her. 'You are concerned for your companion. That is perfectly natural.' He reached across and gently squeezed her arm.

'My lord, I care about her very much.'

'So I see. My lady, I haven't forgotten my promise. I have sent a detachment of scouts to look for her, they are to scour the route that we believe Enrique took. If your duenna is anywhere near the boundary, my men will find her.'

'Your men will enter my father's kingdom?'

'If necessary.'

Some of the anxiety left her face. 'Thank you, my lord. I shall pray that your men come to no harm.'

Rodrigo's throat tightened. This woman was a jewel, she cared, genuinely cared, for everyone who came within her orbit. She was nothing like her father. In truth, the gulf between what Rodrigo had seen of her behaviour and what he knew of the Sultan was so vast, it was astonishing Leonor was his daughter.

Water weed was streaming along with the flow of the river. He was watching Leonor when a new thought knocked him back. *What if she isn't the Sultan's daughter?*

His mind reeled, it was like being struck by an old-fashioned broadsword.

If Princess Leonor was struggling to believe that Rodrigo's methods were not those of her father, he was having difficulties of another kind.

Men and women showed their true colours in a time of trial. And what had their flight from the Sultan's palace been, if not a time of trial?

Born and bred in the seclusion of the harem, Leonor must have felt like a fish out of water from the very start. Yet she'd held up astonishingly well. She'd been calm and dignified; she'd been kind and thoughtful.

Rodrigo enjoyed her company. In truth, Princess Leonor was so unlike Sultan Tariq, it was almost impossible to see her as his daughter. What if she wasn't a princess after all? Was she a cuckoo?

Questions raced back and forth in his mind,

dizzying in their speed. Staggering. Could it be true? Was that even possible? Of course it was. If—

'My lord, is something amiss?'

Rodrigo came back from his thoughts with a jolt. Clearing his throat, he forced a smile. 'Nothing, my lady.'

She bit her lip. 'You fear for Inés?'

'No, no.'

I fear for you.

Think.

Suppose Leonor wasn't the Sultan's daughter, suppose the Princesses were indeed cuckoos and the Sultan knew it…

It would explain his cruelty towards Leonor in exiling her. Sultan Tariq knew he was not her father. Rodrigo's thoughts raced on. There was no question that the Sultan had abducted Leonor's mother, Lady Juana. Could Lady Juana have been with child when she was abducted? It was possible. What was the truth?

Before her abduction, Lady Juana had been betrothed to Lord Jaime of Almodóvar. Had Lady Juana—famed throughout Castile for her modesty and chastity—anticipated her wedding vows? In short, had Lady Juana and Lord Jaime had their pleasure of each other before she was captured? Until today, such a thought wouldn't have crossed Rodrigo's mind. But now…

'Lord Jaime,' Rodrigo muttered under his

breath. Lord Jaime would have answers. Provided Rodrigo had the gall to ask him.

Leonor tipped her head to one side. 'Who is Lord Jaime?'

'Lord Jaime of Almodóvar's estate marches closely with mine.' *And I want to know if he is your real father.*

Saints, this wasn't a question he could pose in a letter, such a question would have to be asked, face-to-face. There was nothing for it, Rodrigo was going to have to visit Lord Jaime in person. And if he went to Almodóvar, he'd probably see Sancha again. His mouth twisted.

Why was it that life had a way of forcing you to do what you least wanted to do?

Leonor was smiling at him, open and interested as ever. His heart warmed and he was startled to discover that his decision was made. He was going to Almodóvar and he would speak to Lord Jaime. He would exchange greetings with Sancha. And the dread he had been expecting to feel?

Gone. Thought of seeing Sancha again usually filled him with disquiet. It had simply evaporated. Rodrigo didn't begin to understand it, but Leonor had, in some mysterious way, exorcised that particular demon. He wanted, more badly than he cared to think about, to prove to this woman that he was not cast in the same mould as Sultan Tariq. What better way than to go to Almodóvar?

'I haven't spoken to Lord Jaime in years, a visit

is long overdue.' He smiled. 'My lady, I have reason to believe that he might be able to help you in your quest to find your family.'

Her eyes went wide. 'Why didn't you mention this earlier?'

Rodrigo looked away. He could hardly admit that he'd not mentioned Lord Jaime because he'd thought Leonor would be returning to Al-Andalus. He temporised. 'It is complicated. Political.'

'Political?'

'In the past, relations between Lord Jaime and I have been strained. Suffice it to say that circumstances have changed.'

'Enabling you to ask him about my family?'

'Aye.'

'Thank you, my lord, a thousand times.' Her eyes sparkled. 'Will you take me with you?'

Rodrigo shook his head. 'That would not be appropriate.'

Her face fell. 'My lord, if this touches on my family, I have to go with you.'

'No, my lady, you do not,' Rodrigo spoke firmly. 'There are other considerations I am not at liberty to discuss with you.'

He couldn't ask Lord Jaime about Leonor's parentage with Leonor present! More importantly, it could be dangerous for Leonor to go with him. With the Sultan's threat burning into his brain, Rodrigo wasn't going to let her travel any distance until he knew she was safe. Did the Sultan's threat have bite? He couldn't be sure.

Her brow wrinkled. 'Political considerations?'

'My lady, I'm asking for your trust and patience. There's more at stake than I'm prepared to say at this moment.'

She leaned back in the saddle, eyes so wary he ached inside. 'I see.'

'My lady, I would be honoured to act on your behalf.'

'You really believe this Lord Jaime will know about Mamá's family?'

'Definitely.'

'Very well, my lord, you may act on my behalf.'

Thank God.

Lord Jaime would help him find Leonor's lost relations, and he would also be able to confirm, once and for all, her true parentage. If Lord Jaime proved to be Leonor's father, Leonor had the right to know about it, and she would wish to meet him.

It would certainly be a challenge asking Lord Jaime whether it was possible that Lady Juana had been with child when she had left Castile. Still, it had to be done, and once that was settled, all that remained would be for Lord Jaime to confirm the whereabouts of Lady Juana's family.

Further, knowing the location of Lady Juana's family might lead them to Leonor's duenna. If Inés had escaped Al-Andalus without running across his scouts, she'd be bound to head home.

'Child's play,' he murmured. If he wasn't skewered for asking Lord Jaime if he'd carnal knowledge of Lady Juana, the rest should be straightforward.

Rodrigo's gaze strayed back to Leonor, she was so lovely, he couldn't help it. Yet it was more than that. Leonor brought out impulses he'd lost when Sancha had married Lord Jaime. He wanted to help and protect her. He wanted to make her happy.

'It would be wonderful to hear about my Spanish relatives,' she murmured. 'Are you quite certain I may not accompany you?'

'Quite certain. My lady, I will do my utmost to help you.'

'Very well.' With a sigh, she turned her attention to the willow-cloaked island that sat midstream. 'That island looks pretty, my lord.'

Rodrigo followed her gaze. 'So it is, I played there as a boy many times.' Out of nowhere, pain ripped through him. It seemed impossible that he'd never see his brother again.

She read his thoughts as though he'd spoken aloud. 'Diego used to go with you.' Her voice was soft.

'Aye.' He cleared his throat. 'We liked to escape the castle. However dry the summers, the willows never die. There are geese and ducks and...'

She was studying the water. 'It doesn't look very deep. Show me. Where do we cross?'

He reached for her reins. 'Allow me, this is the best place.'

They forded the river. On the island, Rodrigo helped her dismount and tethered their horses to the branch of a tree. Swifts hurtled this way and that above them; swallows swooped low over the reed beds.

She let out a sigh. 'It's beautiful. I can see why you came.'

Rodrigo took her hand and led her to sit on the trunk of a fallen tree.

'Diego loved it. He was always a bit of a rebel.'

'Was he?'

'Aye.' Rodrigo stared into the branches of a willow that lay half in, half out of the water. 'He was impulsive too, but it is a dangerous trait in a warrior.'

'Oh?'

'Diego and my cousin Enrique were close. I never understood it myself, but Diego followed him everywhere.'

'I recall you telling me your brother was younger than you. Perhaps his judgement was untried.'

Rodrigo looked at her, startled at her perception, though perhaps he shouldn't have been. For a girl who had spent her days stuck in a harem, she was extraordinarily wise.

'That is true. It was hard to watch him when he grew older. When we were young, we were never apart, and then one day he seemed to shut himself off. The river bored him. I bored him. Enrique on the other hand—he and Enrique would disappear into the back alleys of Córdoba. They'd return reeking of wine.'

'Your cousin led him astray.'

'My cousin led him into battle. If it weren't for my cousin, Diego would still be alive.'

Leonor drew a shaky breath. She was looking at their linked hands. Rodrigo hadn't released her after they'd sat down and he found the fact that she hadn't tried to free herself oddly pleasing.

'I am sorry about your brother. Truly sorry,' she whispered.

He rubbed his thumb over the back of her fingers. 'It's not your fault.' His chest heaved, his throat was horribly tight. 'Grief is not easy to overcome. Back in your father's kingdom I thought I was over the worst of it, but coming home seems to have brought it back.'

'I doubt that one overcomes grief. Perhaps the best that we can hope for is to learn to accept it.'

Her words seemed to sink into Rodrigo's soul and something eased deep inside. 'You're right. There are memories of my brother everywhere here.'

'Was your brother buried in Al-Andalus?'

'No. His body was sent to my mother along with the ransom demand. There's a cemetery in the village next to the castle. He rests there.'

Shoulders stiff, she stared at the reeds. Talking about Diego had put shadows in her eyes, even as it had eased Rodrigo.

She glanced at him. 'If you please, my lord, I should like to return to the castle now.'

'We're almost home,' Lord Rodrigo said as they passed a small orchard and approached the castle walls.

The gatehouse came into view and Castle Álvarez loured over them, solid and imposing. It was the Count's home, not hers, but Leonor simply nodded and wondered how long it would be before she found somewhere she could genuinely call home.

Lord Rodrigo's squire was outside the stable, talking with a couple of grooms.

'Miguel is back, I see,' she said.

'Aye, he returned earlier.'

'Your stallion is fully recovered?'

Lord Rodrigo's dark eyes were, for an instant, utterly blank. Leonor's stomach lurched. This man was no dissembler, and though she'd not known him long, she knew her question had caught him off guard.

'Recovered?' He cleared his throat. 'Oh, aye, Eagle is well.'

'I'm very glad to hear it.'

Puzzled, Leonor handed Amber to a waiting groom and turned towards the keep. Lord Rodrigo was hiding something. She stifled a sigh. She liked this man more than any other and it irked her to realise he was keeping things from her.

Admittedly, her experience of men was limited, but he'd surprised her from the first. Even in Salobreña prison, he'd seemed kind. And later, after she'd fled the palace, he'd looked after her. He'd treated her with great respect, save for that one time when he'd kissed her, and she could hardly hold that against him. That kiss, dangerously pleasurable, had been both a warning and an education. It had taught her that men could give pleasure as well as bring confusion and misery.

Unfortunately, the Count was being evasive. It was extremely disappointing. She gripped her skirts and mounted the stairs, more upset than she cared to admit. The part of her that had enjoyed kissing him at his house in Córdoba wanted, no, longed, to consider him her friend. Something which wasn't possible if he couldn't be completely truthful with her.

I haven't known him long, she reminded herself as she nodded at a sentry and entered the great hall. It was such a pity. She really liked him, and she desperately didn't want to discover that he was just like her father.

She must be strong. She must wait and watch and not be precipitate. Lord Rodrigo seemed kinder and more thoughtful than Father, but she mustn't forget that when it suited him, even the

Sultan was capable of kindness. She scowled at a tapestry at the far end of the hall and wished she understood why her father had shut his daughters up in that tower. Why had he taken away their ponies?

She felt a light touch on her elbow. Lord Rodrigo gave her a charming smile and she steeled herself against it.

'Allow me to accompany you to the solar, my lady.'

She gave him a brusque nod and preceded him to the stairwell.

'Lord Jaime will be with you shortly, Lord Rodrigo,' the maidservant said. She waved at a tray of pottery goblets on a side-table. 'Would you care for some wine?'

'Thank you.'

The maidservant poured him his wine, whisked out of the solar and closed the door. Rodrigo was alone. Since his conversation with Lord Jaime was of a delicate nature, he had left Miguel in the great hall, deep in conversation with Lord Jaime's falconer.

This was Sancha's solar.

It was as large and airy as the solar at Castle Álvarez. Daylight flooded through a wide window glazed with coloured glass. Bright spots of colour—blue, red, green—splashed over the walls and floor. The roof beams were heavy. Decorated with exquisitely intricate patterns, they put Rodrigo in mind of Arabic designs in the cathedral at Córdoba. The solar hearth was empty. It was too hot for a fire.

Rodrigo was staring at a heap of cushions on a wall bench, wondering whether he was looking at Sancha's work, and puzzling over how it was that he felt nothing more than idle curiosity, when the door opened and Lord Jaime walked in.

'Lord Rodrigo, it's a pleasure to see you. I am honoured by your visit.' Moving to the side-table, Lord Jaime helped himself to wine. His eyes danced. 'It's been a long time, my lord. I confess I'd hoped to see you years ago.'

Rodrigo grimaced. 'Aye, it's been far too long. Past time to bury the hatchet.'

'Sancha will be delighted. She's talked about you over the years, and it pained her when you refused to see her.' Lord Jaime fixed him with a look. 'She'll be joining us later.'

'I look forward to it,' Rodrigo said. He was startled to realise he meant it. Once, the idea of seeing Sancha with Lord Jaime would have been nothing less than torment. Now—nothing, he felt absolutely nothing. 'Lord Jaime, before Sancha arrives, there's something I must ask you.'

'Go on.'

'It concerns a scandal that took place years before you met Sancha.' Rodrigo leaned his hip on the side-table. 'When you were betrothed to someone else.'

Lord Jaime's jaw slackened. 'Juana? You've come to ask about Juana? Lord, she disappeared when you were a boy, I'm surprised you even remember her.'

Rodrigo's smile was crooked. 'You are my senior, my lord, but only by six years. The gossip certainly did the rounds. To be honest, I never heard much, as there was little in the way of detail.'

With a sigh, Lord Jaime rested his boot on a fireguard and gazed into the empty hearth. 'That was a blessing.' He lifted his head. 'Lady Juana and I were the same age, we were sixteen when we were betrothed. We loved each other. Lady Juana was quite the beauty.'

Having seen her daughter, Rodrigo could well believe it. He nodded. 'Lord Jaime, the story of Lady Juana's abduction has practically passed into folklore, but in all the tales, I never heard mention of her family. What happened to them? Where did she come from?'

'Baeza. Juana was the eldest daughter of Sir Pedro.'

'Sir Pedro?'

'Aye.'

Rodrigo had heard of Sir Pedro of Baeza and his whole body relaxed. Thank God he had something to tell Leonor. 'Thank you, my lord.'

News that Leonor's mother came from Baeza was priceless. Leonor would be able to visit her relatives. Among family, she would no longer feel alienated, and if all went well, she and her sister would have a base from which to make a home.

And then there was their lost duenna, Inés. If she was still alive and his scouts hadn't managed to track her down, there was a good chance that she'd return to her homeland. Baeza. They had somewhere to go in the search for Inés.

Lord Jaime was watching him, eyes puzzled. 'Rodrigo, you didn't have to come to me to have that question answered. Your mother would know. She would surely remember. When Juana vanished, Spain was turned upside down in an effort to find her.'

Rodrigo made a decisive negative gesture. 'I have another question, my lord, and believe me, it is not one I could ask my mother. I had to come in person to speak to you.'

Lord Jaime waved an expansive hand. 'Please continue.'

'Thank you. This next question is not merely delicate. I fear you will find it impertinent. Be assured, I would not ask it if it were not imperative to do so. In brief, shortly after Lady Juana was abducted, she gave birth to three daughters.'

Silence fell over the solar. Outside, Rodrigo could hear sentries tramping along the boardwalk. A horse whinnied.

Lord Jaime stared. 'You're questioning Lady Juana's virtue?'

'I am.'

Lord Jaime shook his head. His eyes took on a faraway look as he peered down the years. 'My lord, you cannot have heard of Lady Juana's reputation. She was the sweetest girl I ever saw. Fresh. Young. Innocent and loving.' He cleared his throat and his mouth curved in a reminiscent smile. 'Not to mention that she was the most beautiful woman ever to draw breath. You were too young to know, but I was a foolish youth. Wild. Reckless.'

'So are many young men,' Rodrigo murmured.

'That they are. Notwithstanding, all that changed the moment I met Juana.' His voice was earnest. 'She was such an innocent, you see, and she trusted me. I could never have betrayed her like that. When Juana was abducted, she was still a maiden. Innocent and pure.' He gave a heavy sigh. 'We were waiting for our wedding day. It was her wish. It ripped me apart when she vanished, I thought I would never recover.'

'And then, years later, you met Sancha.'

'Aye.' Lord Jaime's expression lightened. 'Sancha captivated me in an altogether different way. She was so unexpected, a blessing that burst into my life like a ray of sunshine on a cloudy day. I never meant to hurt you, lad, but once I'd met her, well, all I can say is that nothing was ever the same.'

Leonor flashed into Rodrigo's mind and it struck him that Leonor had had the same effect on him. This was why his mother's neverending parade of Spanish beauties had left him cold. Until meeting Leonor, part of him had been clinging on to his memories. Today it was blindingly clear that what he had once felt for Sancha paled into insignificance next to his feelings for Leonor. 'I understand,' he said.

Rodrigo almost wished he didn't because he yearned for a woman he could never have. He yearned for a Nasrid princess.

Light footsteps sounded on the stairs and Lord Jaime leaned in, adding quietly, 'We both regretted that our love hurt you, but we hoped that you would come to terms with it.'

The latch clicked and the door swung open to reveal a young woman in a tightly laced red-and-black gown.

'Rodrigo!' Face alight with pleasure, she rushed over and dipped into a deep curtsy. 'Oh, it's such a pleasure to see you.'

Rodrigo took her hand and bowed over it. 'It's a pleasure to see you too, Sancha. You look well, as beautiful as ever.'

'Flatterer.' Skirts rustling, Sancha went to stand by her husband. She tucked her hand into his arm and reached up to kiss his cheek. 'All's well, my heart?'

'All's well.'

A brief exchange of news followed, though Rodrigo scarcely heard a word. It was a relief to see Sancha so happy. Dimly he heard her telling him about three children—Sancha with three children, imagine!—but his mind was elsewhere.

Lady Juana had been a maid when she had been captured, therefore Lord Jaime was *not* Leonor's father. Rodrigo accepted Lord Jaime's testimony completely. If Lord Jaime said that Lady Juana had been innocent when she was captured, then that was the truth.

It was extremely disappointing. Rodrigo had been certain that Lord Jaime must be Leonor's father. Leonor would doubtless find it easier to settle in Castile if she felt wholly Spanish. She would feel she had more of a right to belong.

And if I had been able to prove that Leonor wasn't a Nasrid, there could be no objections if I offered for her hand. There would have been no political ramifications; his mother would have raised no objections...

It was a pity in other ways too. Leonor's feelings for Sultan Tariq must be hideously confused. On the one hand, she must hate him for confining her and for refusing to allow her to explore her Spanish heritage. On the other hand, she was bound to feel love for him, he was her father.

Rodrigo had hoped to lift her out of her confusion. It wasn't to be. Lord Jaime wasn't her father, that honour went to Sultan Tariq. In time, Leonor might untangle the threads, there was good and bad in everyone. No man was a saint.

As Sancha rattled on, Rodrigo realised that the question that taxed him most was whether Leonor's relationship with her father had spoiled her for all other men.

He came back to the present to find Lord Jaime and Sancha looking expectantly at him. It was time to take his leave. 'My thanks, both of you, for your hospitality.'

Lord Jaime clapped him on the shoulder. 'You are most welcome.' He raised an eyebrow. 'Next time, perhaps you will be free to tell me why you were so curious about Lady Juana.'

Rodrigo smiled. 'Perhaps I will.'

Chapter Fourteen

'Ana, has Lord Rodrigo set out for Almodóvar?' Leonor asked. She'd been cooped up in the tower bedchamber all morning with Ana and Catalina and she needed to speak to him. Ever since seeing Count Rodrigo's luxurious town house in Córdoba and then this grand castle, she'd been wondering why he'd taken her ruby necklace. He was clearly no pauper, so it made no sense.

Why did he want my necklace?

'The Count rode out when it was barely light. I'm not sure where he went, I am not in my lord's confidence.'

'Very well.' Leonor resigned herself to wait. The question remained, a niggling doubt, a blot on her otherwise good opinion of him. She liked the Count in so many ways, he was kind and open and apparently honest. Yet regarding that necklace, she was certain he was keeping something from her.

There was also the matter of her recent confinement in this apartment, although when she had queried him on it, he'd told her the entire castle was at her disposal. His only proviso had been that, should she leave the castle grounds, she must take an armed escort.

Leonor smiled at Ana, deciding she would put that to the test this very moment. 'Ana?'

'My lady?'

'I seem to recall seeing an orchard outside the castle walls.'

'Yes, my lady.'

'I'd like to stretch my legs; will you accompany me?'

Ana exchanged startled glances with Catalina. 'You would take a walk, my lady? In this heat?'

Leonor tipped her head to one side. 'I'd like to see that orchard. There'll be shade.'

Ana gave her a look that said her wits were wanting if she desired to walk out at noon, but none the less, she shrugged. 'Very well, my lady, I would be delighted to accompany you. My lord mentioned that you must have an escort if you leave the castle. Shall I alert the guardhouse?'

'Please do.' Leonor let out a silent breath. Relief. Lord Rodrigo had not left instructions for her to be confined. The escort was, she prayed most fervently, merely his way of ensuring her safety.

The orchard was divided into sections. Lemons, oranges, pomegranates. Water trickled along stone channels that criss-crossed the ground. At the end of the nearest channel, Leonor could see the water source—a small, walled aqueduct. She had seen similar aqueducts in the gardens of the Alhambra Palace and her heart cramped as she stared at it.

I will never go home.

A bench sat in the shade of an orange tree. Leonor made her way towards it with Ana. The armed escort stood watchfully on the road a few yards away.

It was peaceful. Sparrows twittered in the branches above them. Cicadas hummed. The air was rich with the scent of ripening fruit. A flash of purple in the corner of Leonor's eye drew her gaze back to the road. A Spanish lady was heading purposefully towards the bench. She was tall and gowned in rich purple. Several golden chains hung about her neck, and her ring bore a ruby the size of a pigeon's egg.

Ana jumped to her feet and sank into a deep curtsy. 'Lady Isabel.'

Leonor smothered a gasp. Lord Rodrigo's mother!

Lady Isabel made a twitching motion with her hand. 'Thank you, Ana. You may leave us.'

Mind spinning, Leonor scrambled to her feet. She had no clue what to say, it was as though her tongue had stuck to the roof of her mouth.

Has Lord Rodrigo told his mother about me?

Does she know who I am? Does she hold a grudge against me because of Diego's death?

Lady Isabel's eyes were disturbing, they were brown like her son's, but there the resemblance ended. Her expression was cold and more distant than the far mountains. Leonor swallowed.

Curtsy.

She wasn't used to curtsying, but somehow, she managed it. Lord Rodrigo's mother was surely due some respect. Her curtsy wasn't returned.

Lady Isabel's lips thinned. 'Catalina told me you were in the orchard. I came to see what my son had brought home with him.'

Leonor stiffened, never in her life had she been addressed in so insolent a manner. 'I don't care for your tone, my lady.'

Lady Isabel snorted. 'Your opinion is of no moment.' Slowly, insultingly, she looked Leonor up and down. 'I don't think I like you. What are you that my son brings you home and installs you in the family apartments without introducing us? Are you his mistress?'

'His mistress?' Leonor wasn't sure what to say, her duenna's tutelage had only gone so far, and she was unfamiliar with some Spanish terms and customs. However, she knew her father had many concubines. 'Is a mistress the same as a concubine?'

Lady Isabel's face froze. 'Don't be insolent.' Her voice dripped poison. 'Are you sleeping with him?'

Anger balled in Leonor's chest. 'I would have thought that is the Count's business, not yours.'

'Let us be frank.' Lady Isabel drew closer and her lip curled. 'Whatever you are to him, he won't marry you.'

Again, that hard gaze raked Leonor from head to toe. Leonor's skin crawled, it was as though her clothes were being peeled away. It was humiliating.

'I can see you might have a crude appeal,' Lady Isabel continued. 'You look like a concubine, a girl like you will never marry.'

Leonor crushed down a surge of anger and stepped sharply on to the path. With Lady Isabel in this mood, there was no point talking to her. What had Lord Rodrigo told her? Surely he wouldn't have admitted to bringing a Nasrid princess into the castle, yet what other reason could there be for this intense hostility?

Lady Isabel blames me for Diego's death.

The sound of hoofbeats was a welcome distraction. Two riders were headed towards the castle, one had a stallion on a leading rein. With a jolt, Leonor recognised the stallion. A fine animal, it was unmistakeably the horse that Lord Rodrigo had left back at the first inn. Eagle, he was called.

Utterly bemused, Leonor stared after Eagle as he was led to the gatehouse. She distinctly remembered the Count leaving Eagle in Miguel's care. Back at that inn, he'd said he hadn't wanted him lamed. What was going on? Miguel had returned the day before, and the Count had implied that Eagle had returned with him.

Or had he? Leonor didn't want to speak to Lady Isabel longer than she had to, but this she must ask. 'I thought Lord Rodrigo's squire brought the stallion back yesterday.'

Lady Isabel's veil shifted as she shook her head. 'See for yourself, Eagle is only now come home. If you need chapter and verse, you must speak to my son.'

'Thank you, my lady, I will.'

'You'll have to wait until he is back from Almodóvar. Likely you won't have been told, but Almodóvar is the home of Lord Jaime and his wife, Lady Sancha.' Lord Rodrigo's mother held out her hand and made a play of examining her nails. The ruby in her ring flamed, angry as fire. 'Lord Jaime's wife and my son were once betrothed. My son is particularly fond of Lady Sancha. They remain close.'

An ache bloomed in Leonor's chest. Telling herself it didn't matter if Lord Rodrigo had been betrothed and was fond of the woman, she tore her gaze from Lady Isabel and pointedly followed the horses' progress. After a moment, realising her hands were bunched into fists, she slowly uncurled her fingers. He was probably conversing with Lady Sancha this very moment. It mattered not.

What did matter was that Lord Rodrigo's stallion was only now returning. If Miguel hadn't been caring for Eagle, where had he been all this time? Had he been sent on another errand?

My necklace! The heat left the sun so sharply, it felt like midwinter. Goosebumps ran along her arms. *Count Rodrigo must have sent Miguel to speak to my father. He sent him with my pendant. Why?*

The answer dropped into her mind like a stone. Revenge. He was using her for revenge. Her necklace was being used to demand a ransom for her safe return.

The ache in her chest intensified. No, no, this could not be.

Yet it was the only explanation. The entire time she had been in Lord Rodrigo's company, he'd been planning to send her home. She'd told him what life had been like in the palace and he hadn't listened. He didn't care. He'd sent his squire back to the Sultan with a view to sending her back to captivity.

He'd been clever. Lulling her into thinking she was free to wander at will about his castle. She frowned at the guards on the highway and wondered what their orders really were. To protect her, as the Count had implied? Might they be there to ensure she didn't stray? He wouldn't want to lose his opportunity for revenge.

'Excuse me.' Lady Isabel brushed past and

stepped on to the highway. Veil a-flutter, she stalked after the horses towards the gatehouse.

The gatehouse seemed to blur. Blinking rapidly, Leonor stumbled after Lady Isabel. She'd been deceived. Lord Rodrigo had let her assume that Miguel had brought Eagle back the day before. Miguel had done no such thing. He had surely returned from Granada bearing a message from her father.

Lord Rodrigo took that pendant as proof I was his captive. He wants to ransom me.

A wave of nausea swept over her. The feeling of warmth she'd experienced between them had existed only in her mind. It was an illusion. She'd wanted to feel a bond with him so badly that she'd imagined it into being. She had dreamed about her perfect knight and it had suited him to play along.

He'd never intended to help her. His brother's death filled his mind and there was room in it for nothing save revenge.

Hollow inside, she set her teeth. As soon as Lord Rodrigo returned, she would have it out with him.

She wanted to believe the best of him, but it wasn't possible. Clearly he had a heart of stone.

Leonor hesitated in the chapel doorway. The interior was brighter than she had imagined. Light was falling through two rows of arched windows;

candles in glass lanterns gleamed on a table covered in a green cloth. That table is the altar, Leonor reminded herself, recalling what Inés had taught her. The cloth glistened with gold thread.

'Enter, my child,' a soft voice said, as a man—a priest by his garb—stepped out from behind a pillar. 'This is God's house and all are welcome.'

The priest's expression was earnest and his eyes kind. Wondering what he would say if he knew Leonor had never been in a church before, she crossed the threshold.

'Thank you, Father. I came here to think.'

'Please, you are most welcome.'

The floor was covered in patterned tiles and stone benches ran along the walls at either hand. It was quiet and, after her encounter with Count Rodrigo's mother, a balm for her wounded soul.

'This is the right place for meditation,' the priest said. 'Your prayers will go straight to God.' Nodding pleasantly, he left the chapel.

Leonor was content to wait. She'd left a message for Lord Rodrigo with Ana. As soon as he returned from Almodóvar, she would speak with him.

Her contemplation didn't last long, and she was staring at the silhouette of a lion on one of the floor tiles when a clop of hoofs in the bailey announced his return. Shortly afterwards, brisk footsteps sounded in the chapel porch. On the altar, the candles flickered in their glass lanterns.

'Leonor.' Lord Rodrigo took her hand and brought it briefly to his lips. 'You asked to see me?'

'Aye.'

Whenever he touched her, it felt as though he was taking possession of her. Carefully, Leonor reclaimed her hand and watched his expression grow wary.

'What is it? My lady?'

Leonor hesitated. She'd come to like this man, yet after that interview with his mother, she was filled with doubts. Despite his many kindnesses, she no longer trusted him. It wasn't easy knowing where to begin.

'My lord—'

He tucked his thumbs into his belt. 'I would be honoured if you called me Rodrigo.'

She looked him full in the eye. '*My lord*, your stallion returned this afternoon.'

He gave her a charming, if rueful, smile. 'Ah. Did he?'

'Seeing him made me wonder—if Miguel didn't bring him back yesterday, what has your squire been doing these past few days?'

Another charming smile came her way, Leonor steeled herself against it.

'My lady, that is a question you don't need to ask.'

'I disagree.' She closed the distance between

them so they were standing toe to toe. 'Where was he all this time?'

Warm hands enfolded hers, setting off a pleasurable tremble in her belly. Ignoring the tremble, Leonor shook him off. 'Answer me, if you please.' She looked pointedly towards the altar. 'We are in God's house. I would appreciate the truth.'

His face fell, and he looked appalled. 'You think I'd lie to you?'

'You lied to me yesterday when you said Miguel had brought your horse back.'

Lord Rodrigo released her and ran his hand round the back of his neck. 'I misled you, I admit it. It was for your own good.'

She narrowed her eyes at him. 'For my own good?'

She had never felt so confused. Brown eyes held hers. Steady eyes. Warm eyes that held comfort and—something else. Uncertainty? Regret? Longing?

'My lord, you sent Miguel to my father, did you not?'

A muscle flickered in Lord Rodrigo's cheek. He strode to the altar and a heavy sigh filled the chapel. 'You worked this out for yourself?'

She gave a jerky nod.

'How?'

Leonor's mouth dried, and she almost moaned out loud. She had hoped—so much—that he would deny it and that she could believe him.

Her fingers curled into her skirts and she forced out the words. 'When I gave you my necklace at the inn, I thought that paying your ransom had impoverished you. I was mistaken. Your house in Córdoba and this castle make that plain, you're a very wealthy man.' Tears stung at the back of her eyes, irritably, she brushed them away. 'My lord, how could you? I begged you not to send me back to my father. I explained what my life at the palace was like. And you still tried to ransom me?'

He was at her side in an instant, strong fingers closing round her wrist.

'Ransom?' His voice was choked. 'You think I asked for ransom money?'

Leonor stared at the brown fingers encircling her wrist. 'I suppose you thought to avenge your brother's death.'

He dropped her wrist. 'It grieves me that you think so ill of me.' His voice was harsh. 'God help me, I thought to serve you well.'

'Returning me to my father would serve me very ill. My lord, wild horses wouldn't drag me back to the palace.'

'Aye.' His voice was softer again. Regretful. 'My lady, believe me when I say I meant you no harm. You are the loveliest of women. Your heart is true, and you are kind and thoughtful. But you are also impossibly innocent—life in the harem has not prepared you for life in Castile. When I sent Miguel back to Granada, I didn't ask for money. I believed the best place for you was back with your father.' He swallowed. 'I now see I was mistaken. You have my sincere apologies.'

She stared, jaw slack with disbelief. It was as though the ground had dropped away beneath her feet. 'I beg your pardon?' Lord Rodrigo was apologising? She couldn't believe her ears. Even more astonishing, he seemed to be admitting he'd made a mistake. 'You…you are apologising?'

Men never apologised, they never admitted they were wrong.

He laid his hand on his heart and smiled—his familiar, heart-stopping smile. 'Forgive me?'

Leonor's response was slow in coming. The Sultan never apologised, he believed himself incapable of making a mistake. Lightly, she touched Count Rodrigo's sleeve. If his apology was heartfelt, this man was a miracle and she owed it to him to hear him out.

'You tried to send me home, but clearly I have not gone. What did Father say?'

Lord Rodrigo's jaw tightened. 'He convinced me that returning you to Granada was not in your best interests.'

'Father disowned me?'

'I didn't say that.'

'It's true, though, isn't it? My lord, will you show me Father's reply? I need to know exactly what he said.'

Lord Rodrigo simply stared at her, an unfathomable look in his eyes. 'Do you read Spanish?'

'No.'

'In that case, there'd be no point you seeing it.'

'Very well.' Leonor held his gaze. 'Then I trust you to tell me its contents.'

He took her hand. 'It's not pleasant.'

'Please, my lord.'

He nodded. 'In brief, Sultan Tariq no longer acknowledges you as his. He claims he only has one daughter, Princess Zorahaida.'

'That's Constanza,' Leonor murmured.

'So I surmised. My lady, you will not be going back to Al-Andalus. It would be dangerous.'

'Father made threats against me?'

He grimaced. 'I shall simply say that if you are caught in his territory, his soldiers have permission to punish you. In effect, you are banished.'

Leonor swallowed. Banished! Bile rose in her throat and she felt slightly dizzy. It struck her that being proved right was far worse than she had imagined. She felt the soft movement of his thumb against her palm, and it was extraordinarily consoling. 'Thank you for telling me. I assume that Alba is also banished.'

'Princess Alba's name wasn't mentioned, but I fear so. I have sent a warning to that effect to Lord Inigo's town house.'

'They have arrived there safely?'

'Thus far, I've heard nothing. My lady, rest assured, Inigo will contact me as soon as they reach the town.' Warm brown eyes held hers. 'I don't want you to worry. You will be safe in Castile.'

She stiffened. 'You've no need to feel responsible for me.'

'Need has nothing to do with it.' His lips formed a crooked smile. 'It is my pleasure to see you safe.'

'Pleasure,' she murmured, recalling that brief and moving exchange of kisses in Córdoba. She pushed the memory aside and looked sadly at him. 'My sister Alba and I have plans.'

'Ah, yes, to find your mother's relatives.' Lacing his fingers with hers, he led her to the wall bench. 'Please, my lady, be seated. Allow me to tell you what happened when I met Lord Jaime.'

He took his seat beside her and the conversation with his mother in the orchard rushed back at her. Lord Jaime was married to Lady Sancha, whom the Count once loved.

'Did you see Lady Sancha?'

The Count stilled. 'You've been talking to my mother?'

'We met in the orchard.'

'She was courteous, I trust?'

Leonor felt her face freeze. She fixed her gaze on the wall behind him.

'My lady?'

'Your mother was...wary.'

An eyebrow lifted. 'Wary?'

'Lady Isabel is uncertain what to make of me. She mentioned that you were once betrothed to Lady Sancha.' A tight ball formed in Leonor's stomach. It was horrible to think that he was still fond of Lady Sancha. She pressed her lips together, she shouldn't have spoken. Any more and he'd be thinking she'd grown fond of him herself. Any more and—

He reached for her hand and the instant their skin touched she felt it again. That warmth, that sense of comfort, of coming home. Was it a lie?

Her cheeks were on fire with embarrassment and she had the sudden realisation that she wasn't the only one to be so moved. A pulse was beating in the Count's neck and his breath wasn't quite steady. Her thoughts tangled.

He cleared his throat. 'I may have mentioned that Lord Jaime of Almodóvar is half a dozen years my senior. He is well respected throughout Castile and he married Lady Sancha of Iznájar. It is true, that in my youth Lady Sancha and I were betrothed.' He gazed towards the altar, his smile reminiscent. 'We were very young. I was besotted. A callow youth, you might say. It wasn't quite the same for Sancha, and the instant she laid eyes on Lord Jaime, it was over for me. I took it hard.

'All this happened over a decade ago. I can't deny that I still hold Lady Sancha in deep affection, but what I felt for her wasn't lasting.'

'It was a boy's love?'

'Aye.' He leaned closer and ran a lean forefinger gently down her cheek. 'My lady, you know I didn't go to Almodóvar to see Lady Sancha. I went on your behalf.'

Leonor's pulse jumped. He had found out about Mamá! 'Pray continue, my lord. What did you discover?'

'Lady Juana was born in Baeza, Lord Jaime knows your family well. He tells me they still live in Baeza.'

'My family,' she murmured. 'I have family.'

For years Leonor had wanted to learn about her Spanish relatives, and it was something of a shock to realise that, should she wish, she could meet them. She bit her lip, suddenly uncertain. How would Lady Juana's daughter be received after so many years had gone by? Her new-found kin might not welcome her, they might view her as the product of a misalliance.

'They...' Her voice was weak. 'They might not wish to acknowledge me.'

Lord Rodrigo's hand tightened on hers, secure and certain. Reassuring.

'They will want to meet you, I am certain. You can send them a message. Indeed, you ought to write without delay and not simply on your own account.'

'Oh?'

'It strikes me that if my men don't find your duenna, she may well return to Baeza.'

Leonor stared at their linked hands. Her head was whirling, but Lord Rodrigo was in the right, Baeza would be home to Inés as well as her mother.

'You can't lose anything by writing,' he added.

'Who should I write to?'

'Sir Alfredo de Baeza, I believe he is a cousin, of sorts.'

'Sir Alfredo de Baeza,' she murmured. 'Thank you for this intelligence, my lord, I appreciate you going to such trouble. I shall write immediately.'

'You are very welcome.'

'There is one slight drawback.'

'Oh?'

'I can write Arabic, not Spanish. I shall need a scribe.'

He smiled. 'That isn't a problem, you may use one of my scribes.'

'Thank you, my lord.'

'When your letter's finished, you may give it to me, I shall deliver it personally.'

Leonor felt herself frown. 'Surely someone else can deliver it?'

'It will be my pleasure. I can explain fully then and answer any questions they may have.'

Leonor returned to the keep, her mood shifting like quicksilver as she sorted through her thoughts. Her father's hateful letter—she and Alba were banished!—had crushed her. It was one thing to suspect the Sultan capable of behaving in such a way, and quite another to have it confirmed.

On the other hand, news that the Count had found their Spanish family did much to redress the balance. She couldn't wait to tell Alba, her sister also needed to know that they weren't alone in Spain.

Thank God for Count Rodrigo. She'd been a fool to think so ill of him. It was a relief to be proved wrong. Ransom hadn't been his intention, he'd written to her father because he'd truly believed she'd be better off in the palace. What was passing strange was that he had admitted his mistake.

Leonor wasn't planning to marry, ever, but if she did, it would be to a man like Count Rodrigo. Her chest ached. It was a shock to realise that what she was feeling was sadness, longing for something that would never be.

Lord Rodrigo was fair and even-handed in his dealings with everyone. He considered her interests, he'd gone to Almodóvar specially to ask about her lost family. He was also devastatingly handsome, not that that signified.

None of it signified because Leonor had vowed never to place her person in the custody of a man again. There would always be that doubt in the back of her mind—the fear of the control a husband could exercise over his wife. Lord Rodrigo might change, he might—unlikely though that might seem now—turn into her father.

She thought about her father's generosity, of the way he'd smiled at her when she'd amused him. That smile had been genuine, she would swear. She could also recall the sound of the key to the tower as it grated in that lock. And now—banished.

She could never marry. Never again would a man have such power over her. Never.

Besides, Rodrigo de Córdoba deserved someone who could give herself to him wholeheartedly. He didn't need a wife who doubted him at the first hurdle. He didn't need a wife who would box him into a marriage that his mother hated.

He'd want children, heirs to inherit all this. Every muscle in Leonor's body went rigid. Children.

Inés had been instructed to keep the Sultan's daughters innocent. Unlike the women in the Sultan's personal harem, the Princesses hadn't been taught how to pleasure a man. But Leonor and her sisters had eyes. Before their freedom had been curtailed, several of the rides around Salobreña had been most enlightening. They'd seen dogs and horses and—well, they'd seen enough to work out what might be involved in begetting children. And if what Leonor suspected was true, she didn't think she could do that, not even with a man who kissed as sweetly as Count Rodrigo.

No, she couldn't do that, not even for him.

And then there was Lady Isabel. Leonor walked blindly towards the stairwell. She couldn't come between a mother and son. Even with the best will in the world, if she were to marry Lord Rodrigo, his mother's bitterness and rage would know no bounds. Diego's death cast a long shadow.

I shall never marry.

Chapter Fifteen

Rodrigo sat at the high table in his hall, a scroll in hand, another at his elbow. Inigo's message was brief. Inigo and Princess Alba had arrived safely in Córdoba and Inigo had received his warning. Inigo agreed that the Sultan's reach couldn't extend as far as Córdoba, but none the less, he'd taken the precaution of increasing the guard on his town house. He promised to write again when there was more to report.

Rodrigo set Inigo's letter aside and glanced at the other scroll. Intended for Princess Leonor, it was written in Arabic, so there was no chance of Rodrigo understanding a word. Not that he would have dreamed of breaking the seal on anything addressed privately to Princess Leonor.

Doubtless it concerned the sisters' plans to find their mother's family. Soon, the Princesses would be moving on with their lives. Rodrigo rolled his shoulders, the thought left him hollow.

He glanced towards the passage that led to his estate office. Leonor was in there, dictating to his scribe. As soon as she emerged, he would give her Princess Alba's letter. The hollow feeling intensified. Rodrigo drummed his fingers on the white cloth and took stock of his surroundings. Best not think about Leonor.

Everything was in order in his hall. Brightly painted jugs and bowls were displayed on the side-tables; polished weaponry gleamed on the walls. Higher up, the painted roof beams were almost obscured by the banners of his household knights. Banners of every hue imaginable hung in rows along the walls—green, blue, gold, silver...

Inevitably, Rodrigo's gaze was drawn to the opposite wall where his standard was displayed—a black horse racing across a crimson field. It was most distinctive, and he'd always liked it. As he studied it, he was struck by an odd coincidence. Crimson was also the colour of the field on the Sultan's standard.

Why had he not remarked on it before? Had Leonor noticed him on the Salobreña quayside because of his crimson tunic?

He was staring at one of the more faded banners thinking about how the longing he used to feel for Sancha had paled into insignificance before his desire for Leonor.

Leonor. *Dios mío*, she was fast becoming an obsession. It wasn't healthy. Leonor wouldn't be with him for long, all she wanted was to meet her relatives. She'd scrambled on to his horse outside the Alhambra Palace with that one goal in mind.

I don't want her to leave.

Impatient with himself, he shook his head. His wishes were unimportant. He must set them aside and help her. And pray that she would learn that caring for someone wasn't the same as imprisoning them because what he really wanted…

'My lord?' The fragrance of orange blossom teased his senses, and all at once she was at his elbow, scroll in hand. 'Here's the letter for Sir Alfredo.'

Rodrigo rose, took the letter and tucked it into his tunic. 'Thank you, I leave for Baeza at first light tomorrow. I may be away a few days; should you need anything, please apply to Miguel or my castellan, Sir Sebastián.'

Her eyebrows lifted. 'Miguel doesn't ride with you?'

'I'm taking another squire, Joaquin, with me this time.'

Leonor murmured something non-committal about not realising he had more than one squire, and Rodrigo gestured at the table. 'We have news from Córdoba.'

Her face lit up. 'A letter from Alba!'

'Aye. My lady, please sit while you read it.'

Leonor sat beside him and cracked the seal. Rodrigo reseated himself.

'They're safe,' she said with a sigh of relief.

'So Lord Inigo told me.'

She read on and then looked up. 'I really need to see her. May I go tomorrow?'

Rodrigo hesitated. 'I'd prefer you to wait until I return from Baeza. You'll have more to tell her then.'

A pleat between her eyebrows, she clutched the letter to her breast. 'You're thinking about my father. You're concerned for my safety. I understand, my lord, but I can't wait. My sister and I have been too long apart as it is. Send someone else to Baeza and then you can come with me.'

Rodrigo hid a smile at her imperiousness. The habit of command, it seemed, was deeply ingrained. He shook his head. 'That's not possible, I need to go in person.' If Leonor was truly planning to make her home with her relatives, he wanted to make sure she'd be welcome. He couldn't leave her with simply anyone.

'In that case, would you grant me an escort?' Leonor asked. 'Might Sir Sebastián accompany me?'

Rodrigo thought quickly. A large escort marching through Córdoba would attract far too much attention. Questions might be asked, and until matters were resolved with Sir Alfredo, he'd prefer to keep quiet about Leonor's presence in Castile. A small party of guards might serve, if she dressed simply. She'd be taken for a merchant's daughter. Yes, that might work. 'On one condition.'

She leaned forward. 'Anything.'

'You must wear your plainest gown, and you must promise not to do anything that will draw the eye. You must obey Sir Sebastián's orders.'

'I swear.'

Rodrigo didn't like the idea of her travelling to Córdoba without him, but the joy on her face was its own reward. She reached for his hand, pressed it briefly against her forehead and kissed it.

'Thank you, my lord, a thousand thanks.'

Rodrigo couldn't help it. He looked at her mouth. And found himself wondering if she would ever be able to contemplate marriage without fear that her husband would box her in.

'Have you had any news of Inés, my lord?'

'No, my men have not yet returned. I think it likely she has made her own way to Baeza. If she has, I will know soon enough.'

Leonor woke early. She was finally going to see Alba! There was much to talk about, good and bad. Her smile faded. Alba needed to know about their banishment. However, what mattered most was that they had escaped their father and their Spanish relatives had been found.

Inés remained a problem, as there'd still been no sign of her. God willing, their duenna would find her way to Baeza and they would eventually be reunited. Constanza was also a worry. Was she locked in that tower alone? Leonor sighed. She still wasn't sure why her youngest sister had chosen to stay behind.

Ana was sleeping on a mattress beside her bed. 'My lady, is anything amiss?'

'I'm in a hurry.' Leonor strode to the washbowl. 'I'm visiting my sister today.'

Ana knuckled sleep from her eyes and groaned. 'It's barely light, the larks are surely asleep.'

'I can't wait, I need to see her without delay.' Dragging on her plainest gown, for Lord Rodrigo's instructions regarding her attire made sense, Leonor turned her back and gestured for Ana to lace her up.

Her spirits lifted as it occurred to her that in Córdoba, she could spend the entire day without running into Lady Isabel. Lord Rodrigo's mother clearly loathed her.

Would Lord Inigo permit her to stay as his guest until Count Rodrigo returned? It would be wonderful if he did.

Three days later, Rodrigo returned to Castle Álvarez. He was sticky, dusty and irritable after a hard ride from Baeza and he intended to visit the bathhouse before giving Leonor her news.

His interview with her relatives had gone better than expected. Lady Juana's nephew, Sir Alfredo, had been intrigued to learn that two of his aunt's daughters had fled the Sultan's care and might seek sanctuary at Baeza. Sir Alfredo had professed himself eager to meet them, even going so far to say that the Princesses need expect no prejudice under his roof. Sir Alfredo came across as straightforward and no-nonsense, and Rodrigo believed his assurances.

Even better, when Rodrigo had hinted at the possibility of an alliance between his family and Sir Alfredo's, the suggestion had been met with interest, even warmth.

All in all, it had been a worthwhile journey, with one proviso. No one at Baeza had seen Inés, who seemed to have vanished from the face of the earth. That would certainly distress Leonor, and Rodrigo could only pray that her duenna had gone into hiding and would eventually emerge, safe and sound.

Miguel was outside the forge, lobbing rusty horseshoes at a pin hammered into a board. Under the awning, a black mare was being shod. Miguel dropped the horseshoe and crossed the bailey as Joaquin took charge of the horses.

'Well met, my lord.'

'Miguel.' Rodrigo smiled. 'Is Lady Leonor in her chambers?'

Miguel gave him a blank look. 'Lady Leonor? No, my lord, I thought you knew. She went to Córdoba.'

A chill ran down Rodrigo's neck. 'Yes, yes, but that was days ago, she can't still be there.'

'She is, my lord. She went to visit her sister. She didn't come back. As I understand it, she is Lord Inigo's guest.'

Rodrigo couldn't seem to take in what Miguel was saying. 'Lady Leonor has left the castle?'

'Yes, my lord.'

'Did she take her belongings with her?'

Miguel gave a thoughtful frown. 'I don't think so, my lord.'

The blood drummed in Rodrigo's ears. Had she gone for good? Had he lost her already? He glanced up at the window of Leonor's apartment. 'Is Ana about?'

'She's in the tower apartment.' Miguel's eyes were full of understanding. 'My lord, I expect Lady Leonor will soon be back.'

Rodrigo grunted. 'Attend me, if you please. After a bath and a change of clothing, I shall be needing a fresh horse.'

'Yes, my lord.'

Rodrigo rode swiftly with Miguel to Inigo's town house, although he was aching in every bone. He would have preferred to find Leonor waiting for him on his return. It wasn't that he was concerned for her safety, as Inigo would be sure to guard her well. What bothered him was not knowing whether, when she'd left his castle, she'd been planning to return.

Had his mother upset her? Leonor had mentioned speaking to her. He thought back to their meeting in the chapel. He'd asked if his mother had been courteous and all Leonor had said was that his mother had been wary. Wary.

He swore under his breath. Leonor had temporised. His mother was many things, but wary was not one of them. What had she said to Leonor? He would have to make it clear to her that Leonor would always be welcome in his castle. Always.

Ana had assured him that Leonor had taken only the gown she was wearing. That sounded promising, as if she intended to return. Most likely, her decision to stay in Córdoba had been made on impulse. Yes, she'd been so overjoyed to see her sister that she hadn't wanted to leave again so soon. She'd bent Sir Sebastián to her will and convinced him to allow her to stay in Inigo's town house. It was perfectly natural. Perfectly understandable.

'Miguel, remind me to have words with Sir Sebastián.'

'Yes, my lord.'

Madre mía, Leonor was a tricky woman.

So, here he was, riding to Inigo's house as fast as he could with his guts in a tangle because a headstrong princess had taken it into her head to stay with her sister in Córdoba rather than return to his castle, to him.

What were they talking about? Their journey to Baeza?

The sisters were walking around a sparkling fountain in the central courtyard of Lord Inigo's town house, their arms about each other's waists. They dressed in Spanish fashion, Leonor had borrowed one of her sister's new gowns. It was fashioned from a marvellous rose-coloured damask that was every bit as sumptuous as the fabrics Lord Rodrigo had given her.

'Lord Rodrigo is certain that Father banished you for ever?' Alba asked, not for the first time. In the three days they'd been together the sisters had talked of little else.

Leonor didn't blame her. It was hard to accept. 'Yes. As I said, Father has told his men that they are at liberty to punish me if I am caught in Al-Andalus. The letter didn't mention you by name, though Father did say that he only has one daughter, Zorahaida.'

'So I must accept that I too am banished.' Alba sighed. 'I can't say I'm surprised, but what does surprise me is how upsetting it is.'

Leonor smiled sadly. 'I agree, I feel like an orphan. The only brightness in this is that we are reunited. And of course, there's Lord Rodrigo, I've enjoyed coming to know him.'

Alba gave her a thoughtful look. 'You seem to understand him extraordinarily well.'

Leonor fixed her gaze on the fountain. 'He's kind and unexpectedly patient.' She turned to Alba. 'Promise me you'll never go home.'

'I shan't go back. I'm looking forward to meeting our Spanish family.' Alba flushed. 'Before that, however, there's something I need to do.'

Leonor lifted an eyebrow. 'That sounds intriguing.' When Alba didn't continue, Leonor nudged her. 'Well? You've whetted my curiosity. You can't stop there.'

'Ah, but I can. If I succeed... No, *when* I succeed, you'll be the first to know.' Alba lifted her shoulders in a careless shrug. 'Rest assured, if I live to be a hundred, I will never set foot in Al-Andalus again.'

'I'm glad.' Leonor took in a breath to brace herself. 'I thought the same. At first.'

'What are you saying?'

'I need to return home, and before you object, it will be the briefest of visits.'

Alba's mouth fell open. 'What? You can't warn me not to go home because Father has banished us only to announce that you're going back yourself. The heat must have addled your brain.' She searched Leonor's face and her expression clouded. 'So help me, you're serious. Why?'

'Constanza. We can't abandon her, and if anyone goes back, it must be me. It's my fault we were separated.'

'Leonor, it's not your fault.' Alba's eyes were sad. 'Constanza's always been timid, we were deluding ourselves to think that she would come with us.'

'Aye, she hates confrontation. I've been thinking about this a lot the last few days and believe I know why she didn't come with us. As much as Father terrifies her, she's more afraid of the unknown.'

'I can't blame her for that,' Alba said. 'I was nervous myself.'

Leonor frowned at the fountain. 'Constanza needs to know life is waiting for her outside the palace walls. She needs to know Mamá's family has been found. Then, when she's ready, she can follow us. She will be free.' Leonor clutched Alba's hand. 'I have to tell her. Outside Al-Andalus, Constanza will be safe. Father won't follow her beyond the boundaries, so there'll be no more living in fear.'

Alba shook her head. 'It's far too dangerous. Moreover, it won't work. Constanza had her chance and made her choice, it's too late for her.'

'I can't accept that. What will her life be like? We did everything together. She will surely be miserable on her own. Alba, the three of us belong together.'

Alba gave her an odd look. 'Do we?'

Leonor couldn't believe her ears. 'Until we ran away, we were inseparable. It's not right that we have our freedom while Constanza still moulders in that tower.'

Alba opened her mouth to respond when a disturbance drew their attention to an arched doorway leading off from the courtyard.

The door swung wide and Lord Rodrigo stepped through it, spurs chinking on the stone flags. A slight sheen of sweat on his forehead told Leonor he'd been riding hard. Face set, eyes belligerent—something had clearly angered him— his gaze homed in on her.

'Lady Leonor, why are you still here?'

Leonor lifted her chin. 'As you see, my lord, I am visiting my sister. Lord Rodrigo, may I present Princess Alba?'

Lord Rodrigo gave Alba a cursory glance. His bow was so brief it bordered on rude. 'Delighted, Lady Alba, I'm sure.' He transferred his attention back to Leonor. 'Were you planning to ever return to Castle Álvarez?'

'Naturally, my lord, I—' Leonor broke off, blinking in shock. 'You can tell us apart!'

'Don't be ridiculous.' Rodrigo ran his hand through his hair. 'Of course I can.'

Alba stepped forward, she had watched this exchange with great interest. 'Lord Rodrigo, what my sister is trying to say is that most people cannot.'

Lord Rodrigo snorted. 'Clearly, most people are blind.' Imperiously, he held out his hand. 'Come, Lady Leonor, I have news from your family in Baeza.'

Leonor shot Alba an apologetic look—really, the Count was behaving very oddly. She permitted him to take her hand and willed herself to ignore the way her heart leapt at his touch. 'News of our Spanish family?' She nodded pointedly at Alba. 'Then I am sure my sister would also like to hear what you have to say.'

The instant Rodrigo's fingers closed over Leonor's, the tension that had been driving him since he'd returned to Castle Álvarez and found her absent simply melted away. Leonor hadn't walked out of his life, she was still here, talking to her sister.

The Princesses were remarkably alike. Two pairs of beautiful dark eyes were gazing at him through luxuriant eyelashes. Both sisters had glossy black hair and slender, feminine bodies. Princess Alba's delicate form was almost as tempting as Leonor's. Almost. There the similarities ended.

Leonor's eyes were surely livelier and she was slightly taller. As Rodrigo bowed over her hand, he inhaled surreptitiously. Leonor. That sensual, womanly scent was as unique as Leonor herself.

He could tell them apart at a thousand paces. Was this love?

He straightened. *I love her?*

He couldn't stop looking at her. He searched for the tiny grey flecks in her eyes and smiled at his capacity for self-delusion. It hadn't been a chivalrous desire to aid a princess in distress that had led him to Sir Alfredo. That had been true at the beginning, but it was true no longer. Nor had he been driven by the desire to further a propitious alliance; Princess Leonor would bring him nothing save her lovely self.

Love had driven him to Baeza.

Love had tied his guts in a tangle when he'd returned home to find her missing.

I love her.

'Very well, my lady,' he said, gesturing towards a low divan positioned in the shade under one of the arches. 'I will share the news from Baeza. But first, where's Inigo?'

'He's not here, my lord,' Princess Alba said. 'He went to the horse fair.'

The next half hour passed with Rodrigo telling the sisters about their cousin. 'Sir Alfredo's looking forward to meeting you. He told me you would be more than welcome to stay at Baeza.'

Leonor looked at him, frowning slightly. 'And Inés? Has he heard from Inés?'

'I'm afraid not. However, Sir Alfredo has

strong hopes that your duenna will find her way to Baeza if my men cannot locate her. So, as soon as arrangements can be made, the two of you may visit him.'

Leonor fiddled with the fringe on her veil. 'Thank you, my lord. It was kind of you to go to such trouble.'

Alba leaned forward. 'My lord, you have my thanks too. After I have consulted with Lord Inigo, I will let you know my decision.'

Rodrigo blinked. 'You're not certain you'll go?' He glanced Leonor's way. 'I thought you were set on meeting your family.'

'We are.' Princess Alba smiled. 'However, I have matters to attend to in Córdoba first.'

Leonor cleared her throat. 'Speaking for myself, I've decided I would prefer to meet our Spanish relatives on neutral ground.'

Alba murmured agreement.

At a loss, Rodrigo stared at them. The Princesses had braved much to meet their Spanish family. Yet as soon as their goal was within reach, they balked. Perhaps it was understandable. Leonor was, as Rodrigo knew to his cost, deeply wary of putting herself in a vulnerable position. The Sultan's letter had obviously unnerved her.

'You think your family will take advantage of you?' he asked, looking at Leonor. 'My lady, I assure you Sir Alfredo is anxious to meet you, both of you. You need have no fear of him.'

Leonor's smile was strained, a mirror of Alba's. 'None the less, my lord, we prefer to meet our cousin on neutral ground.'

Rodrigo had little option but to agree. Locking horns with her would achieve nothing. As for the rest—his declaration of love and acceptance as a potential suitor by her Spanish relatives—all that could wait until she'd learned that not all men maltreated their women.

Until that day dawned, he must bide his time. In Leonor's present unsettled frame of mind, a declaration of love would surely only make matters worse.

He gave her a wry smile. 'Have you and your sister talked yourselves to a standstill?'

'My lord?'

'You've had three days together, so are you ready to come home yet?'

Leonor laughed and came gracefully to her feet. 'Yes, I think we've caught up.' Her voice warmed. 'It's a relief to know we can see each other whenever we want.'

Rodrigo helped Leonor into the saddle and they rode through the straw-strewn streets at an easy pace. Leonor's eyes were, as ever, alight with interest as she looked about her. She hadn't the slightest idea that she'd put him on the rack when he'd returned to find her gone and he wasn't about to admit it to her now.

The streets around the cathedral were lined with market stalls. Goods sweltered under canvas awnings. The heat was at its height, so the crowd had thinned, though a few brave souls were picking over the merchandise.

As they wove steadily through the townsfolk, Rodrigo watched her drink it all in. She smiled at children eating sweetmeats on the steps of the cathedral; her gaze lingered on the brocades gleaming from a cloth merchant's stall...

Leonor wasn't made to be immured in a palace—thank God, she'd escaped. It would be a crime to cage a woman like Leonor.

They reached the goldsmiths' quarter. Here, the whitewashed houses had shutters that could be let down to form stalls. Several were closed until it was cooler, but a handful remained open. Leonor's attention fastened on an array of bracelets displayed on black velvet.

'You like these?' Rodrigo found himself thinking that if she wanted the stars he would try to give them to her. Saints, what was wrong with him? He'd never felt like this with Sancha. Unable to help himself, knocked back by the intensity of his need to make her his, he reined in. 'If you wish, we can dismount so you can look more closely.'

She gave him an abstracted smile. 'No, thank you, my lord, I still have the jewellery I brought with me. I was simply wondering what price such things fetch, here in Córdoba.'

He felt a flicker of unease. 'You're not thinking of selling your jewellery?'

'Not at present.' She turned her gaze back to the goldsmith's stall. 'However, that time might come. I have observed that, outside the palace, money is more useful than jewellery and my store of coins is small. I'm glad to know where to come, if I need to exchange my jewels for money.'

Suddenly, at the forefront of his mind, was the memory of Leonor in that squalid prison, handing over her bracelet to pay for Inigo's treatment. Rodrigo's skin chilled. It had never occurred to him until now, but it seemed likely that the Nasrid royal family were in the habit of gifting their servants and subjects with jewels to reward them for services. When under their father's roof, the Princesses wouldn't have needed money.

He stared at her profile, unable to read her. She was a mysterious woman and something in her tone had set alarm bells ringing. What was she up to? He gripped the reins. Undoubtedly, his Princess—and, yes, she was his, though she had yet to accept it—placed a high value on her independence. Rodrigo had no wish to curtail her freedom, but she must be made to understand that here in Spain, naivety could be dangerous.

Dios mío, she couldn't wander about offering gold bracelets to all and sundry. She was so vulnerable. He felt fiercely determined not to let anyone take advantage of her. For her safety, he must discover what she had in mind.

'My lady, you must ask if you need assistance, I'd be honoured to help you.'

Her head turned, but her eyes were filled with suspicion and his heart sank.

'My lord?'

He drew in a steadying breath, it was obvious she wasn't ready to trust him. Had her father ruined her for all time?

I will teach her to trust me. I will win her.

'You need not sell your jewellery. My lady, I will give you all the help you need.'

She stiffened. 'Thank you, but I do not require help.'

Smiling, he shook his head. 'Leonor—my lady—you are thinking of selling your jewellery.' He lifted an eyebrow. 'Why is that?'

She gave a tight smile. 'I am uncertain whether to tell you.' Her smile faded and she bit her lip. 'In truth, I do need help. However, I'm confident you won't give it.'

They'd reached the end of the goldsmiths' street. The city wall was in sight. They'd almost reached the gate.

'Try me. Please, my lady, go on.' She was, he noted, sitting very stiffly in the saddle.

'Very well, my lord.' She squared her shoulders. 'I need to return to the Alhambra Palace and I'd be eternally grateful if you would serve as my escort.'

It took a moment for Rodrigo to digest what she had said, and when he understood, he couldn't believe his ears. Leonor—return to the palace?

No! Every fibre of his being rebelled. 'That's impossible.'

'Is it? You brought me here, surely you can take me back?'

'Holy Mother, you've been banished. You're an exile. Leonor, you feared your father before he banished you, and now—what will his men do if they catch you? Think. Al-Andalus is lost to you for ever. Lost. Saints preserve us, you fought for your freedom and you've won it, why the devil would you go back?' Words failed him. And then he couldn't help himself, he reached for her mare's reins and hauled her horse close to his. He leaned towards her. 'I forbid it.'

Her eyes flashed. 'Forbid? My lord, you forget yourself. You have no authority over me. Unhand my mare.'

'Not until you put this foolhardy idea aside. You cannot go back. I won't let you.' If she returned, her father would kill her, just as she had told him at the outset.

Her jaw set. 'I shall go back, my lord, with or without your blessing.'

Her voice was icy and for the space of a heartbeat it was like looking at a stranger. Did he know her at all? Why risk her hard-won freedom to return to a place she loathed? What had she said, that wild horses wouldn't drag her back to the palace? What was going on? If only she would confide in him.

She is desperate. Desperate and afraid.

'My lady, why are you even thinking about this?' Rodrigo was struggling to sound calm. 'Your father is a vengeful man. What's so important that you would risk your freedom for it?'

'My sister.'

'You mean Princess Constanza, the one who remained behind?'

'I have to speak to her.' And then the words tumbled out in a rush. 'My lord, Constanza has a nervous disposition, she fears the unknown. I must tell her that if she can get to the borders of Father's kingdom, he will not pursue her. She needs to know that Alba and I are safe, and that our Spanish family has been found. She needs to know that a refuge awaits her, if she needs it.'

Relief filled him, Leonor wasn't trying to return to life in the Sultan's palace, she was simply trying to help her sister. Sisterly affection notwithstanding, Leonor had to understand that her plan was far too dangerous. 'My lady, Princess Constanza chose to stay behind.'

'We belong together.'

She sounded so mournful an ache bloomed in Rodrigo's heart. 'Princess Constanza didn't want to leave when she had the opportunity. Therefore she must be content to remain there.'

Her nose lifted. 'I have to go back, I have to know Constanza is well, and she really needs to know that our cousin has been found in case that makes a difference.'

'You are not your sister's keeper.'

'My lord, you don't understand. Please consider—'

'I will consider nothing. You will not be returning to Granada. This conversation is at an end.'

'I want to save her.' Her eyes flashed, dark as obsidian. 'You, my lord, are a hypocrite. You went after Diego.'

Rodrigo's nostrils flared. He felt as though she'd punched him in the gut. 'That was a different case entirely.'

'Was it? I thought you'd understand. Clearly, I was wrong.' Her mouth tightened. 'Thank you, my lord, you have fulfilled my every expectation.'

Jerking her reins free, she set her heels to her mare's flanks and cantered towards the city gates, her veil trailing behind her like a banner.

Rodrigo spurred after her, jaw tight. Clearly his Princess didn't like to be crossed. That comment about Diego had been particularly low. Although—he grimaced—perhaps he had expressed himself rather strongly. He hadn't been able to stop himself, the idea of her falling into her father's clutches was torture.

She needed time to cool down. They both did. They'd talk again when they were calmer. Leonor must see sense.

Chapter Sixteen

Leonor slipped quietly up the winding stairs to her bedchamber. Thankfully, there was no sign of Ana. Finding the most practical gown, she bundled it up in a cloak and shoved it beneath the bed. She removed her jewels from the box Lord Rodrigo had lent her and, hands shaking only a little, stowed them in a purse ready to tie about her waist.

Images flitted through Leonor's mind like butterflies in the gardens of the Alhambra—the lacy plasterwork ceilings; the pools silvered by moonlight; the delicate fretwork on the shutters. Shutters that closed out the world.

Sinking down on the edge of her bed, she hugged her middle. This was terror, she felt sick with nerves.

I must go back. Without Count Rodrigo's knowledge.

The palace was a gilded cage and the idea of

Constanza stuck there for the rest of her life was intolerable. Constanza deserved another chance to choose freedom.

It's my fault she stayed behind.

Leonor should have known Constanza needed coaxing. She was determined to make amends.

Constanza must be told that the Sultan's reach ended at the borders of Al-Andalus; she must be told that there were knights in Córdoba capable of protecting them as diligently as their father—chivalrous knights who had no need to browbeat women to force them to their will. Furthermore, it would surely give Constanza an extra push to learn that their mother came from Baeza and that their Spanish kin had been found.

In Castile, Constanza need never feel alone. In Castile, the three of them could be together.

Once Constanza understood that she would be safe in Spain, she would surely find the courage to escape.

Leonor pushed to her feet. Constanza wasn't going to moulder for the rest of her life behind the palace wall, not if she could help it. However, she wasn't fool enough to attempt the journey on her own. Rodrigo had refused to help her; would Miguel do the same?

There was one way to find out.

Miguel was talking to Lady Isabel in the courtyard. The warmth and affection on Lady Isabel's face gave Leonor pause. With no sign of the hostility Leonor had witnessed in the orchard, she looked a different woman.

Discreetly gesturing at Miguel to let him know that she needed to speak to him, Leonor ducked into the stable.

Constanza had to be told that the skies wouldn't fall if she ran away.

She prayed for the words to convince Miguel to help her.

Shortly after noon the following day, Rodrigo was preparing to ride out on patrol when his mother approached him in the bailey.

'Rodrigo, a moment, if you please. Miguel asked me to give you a message.'

Rodrigo set his foot in the stirrup. 'I wondered why he missed breakfast, it's not like him. Has he gone into town?'

'I… No.' Lady Isabel clasped her hands at her waist. Her colour was unusually high and her gaze was firmly focused on the cross on the chapel roof.

Ice trickled down Rodrigo's spine. He knew that expression. His mother looked guilty of all things, not to mention edgy. Slowly, he removed his foot from the stirrup. 'Mamá?'

'Miguel sends his regrets and asks that Joaquin squire you for the next few days.'

Still she wouldn't look at him. What the devil

was going on? 'Very well. Miguel's a free man, he's served me faithfully and is loyal to the bone. I am content for him to have some time for his own affairs.'

His mother gave a shaky sigh and finally met his gaze. 'I doubt you will be content when you hear where he has gone. And with whom.'

Dread filled him. 'This concerns Lady Leonor?'

His mother gave a jerky nod. 'They set out together before first light.'

Rodrigo gripped his mother's arm. 'Where have they gone?'

Even as the words left his mouth, a sick lurch gave him his answer. Leonor had persuaded Miguel to take her back to the Alhambra Palace. Merciful heaven, ever since their disagreement, Leonor had been on his mind. He'd been waiting for her to cool down enough to have a rational discussion about the best means of getting a message to Princess Constanza. He'd left it too long.

'They've gone to Granada,' his mother said. 'To the palace, I believe.'

Rodrigo glared at her. '*Dios mío*, why didn't you tell me immediately?'

His mother's gaze was keen as a hawk's. 'She's a Nasrid princess, isn't she?'

Rodrigo struggled for control. 'Mamá, Lady Leonor's mother was Spanish. And even if it were otherwise, I would ask you to accept her as you accepted Miguel.'

His mother's mouth looked pinched. 'There's no comparison between Miguel and that woman. Miguel is not a Nasrid. That woman's father is responsible for Diego's death.'

'That woman's name is Lady Leonor and I'd be grateful if you would remember it.' He sighed. 'Be reasonable, Mamá, you cannot lay Diego's death at Leonor's door. It was not her fault.'

His mother gasped. 'She's Leonor to you, I see. Saints preserve us, you're in love with her. A Nasrid princess!'

'Yes, Mother. I love her. Forgive me for believing that your heart was big enough to accept her as you accepted Miguel.'

His mother's eyes glittered, hard as jet. 'It is you who is unreasonable. Miguel was a little boy when you brought him here, that woman is a Nasrid.'

Rodrigo turned away, he was furious, mainly with himself. He couldn't blame his mother for allowing Leonor's departure. A princess wouldn't be in the habit of taking no for an answer, he should have worked out what she would do.

'If you'll excuse me, Mamá, I must prepare for another journey.'

His mother went chalk white. 'Rodrigo, no! I cannot lose another son.'

'You should have thought of that before allowing Leonor and Miguel to set out.' Then, seeing the stricken expression on his mother's face, he relented and softened his voice. 'Mamá, you are not going to lose me.'

Rodrigo led a small contingent of knights into Al-Andalus. They reached the foot of the gully that ran alongside the palace wall under cover of darkness. Long hours of riding, when day had blurred into night, meant they were, to a man, exhausted.

Fear for his Princess had given Rodrigo a tightly clenched belly and an incessant pounding in his brain that had beat in time with the horses' hoofs. Was she safe? What would her father do to her if she fell into his clutches? The entire ride had been a nightmare in which Rodrigo could think of little else.

His eyes were gritty and his throat burned. Thirst. Longing. Fear. In truth, he couldn't recall ever feeling such fear. His thoughts had been painful from the moment he and his knights had cantered away from Castle Álvarez.

Leonor asked for my help and I refused her.

She'd confided in him. She'd trusted him enough to tell him she wanted to get a message to Princess Constanza and what had he done? He'd lost his temper. In short, he'd behaved just like her father. As soon as Rodrigo had done it, he'd regretted it. And then he'd made matters worse, he'd decided they needed time to cool down.

He'd underestimated the strength of the bond between the three sisters. He'd been blind, it was obvious Leonor ached to see Constanza as much as he ached to see Diego. Maybe Leonor's hurt was greater. She'd been swift to confess that the Princesses had been everything to each other. In not listening, he'd failed her.

I refused to help and this is the result.

'Well done, men, you rode like demons,' he murmured as they dismounted. 'Sir Esteban, you're with me. No torches.' He gestured at the spangled heavens. 'We can rely on the stars.'

Sir Esteban nodded. 'Understood.'

'The rest of you, stay here. The danger signal is three long whistles. If you hear it, flee for your lives. Other than that, don't move.'

Rodrigo and Sir Esteban started up the gully. Black shapes reared up before them, trees with dark branches clawed at the stars. Night filled every crevice, the rocks looked grey.

Rodrigo was wearing a leather gambeson and sweat prickled at the back of his neck; the night was warm. Unseen animals rustled in the under-growth. Somewhere in the palace grounds a pea-cock shrieked. The sound knifed through him and the pain of Diego's death was suddenly as fresh as though his brother had been killed only a few hours ago. Being near the palace had brought it all back. Rodrigo forced himself on.

They were halfway up the gully when he saw her. A pale figure in the moonlight, she was standing alone on a rocky outcrop, staring at the palace wall. Her clothes looked out of place. In his mind Rodrigo had clothed her in her harem silks, yet here she was in a Spanish gown. She looked nothing like the mysterious woman he'd encountered in that stinking prison yard.

Quietly, he moved towards her. She whirled about and her sharp, indrawn breath was loud in the dark. Starlight glistened on the moisture on her cheeks; she was crying. A knot formed in Rodrigo's throat.

'Rodrigo!' Shooting a last, fearful look at the palace wall, she was at his side in a trice. Delicate fingers gripped his. 'You shouldn't be here. Come away.'

He let her draw him behind a scrubby tree, wrong-footed by the realisation that she had finally—*finally*—dropped his title when addressing him.

She called me Rodrigo.

He paused to wipe a tear from her face and pulled himself together. 'I might say the same of you. Why are you alone? Where in hell is Miguel?'

She dashed away another tear. 'Bless him, he's checking the tower.'

'What happened?'

'It's as quiet as the grave and there has only been the faintest of lights. No music.' Her voice broke. 'No movement.'

He felt himself frown. 'Constanza's not there?'

'I don't know. We've been hiding, waiting for signs of life. I even sang.'

He flinched. 'That was foolish, not to mention incredibly dangerous. Your father banished you, think what will happen if you are caught.'

She stared up at him, face grim in the moon glow. 'I don't care. I must get a message to her.'

He drew her deeper into the scrub. 'Come, we're in sight of the guards on the walkway.'

When she opened her mouth to object, he pulled her close, silencing her with a deep, thorough kiss. It was heaven to have her safe in his arms.

She called me Rodrigo.

It was a small step, yet it symbolised so much. Despite their disagreement, she'd spoken to him as one would to a trusted friend, to an equal. The distance between them was dissolving.

Their kiss deepened and her lips warmed, softening to such an extent that when he finally drew back, he was breathless and so lost in longing it took a moment to remember where he was.

'Leonor, I should have told you this before— I'll help get a message to your sister.'

In the starlight, her face seemed to shine. 'You will? How?'

'Mind that you are to obey me. One argument and we head straight back to Castle Álvarez.'

She shot him a look from under her eyelashes and gave a jerky nod. 'There won't be any arguments.'

He squeezed her hand and grinned. 'Excellent. After we find Miguel, we'll go to the Vermillion Towers, I need to speak to the overseer.'

Leonor dug in her heels. 'Rodrigo, no! He'll have you in chains in a trice.'

'I doubt that.'

She called me Rodrigo again.

He pulled her back into his arms and smiled into her eyes. Eyes that were filled with anxiety— for him as well as for her sister. 'Leonor, you can't have forgotten your promise already. Trust me.'

'I don't want you walking into danger on my account.'

She twisted around, peering into the dark. Clearly, she believed an attack was likely, if not imminent. His spirits lifted. She didn't want him hurt.

'Leonor, I give you my word, no one will be in any danger.' Lightly, he kissed her cheek. 'The overseer at the Vermillion Towers is susceptible to bribes, though I suspect you know that already.'

'Aye, I remember how Inés paid him to let you and your comrades rest beneath our tower.'

'Exactly.' Rodrigo tapped the purse on his belt. 'I've brought enough gold to ensure he can build a new life elsewhere.'

'*You're* going to bribe him this time?'

He kissed her nose. 'Aye. He will see Constanza gets your message. Leonor, you must agree. I will not permit you to remain here a moment longer.'

Her sigh melted into the night. 'Very well. After we've spoken to the overseer, we will return to Castle Álvarez.'

He blinked, he hadn't expected so swift a capitulation.

She noticed his surprise and shrugged. 'I don't want Father to get hold of you or Miguel.'

Heart warm, Rodrigo leaned in and kissed her again. On the mouth. This time he lingered for as long as he dared. It was impossible not to. 'You're a treasure; you know that? So, we return to the castle, there to await your sister's reply.'

She scuffed the ground with her boot. 'I foresee a couple of drawbacks.'

'Oh?'

'What if we never hear from Constanza?'

He cupped her face with his palm. 'We will.'

'And if we don't?'

He lifted his shoulders. 'We'll think again. On my honour, I swear we'll get a message to your sister, even if it means learning to fly to get into the palace gardens.'

She gave a slight smile. 'Thank you.'

He raised an eyebrow. 'And the other drawback?'

'What's to stop the overseer simply taking your money and walking away?'

'We give him half the gold now, and half after you hear from Princess Constanza.'

Another silence was followed by a quiet sigh. Leonor leaned her head briefly against his chest. When she lifted it, she was smiling. 'Your plan has promise. The overseer has to have contacts in the palace if Inés found a way to bribe him.'

'You approve?'

'I do, thank you.'

'In that case…hush, what was that?' Rodrigo focused on the top of the palace wall where, briefly, a light had gleamed.

'The guard,' Leonor hissed, pulling urgently at his hand. 'Come away.'

Rodrigo set his jaw. 'This way.'

'What about Miguel?'

'Miguel can look after himself.' Rodrigo knew it sounded harsh, but Miguel knew the risks and he must have known Rodrigo would never have agreed to him bringing Leonor anywhere near the palace. Sultan Tariq must not be permitted to get his hands on Leonor. Her safety was paramount. Only when Leonor was safe, would Rodrigo approach the overseer at the Vermillion Towers.

Brambles snatched at his clothes as they navigated their way down the crevasse.

The peacock's shrieks followed them down the gully.

Castle Álvarez, several nights later

Hushed voices pulled Leonor from sleep. It was pitch dark. Bedcovers rustled and the latch on her bedchamber door gave a soft click. Across the chamber, a soft light wavered and a tall figure—Rodrigo—turned to face the bed. He was carrying a glass lantern and there was no sign of Ana, he must have dismissed her.

Leonor let out a breath and sat up. 'What are you doing? You shouldn't be in here.'

Smiling, Rodrigo set the lantern on a nearby coffer and came to stand at the bedside. He was wearing a long blue tunic, belted loosely at the waist. His hair was ruffled. It occurred to her that he'd been roused from sleep.

'Relax. Leonor, much as I might wish it, I haven't come to seduce you. A messenger has arrived. And before you ask, it's too soon to hear from Constanza.'

Leonor felt herself sag. 'Oh.'

'I feel confident we shall hear from her before long.'

Leonor nodded. She hadn't seen much of Rodrigo in the last few days. After racing down that crevasse near the Princess's tower, he'd handed Leonor into the care of his men, giving orders that they get her back to Castle Álvarez with all speed. He'd found Miguel, and he'd spoken to the overseer at the Vermillion Towers.

Constanza's message should have reached her by now.

It is too soon to hear from her.

Determined to hide her disappointment, Leonor flicked her braid over her shoulder. 'Who would wake you at this hour? It must be well past midnight.'

'Sir Alfredo has sent an envoy from Baeza. Leonor, Inés has reached your family, your duenna is safe.'

Inés was safe? The relief was so overwhelming, at first all Leonor could do was stare. Reaching for Rodrigo's hand, she gave it a slight tug and he sank on to the edge of the mattress.

'God be praised. Is there other news? Was she hurt? When did she get there?'

Dark eyes held hers and Rodrigo's thumb moved gently against her palm. Gold threads glinted in his tunic. 'She's well, if somewhat exhausted. I believe she reached Baeza at about the same time I was chasing back to Granada to find you. I shall have to recall the men I sent to search for her now she is safely home.'

His hand shifted and slid a little way up her arm before releasing her. A caress. Leonor frowned, she was shamefully aware that she liked it. When his smile didn't waver, her cheeks grew warm. She had a strong sense that his every movement was deliberate. He wanted her to crave his touch.

Slowly, he reached for her braid, pulled it back over her shoulder and fingered the ribbon. His eyes were shielded.

'I'd dearly like to see Inés,' Leonor said slowly. 'But I can't leave here until I hear from Constanza.'

'I thought you might say that.' He cleared his throat and toyed with the ribbon. 'So I've taken the liberty of inviting Inés here.' His gaze lifted. 'My knights shall escort her after she has taken a few days to recover.' Leaning in, he kissed her cheek, lingering to nuzzle her ear and neck. Leonor's heart skipped a beat.

'Thank you, my lord, that is most considerate of you.'

He pulled back. His smile was so tender, Leonor's eyelids prickled and her chest ached.

'Leonor?' The smile vanished. 'What's this? Tears?'

She nodded, heart too full for words.

'Why?'

She swallowed hard. 'I... I don't know.'

'You're happy for Inés, no doubt.'

She nodded. 'Aye, though it's not just that. You.' She sniffed. 'Me.' Another sniff. 'Rodrigo, my thoughts are in knots, and I don't know what to think.'

'Come here, my love.' Shifting, he pulled her into his arms.

The relief, the joy was too much. Leonor stiffened and he shook his head.

'Don't do that, sweet.' His voice was a balm. It was so soothing. It was also dark, exciting and sinful. His voice was everything. He stroked her hair. 'You don't fear me.'

'No.' Her voice was little more than a whisper.

Leonor worried at her lower lip—wondering if, in the half-light, Rodrigo could read her. She didn't fear him—she loved him. And love, as she knew to her cost, was dangerous. Love was deadly. It could turn to hate, just as it had done with her father. A part of her would always love her father, she couldn't help it. Yet another part hated him. She hated the way Sultan Tariq ruled his daughters. Charm and gifts when everything was going his way, and the iron fist the instant he was thwarted. He ruled his kingdom in the same way. She hated that too.

Undoubtedly, this was why the love she felt for Rodrigo didn't feel pure. Tainted by her past, it brought new terrors. Rodrigo de Córdoba could hurt her. He had taught her to love him, and if he discovered it, he would have more of a hold over her than her father had ever had.

Love was dangerous.

'Fear is not what you feel for me,' he said, voice soft and confident.

Her heart lurched. *He knows.*

He went on stroking her hair. 'When we first met, you were, I believe, blinded by your experience with your father.' His voice deepened. 'And I, for my sins, didn't understand. I didn't take you at your word when you told me of your life at the palace—the restrictions, the loss of your ponies, being locked in that tower. I thought your father must surely adore you.'

Rodrigo manoeuvred himself on to the bed and Leonor found herself lying against him, head pillowed on a strong shoulder, hand against his chest. And he was no longer merely stroking her hair, at some point in their conversation he had untied the ribbon and unravelled it. He was trailing her unbound tresses through his fingers, eyes half-narrowed as he watched her.

It was most enjoyable.

With a quiet sigh, Leonor allowed her body to relax against his. She wasn't sure what he would do next, and her will to resist him was weakening. Oddly, her fears were fading. Rodrigo was large and strong and the feel of his body against hers was a blessing, she would enjoy it whilst she could.

'We were both blind,' she said, sliding her hand across his chest. The need to push her fingers into his hair was a deep ache, the most pleasurable of longings.

'Leonor, my lovely Leonor.'

He stroked her waist; his hand was warm and sensual and very tempting. Certain he was about to kiss her, she closed her eyes and angled her mouth to his.

Nothing happened. She opened her eyes to find dark eyes smiling into hers.

'Leonor, my love, will you do me the honour of marrying me?'

Leonor stared. His expression was open and honest and full of hope. 'Marry you? We can't marry!'

He nuzzled her cheek. 'Yes, we can. I care for you more than any woman alive.' He pulled back, eyes soft. 'You entranced me from the beginning, although I didn't realise quite how much you meant to me until you stole my squire and ran back with him to your father's palace. I was utterly sick with fear for you. Leonor, I'll protect you all my days. I'll never hurt you. Put me out of my misery and say you'll marry me.'

Leonor's heart squeezed. She cared for him too, and not just because by following her back to her father's palace he'd proved he'd walk on hot coals for her sake. She loved his steadiness. That unwavering sense of honour. He would care for her, although... Slowly, she shook her head. 'My lord, you do me great honour, but I can't marry you.'

'Can't? Why not?'

She huffed out a breath. 'You know very well why not.'

'No, I don't.'

His gaze held hers. It was calm and oddly confident. He looked as though nothing stood between them, when in reality...

'Rodrigo, if we married, Lady Isabel would never forgive you.'

He grimaced. 'We'll win her round.'

'Will we? Every time she sees me she'll be reminded of Diego's death.' Other objections swirled to the surface. Rodrigo deserved a woman with a pure heart. Hers was tainted by her fears. Marriage was a cage and he deserved better than to be locked inside it with a woman like her. Rodrigo was kind and honourable; he likely felt sorry for her because her father had banished her. He was offering out of duty and chivalry. He hadn't said he loved her.

'We come from different worlds.' Her voice cracked. 'I'm not the woman for you.'

Dark eyebrows snapped together even as his fingers continued weaving their way through her hair. Stroking it, fanning it out over her shoulder. 'I disagree. And I hereby give you fair warning. I've changed my mind about not seducing you. Leonor, with your permission, I should like to try an experiment.'

'Oh?'

'I hope to persuade you that we belong together.' Eyes darkening with what she knew was desire, he cleared his throat and that large warrior's body moved against hers. At her indrawn breath, he gave a rueful smile. 'You're afraid of me physically?'

'No.'

His smile brightened and he shifted more purposefully. 'Then I'm going to kiss you.'

They came together and their lips met in a kiss that melted all objections. Rodrigo's scent—the soap he had used, the scent of the man himself—filled her nostrils. His hair slipped softly through her fingers and his groan mingled with hers.

She drew back, breathless, and gazed into warm brown eyes. His breathing was uneven, it sounded as though he had run all the way from Córdoba.

'All right so far?' he asked, a crooked smile on his lips.

Leonor murmured assent, though in truth, she scarcely knew what she said. Rodrigo's kisses scattered her wits. She did know that Rodrigo was an honourable man, she would come to no harm here. With a jolt, she realised that whilst she could never marry him for his own sake, she would not mind being his lover. In truth, it would be good to be this man's concubine.

'Rodrigo?'

'Hmm?'

He was nuzzling her neck, raining a chain of kisses round her throat. Should she ever anger him, he would never beat her maidservants. He would talk to her and they might argue; he might even shout a little and she would shout back, safe in the knowledge that he would never...

A large hand closed over a breast and she gasped. Sensations swirled through her, heady and far too distracting. 'Rodrigo?'

His head lifted. 'I love the way you say my name,' he said.

He was busy tugging the sheet from her body, eyes dark. Hot.

She caressed his temple. Marriage between them was impossible, but she wanted this man and he wanted her. It would have to be enough. Except—her education about what passed between a man and a woman was so very limited. Now she realised her father must have forbidden Inés to enlighten her. 'Rodrigo, wait. Please.'

He blinked and looked down at her, eyes half-lidded. 'You've changed your mind?'

'No, it's just that I am appallingly ignorant.' Cheeks burning, she touched his mouth with her thumb. 'There were certain topics that we were not allowed to discuss.'

'No matter, I am honoured to instruct you.' Eyes dancing, he bent over her once more and she felt his tongue on her breast.

Sliding her hand into his hair, she gripped his

head. 'Really, Rodrigo.' She gasped, the sound was breathy and desperate. 'It is extremely hard to think when you are doing that.'

'You're not meant to be thinking.'

Leonor bit her lip and swallowed down a groan of pure pleasure. 'W-will we make a baby?'

He laughed. 'I hope so.'

'How…how does that work?'

He raised his head and nuzzled her nose. 'Saints, Leonor, you are such an innocent.'

'You're angry.'

'Not at all, you are my joy. However, this would go better if you stopped thinking. Talking is forbidden.'

'Forbidden?'

'Surrender to feeling.' His eyes sparkled in the lamplight. 'Can you do that?'

'I think so.'

I am his joy.

Easing back, he dragged off his tunic and slid between the sheets. Leonor's thoughts scattered as she tentatively reached out her hand and touched his naked skin. He was all warm muscle. Solid. Trustworthy. Beautiful. Leaning forward, she kissed him over his heart.

I love you, she thought. *I love you.*

She could never tell him. Rodrigo deserved someone better than her. Someone whose heart wasn't twisted into knots because of her past. He deserved a woman his mother could look at without seeing the spectre of his brother's death. A woman his mother could accept.

She would give herself to him because she loved him and couldn't resist him. And should there be a child, well, she had her jewels, she had the means to care for a baby. In any case, knowing Rodrigo, he would probably want a hand in the care of his child, he was that sort of man.

She wouldn't marry him though; Lady Isabel would never forgive her. And he, when he came to his senses, would never forgive her either.

Large hands gathered her to him and Leonor took that final, most difficult step, she took pleasure in obeying a man's command.

Words faded until all that was left was Rodrigo. *I am his joy.*

And even though she knew she could never keep him, it was enough.

Chapter Seventeen

The lamplight trembled. Leonor lay, warm and relaxed, in Rodrigo's arms. Her hair flowed over the pillows—dark, swirling tresses that smelt faintly of orange blossom. She was smiling gently to herself as she idly nuzzled his chest.

They'd made love twice and simply looking at her had Rodrigo's loins tightening again. He still wanted her, he'd always want her. Not that he would be so crass as to make love with her a third time. His Princess was new to this, she needed rest, she needed to recover. His desires must wait.

He smiled down at her, happily sated, yet conscious of renewed desire. A desire he knew he would soon—tomorrow, if not tonight—satisfy. His thoughts were pleasantly jumbled. Love was, it seemed, more complicated than he'd believed. After losing Sancha, Rodrigo had guarded his heart. It had seemed easy.

Until Leonor. His Nasrid Princess had stormed

his defences without even trying. She'd had him twisted round her little finger from the outset. If he lost her—his guts tightened—Lord, that was an ugly thought. He'd never felt this strongly for Sancha.

He needed to know Leonor was his. She was still calling him Rodrigo, which was reassuring. And he was pretty certain she would never have given him her body if she didn't love him. Unfortunately, pretty certain wasn't enough. He wanted the words. Did she?

A glossy strand of black hair gleamed in the candlelight. Reaching out, Rodrigo twined it round his finger. Pure silk. Pure Leonor. He couldn't lose her, there was to be no more running away. Their relationship had to be formalised.

He tucked a finger under her chin. 'Leonor?'

She pressed a kiss over his heart. 'Mmm?'

Gently, he placed his palm on her cheek, angling her head so their eyes met.

'I love you, Leonor.'

Her eyes widened and he heard a slight catch in her breath. 'That's good to hear.'

'You realise that you can no longer refuse me.' He gestured at their entwined bodies and the rumpled bed. 'After this, we have to marry.'

Her whole body stiffened. '*Have* to?'

A warning tingle skittered down Rodrigo's spine. 'You know we do. I love you and I flatter myself enough to think that you have a fondness for me; you wouldn't have given yourself to me otherwise.'

'No, of course I wouldn't, but you can't assume I will marry you.'

Rodrigo's blood turned to ice. 'We must marry.'

Eyes sad, she shook her head. 'I am flattered, my lord, but please understand my answer hasn't changed.'

My lord. Just as he'd thought he'd won her, she was distancing herself from him again. Well, he wouldn't allow it. 'Leonor, you have to marry me.' It was a battle keeping his voice even. 'After to-night, we might have a child.'

She frowned. 'So?'

'My children will know their father.'

'I am pleased to hear it,' she said calmly.

Rodrigo was beginning to feel as though he was lost at sea in a small boat which had no oars. 'I will not foist illegitimacy on my children. Leonor, I realise you may not be familiar with our customs, but in my world, illegitimate children do not have the rights of legitimate ones. We need to marry. Our children will bear my family name. Inherit—'

'No, my lord.' She shrugged. 'In any case, there may not be a child. This is only one night.'

Rodrigo wrapped a strand of hair round his wrist and tried for lightness. 'There will be other nights, many of them.'

Placing her hand on his chest, she eased away from him. 'Be that as it may, I shall not marry you.'

He swallowed. 'Why not?'

Dark eyes looked at him. She reached for the sheet and slowly pulled it over herself, shielding her body in much the same way as she shielded her thoughts.

'Leonor, why not? You like me. I love you. Does my love mean nothing to you?'

'It means a great deal.' Her smile was full of regret and she gave a heavy sigh. 'Rodrigo, you must see that we cannot marry. Your mother would never forgive me. Above all, she would never forgive you. Lady Isabel hates me. The looks she gives me! Does she know who I am?'

He clenched his jaw. 'When you ran back to the palace with Miguel, she guessed. I admit my mother has no liking for your father, but she will learn to accept you.'

'Will she?'

'She will.' Earnestly, he leaned towards her. 'Leonor, it was Mamá who alerted me to the fact that you had returned to Granada.'

Leonor stared. 'Truly?'

'She has a warm heart. She was wary of Miguel when he first arrived, but over time, she's grown genuinely fond of him.'

'I don't understand.' Leonor's brow creased in puzzlement.

'Miguel wasn't always called Miguel, his family named him Hakim. I rescued him, a small scrap of a boy, a few years ago, after a skirmish on the border of Al-Andalus.'

'A small boy was fighting as a soldier?'

'His family served the Nasrid dynasty. Hakim had disobeyed his father and followed him into battle. The boy was wounded and his father dead. I brought him home.'

'You saved him.'

'Mamá saved him. It was she who tended his wounds.'

'Saving a small boy is one thing, but watching your son marry a Nasrid princess, an enemy princess, is quite another.'

'My mother will come to love you. I am certain of it.'

'Rodrigo, she holds my father responsible for your brother's death, she'll not forget that.'

'She will if I ask.' He paused. 'Although she will need time. At present, she's struggling to accept that Diego is himself responsible for what happened to him. She was extremely distressed when I pointed this truth out to her.'

'What do you mean?'

'In the past, I warned her that Enrique was becoming increasingly reckless. She didn't want to hear it. Just as today she doesn't want to hear that Diego's death was unnecessary. If Diego hadn't rushed to help Enrique, who'd dashed into battle too soon, he'd still be alive.' He shoved his hand through his hair. 'The truth can be painful.'

Leonor bit her lip. 'I'm causing a rift between you and your mother.'

'It won't last. Mamá will come to understand the truth, and she will accept you.' He ran his fingertips gently down her cheek. 'She loves me. Leonor, she's weighed down with grief right now; you haven't seen her at her best.'

Dark eyes held his. 'When we met, you were weighed down with grief. You accepted me, despite it. You cared for me when I'm sure all you wanted to do was race home. Lady Isabel hates me.'

'Have faith, my love, that will change.' Rodrigo picked up her hand, kissed it and eased out of bed. 'It's almost cockcrow, I have to go. Remember, I'll be sharing your bed again tonight. And tomorrow and tomorrow and for all our tomorrows.'

Leonor lifted an eyebrow. 'Will you tell your mother?'

Rodrigo held down a sigh. It hadn't escaped him that, by focusing on his mother, Leonor had side-stepped his proposal of marriage.

Leonor went to sleep thinking about Rodrigo. The idea of marriage frightened her. Or it used to. She was no longer sure what she thought. If she married Rodrigo, she'd be granting him power over her. She'd have to obey him. And she'd sworn that never again would she find herself in a position of weakness.

Oddly, the idea of marrying Rodrigo wasn't half as frightening as the thought of losing him. That was terrifying.

Rodrigo is a great lord, and he'll be expected to marry. Now that his brother is dead, he needs heirs more than ever. If I don't marry him, I'll lose him to someone else.

Sick at heart, she tossed and turned. She rested her palm on the pillow next to her. His scent lingered on the linens—masculine and musky. Pure Rodrigo. *Safe.*

He'd made love to her so carefully. So delicately. He'd called her his joy, whereas in reality the joy was all hers. It had been a joy to give herself to him. Pure joy.

We are meant to be together.

The astrologer who'd cast her horoscope when she was born had foreseen exactly this circumstance. He'd warned her father, and despite every precaution her father had put in place, she'd still run away with Rodrigo.

Leonor hugged the pillow to her and smiled. She and Rodrigo were meant to be together, it was written in the stars. Except—her smile died—what would the stars have to say about Lady Isabel?

Clearly, the stars didn't know everything. In the morning, she was going to give them a helping hand.

* * *

Directly after breakfast, Leonor went to the chapel. The bread she had eaten sat like a lump in her stomach. Nerves. The omens weren't good, her first encounter with Rodrigo's mother could hardly have been worse.

The priest was kneeling before the altar, lips moving in prayer. Hearing her enter, he pushed to his feet. 'May I help you, my lady?'

'I'm looking for Lady Isabel.'

'She is at the graveyard.'

A lump formed in Leonor's throat. The graveyard. She swallowed. 'Where is that, if you please?'

'It's not far, leave the castle, walk past the orchard and into the village. There's a wall with iron gates, you can't miss it.'

'Thank you, Father.'

Leonor turned to go and the priest's voice called her back.

'My lady, don't forget Lord Rodrigo's orders.'

She looked blankly at the priest. 'Orders?'

'When you leave the castle, you must take an escort.'

Leonor smiled. 'Thank you, I haven't forgotten.'

A spray of lavender in hand, Leonor gave the ironwork on the cemetery gates a brief glance. It was very fine—flowing vines swept across each gate; roses and lilies were growing among the grapes; acanthus leaves spread across each corner. It looked like a depiction of paradise.

She could see Lady Isabel through a gap in the ironwork. She was standing, head bowed, at one of the graves.

Diego's grave.

Leonor stiffened her spine and turned to her escort. 'Wait for me here, if you please.'

'Yes, my lady.'

Pulse thudding like a battle drum, Leonor moved quietly to the other side of the grave and clutched the lavender. Even now, she had no idea what she was going to say.

Naturally, Lady Isabel saw her straight away. She was weeping in silence, huge tears rolling down her cheeks. Leonor's heart went out to her and her own eyes prickled in sympathy. The poor woman.

Leonor said nothing, and she stood motionless as Lady Isabel's attention turned back to the grave. Her lips were moving and she was holding a strand of glass beads. It was a rosary, Leonor recalled Inés mentioning them. At each bead, Lady Isabel paused and prayed.

Leonor waited.

When the beads finally stilled, Lady Isabel looked up. 'You've got gall, I give you that,' she said. Nose to the sky, she picked up her skirts and made to move away.

Leonor held up her hand. 'Please, my lady, I must speak to you.'

'You're a Nasrid princess. The daughter of the Sultan, our enemy.' The rosary beads glittered. 'I have no desire to converse with you.'

Leonor held her ground. A rook called from a nearby tree. 'My lady, please hear me out. I know what it is to love a father and to be rejected; I know what it is to love my sisters.' Bracing herself for Lady Isabel's reaction, she looked pointedly at Diego's grave. 'It must be terrible to lose a son, I cannot imagine the depths of your pain.' She drew in a breath. 'I am truly sorry you lost him and I wish that you could accept my sympathies, but before I ask you to do that, there is something else you need to know.'

Lady Isabel wound the rosary round her palm. Her foot tapped. 'Go on.'

'I love Rodrigo.'

The string of beads snapped and glass beads bounced all over the path. Neither woman moved.

'You, Sultan Tariq's daughter, dare to tell me that?' Lady Isabel's eyes were as hard as her rosary beads.

'I do. I am the Sultan's daughter, and you must know I had no hand in Diego's death. All I can do is regret it. Just as I regret the conflict between my father's people and yours.'

Silence. Then the rook cawed, harsh and loud. Leonor reminded herself that Lady Isabel had warned Rodrigo when she and Miguel had gone back to Granada. She needn't have done that, she could have left well alone. She reminded herself that Lady Isabel was fond of Miguel even though she must recall that his father had served the Nasrids. There was hope.

A deep frown scored Lady Isabel's brow. She tipped her head to one side. 'Tell me, I've been wondering, did your mother come from Baeza? Was she definitely Spanish?'

'Yes, Father captured her and forced her into marriage.'

'Your mother was Lady Juana, then. Sweet Mary, that's why Rodrigo went to Baeza.' Lady Isabel gave a huge sigh and their gazes locked. 'He tells me very little, you know.'

Praying that Lady Isabel's antipathy towards her was weakening, Leonor's gaze flickered briefly to Diego's grave. 'My lady, you have every reason to mislike me.' She gripped the lavender. 'I can only hope that you will one day accept that I had no part in your son's death. I think it is a tragedy. Please accept my sympathies.'

Lady Isabel's eyebrow twitched. 'Rodrigo tells me that what happened at the border was largely Sir Enrique's fault. Diego was drawn into the conflict through his cousin's stupidity.'

'I heard that too,' Leonor said carefully.

'Rodrigo is most insistent that Diego should have known better.'

'As to that, my lady, I cannot say. What I can say is that Lord Rodrigo is as chivalrous and honourable as the day is long. He would never baulk at facing the truth, however unpalatable.'

Lady Isabel gave her a thin smile. 'I am coming to see that you, Lady Leonor, are a wise woman.' She gestured at the lavender. 'Well? Are you leaving that for Diego, or not?' Eyes glistening, she turned abruptly and strode, veil trailing behind her, towards the iron gates and Leonor's waiting escort.

Leonor had forgotten about the lavender. Carefully, she placed it next to the headstone and composed a prayer for Diego. Shortly after that, she followed Lady Isabel out of the cemetery.

Rodrigo tracked his mother to the storeroom, he'd been told she was checking the castle's supply of herbs and spices. He was relieved to see that she was alone.

'Mamá, I'd be grateful if you'd find alternative sleeping accommodation for Ana,' he said.

'Oh? Why's that?' His mother shut the door of the spice cupboard and locked it with a key hanging from her waist.

'From now on I intend to share my bed with Lady Leonor.'

His mother raised her eyebrows and said mildly, 'Every night?'

'Yes, Mamá, every night.' Rodrigo frowned.

Braced for an argument, he was puzzled by his mother's calm response.

'Father Pablo will be shocked,' she murmured.

'So be it.'

'You love her?'

'Very much.'

'Will you marry her?'

'She's refused me.'

His mother drew her head back. 'That does surprise me. Rodrigo, it might be better if you took her to Córdoba. You can't keep her here unless you are wed. My ladies will be outraged and there are those among your knights who will not approve.'

He shrugged. 'I can release them from their service, and they may go elsewhere. Lady Leonor stays.'

Lady Isabel gave him the most searching of looks and her mouth softened. 'Very well. If Lady Leonor is your choice, I will support you. This morning she impressed upon me how deep her feelings are for you.'

Rodrigo went still. 'You spoke to her this morning?'

'Aye, she sought me out. I confess I was pleasantly surprised. She has the look of her mother, you know. I can see it now. Will you ask for her hand again?'

Inés came as promised and stayed for a week. During her visit, she and Leonor were inseparable. In the day, they visited Lady Alba in Córdoba. Occasionally, Rodrigo would accompany them on rides about the estate. In the evening, Rodrigo sat at table in his hall and watched Leonor and her duenna deep in conversation.

Leonor barely spared him a glance. Except at night. When he joined her in her bedchamber, she was as attentive and welcoming as a man could wish. Rodrigo was impatient for more. He wanted to set a permanent seal on their relationship, he wanted her hand in marriage. Unfortunately, though Leonor gave him her body every night, her heart remained guarded. The words he ached to hear remained unspoken.

He couldn't fathom her reasons. Leonor wouldn't give her body to someone if she didn't care for them. Though the words had yet to cross her lips, he was certain she loved him. He told himself that patience was all, Leonor must realise they belonged together.

Then came the evening that Constanza's reply arrived.

Rodrigo took the scroll to their chamber. Moonlight was streaming through the open shutter, bathing their bedchamber in pale light.

Leonor was standing in semi-darkness, combing her hair. Her gaze flew to the scroll and she dropped the comb. 'It's from Constanza?'

'Aye.'

Taking the letter, Leonor broke the seal and moved to sit in a pool of lamplight on the bed. She read greedily, hair tumbling over her shoulders like shiny black silk. She chewed her lip. She gasped. There was more biting of her lip.

Rodrigo rubbed his chin. Clearly, whatever Constanza had written, Leonor didn't like it.

'What does she say?'

Imperiously, she held up her hand. 'One moment.' She hunched over the letter again, and when her gaze finally met his, she looked stricken. 'Zorahaida,' she murmured. 'She will always be Zorahaida.'

'Zorahaida?' Rodrigo asked. Then he remembered, Zorahaida was the name the Sultan had given his third daughter. He looked quizzically at Leonor. 'Do you have two names?'

'Mamá named me Leonor, to my father I am, or rather I was, Princess Zaida.'

'Princess Zaida, I like it.'

'I prefer Leonor.'

'Then that is what I shall continue to call you, my angel.'

'Thank you.' She bent over the scroll. 'Constanza says she's happy at the palace. How can that be?' Her frown deepened and she ran her fingertips over the script as though caressing it. 'I don't understand it, but this is definitely Constanza's own hand.'

'And that surprises you?'

'Given the contents, yes.'

Rodrigo sat down and gently swept her hair back over her shoulders. 'If Constanza wrote it, you have to accept it.'

'She can't stay at the palace! She can't.'

'Leonor, you are not your sister's keeper.'

'No, but...'

Rodrigo stared at the letter. It was written in Arabic, lines of pretty curlicues that were a mystery to him. 'What else does she say?'

'That she belongs at the palace, and if she changes her mind, she knows where to find us.' Leonor looked desolate.

'My love, it's not that bad.'

'Isn't it?'

Her eyes were glassy with unshed tears. She was devastated.

It was then that he realised. Her father wasn't the sole reason Leonor refused to commit to him, her sister was part of the problem. From the moment Leonor had emerged from that sally-port, worry for Constanza had been tearing her in two. Leonor felt guilty, guilty that Constanza had stayed behind when she had won her freedom.

Constanza stands between us.

'Princess Constanza loves you, I'm sure,' he said gently.

She wiped away a tear and glanced at the letter. 'Aye, so she says.'

'There you are, then. Let her go. Give her re-

sponsibility for her own life. Leonor, you feel
guilty that you have escaped when she did not,
and there truly is no need.'

She stared. 'That's exactly what I feel. How
did you know?'

Rodrigo cleared his throat. 'Diego.'

'You mean because you came back from
Granada and he didn't?' She gripped his hand.
'Rodrigo, none of that was your fault, you told
me that Diego chose to follow Enrique.'

'He did.' Rodrigo smiled sadly. 'It doesn't make
it any easier. Diego made a mistake and the rest
of us must live with the consequences.'

'You're saying that Constanza must be allowed
to make mistakes?'

'Aye. Your sister must make her own deci-
sions. Set her free. Allow her to do what she wants
with her own life.' Rodrigo's heart cramped. He'd
learned that lesson years ago, with Sancha too.
God save him, it had taken all his strength and
fortitude. It would kill him to release Leonor if
she insisted on it. Yet he knew he'd do it. 'Love
doesn't come with chains,' he murmured.

She let out a trembling sigh and set the letter
aside. 'It's hard.' She gave a watery smile and
leaned against him. 'If Princess Zorahaida never
leaves the palace, she will never know joy like
ours.'

Rodrigo felt himself go still. 'Joy?'

'Joy.' She turned to him, expression warm. 'I want her to have what we have.'

'Constanza chose the palace,' Rodrigo said, pointedly eyeing the letter. 'She hasn't changed her mind. Release her, Leonor. Give her the privilege of choosing her own path. She may well find her joy there.'

Against his shoulder, he felt her nod. A small arm slipped around his waist. When she hugged him to her, his heart turned over. His Princess wasn't given to initiating gestures of affection and he hoped it meant what he thought it did.

'I am blessed to have found you,' she murmured. 'Rodrigo?'

'Mmm?'

'I love you.'

Carefully, noting absently that his hand was shaking, Rodrigo took her chin and tilted her face to his. He sealed her declaration with a kiss that was very firm and probably far too possessive. Delightfully, she made no objection and, even more delightfully, when he had finished, a faint flush of colour stained her cheekbones. She was the most beautiful woman in creation.

He cupped her cheek and ran his forefinger round her ear, smiling as she pressed against him. 'I have waited a long time for those words.'

'I have loved you a long time, and I'm sorry I couldn't tell you before.'

'I understand. Leonor, you will be my bride.'

She kissed his chin. He was thankful to see the sparkle was back in her eyes. He could see the grey flecks. 'Will I, my lord?'

'You will. And there will be no more talk about moving to Baeza. You may visit Sir Alfredo, but you are not going to stay there.'

Her eyes narrowed and her chin lifted. 'I will if I wish to.' She was trying, not very successfully, to hide a smile.

'You, my lady, are a tease. Confess it, you have no wish to live in Baeza.'

She shook her head and the smile appeared.

'Marry me.'

'Very well, Rodrigo, I will.'

Choked with emotion, he pulled her close, buried his face in her neck and inhaled. Leonor. His joy. And soon, God willing, his Countess. His fingers searched for the ties of her gown.

'One moment.' Gently disengaging herself, she rose and padded to the window. Hand on the shutter, she stared into the night.

Rodrigo came to stand at her side. 'What are you thinking?'

'The stars. The moon. The way the heavens are constantly on the turn. Did I tell you that when my sisters and I were born, Father had astrological charts cast for us?'

Rodrigo looked sceptically at her. 'What did the charts say?'

'They foretold a future away from the palace.'

Her eyes danced and her fingers linked with his. 'Father was told to guard us closely when we reached marriageable age.'

'Truly?'

'Truly. The stars brought you to me.'

Smiling, Rodrigo shook his head.

'You don't believe it.'

'It's a pretty idea, but I believe we make our own destiny.' Rodrigo put his arm about her shoulders. 'Come to bed, my love.'

With a last glance at the moon, Leonor closed the shutter and gave him a dazzling smile. 'I am happy. I am free. Rodrigo, I will love you all my life.'

* * * * *

MILLS & BOON

Coming next month

A KISS AWAY FROM SCANDAL
Christine Merrill

Hope turned back to the mirror, and flashed a smile that would blind a duke at twenty paces. Then, the curtsey. "Good evening, my Lord." This time, she dipped deeper and felt an embarrassing tremble in her front knee. She was nearly one and twenty, but hardly infirm. She could do better. She must do better.

She tried again. "Good evening, my Lord."

"I should think good morning would be more appropriate. It is not yet eleven."

She stumbled at the sound of a voice behind her and raised her eyes to see the reflection of the stranger who had entered the room as she practiced.

It was he.

Who else but the Earl of Comstock would be wandering around the house unintroduced, as if he owned it? In a sense, he did.

"And I have no title."

"As of yet," she said. There was no longer a need to practice her smile. When she looked at him, it came naturally. Who would not be happy in the presence of such a handsome man? Though she had never been one to dote on the male form, his was perfectly proportioned, neither too tall nor too short, with slim hips and broad shoulders on which rested the head of a Roman God. His blond hair was cut a la Brutus, curling faintly at the fringe that framed a noble brow, unmarked by signs of worry. His grey eyes were intelligent, his smile sympathetic.

Praise God, she had been delivered just the man she'd prayed would come: young, handsome, and judging by the twinkle that shone in those beautiful eyes as he looked at her, single. But not for long, if she had her way.

He tilted his head. "You are correct. I have no title, as of yet. Nor am I likely to get one. But they are sometimes awarded to men whose service merits them, and I am not yet thirty. With time and effort, anything is possible, Miss Strickland."

She steadied herself from the shock and turned to face him with as much grace as possible, struggling to maintain the expression she'd been practicing in the mirror. "Then you are not my cousin from America?"

"The future Earl of Comstock?" His smile softened. "Unfortunately, no." He bowed from the waist. "Gregory Drake, at your service, Miss Strickland."

Continue reading
A KISS AWAY FROM SCANDAL
Christine Merrill

Available next month
www.millsandboon.co.uk

LET'S TALK
Romance

For exclusive extracts, competitions
and special offers, find us online:

f facebook.com/millsandboon

⊙ @millsandboonuk

🐦 @millsandboon

Or get in touch on 0844 844 1351*

For all the latest titles coming soon, visit
millsandboon.co.uk/nextmonth